MARINE L: SBS

RAIDERS FROM THE SEA

GW00642947

MARINE L: SBS

RAIDERS FROM THE SEA

Ian Blake

First published in Great Britain 1998
22 Books, Invicta House, Sir Thomas Longley Road,
Rochester, Kent

Copyright © 1998 by 22 Books

The moral right of the author has been asserted

A CIP catalogue record for this book
is available from the British Library

ISBN 1 86238 012 0

10 9 8 7 6 5 4 3 2 1

Typeset by Hewer Text Composition Services, Edinburgh
Printed in Great Britain by
Clays Ltd, St Ives plc

1

The Prime Minister removed the newly lit cigar from his mouth and glared at his First Sea Lord. 'What the devil do you mean, "reluctant"?'

Admiral Sir Dudley Pound was not First Sea Lord for nothing. He had commanded a battleship at Jutland and served with distinction as Commander-in-Chief of the Mediterranean Fleet. He was a sea dog through and through, and as tough as old boots. Yet he had to admit to himself that he found the Prime Minister intimidating. There was something of the schoolboy bully in Churchill, and once he had made up his mind he was implacable. When the two clashed it was a case of an irresistible force meeting an immovable object. When that happened third parties kept well clear.

'The French are our allies, Prime Minister,' Pound said stubbornly. 'They are, like ourselves, a proud and ancient nation. It is not unreasonable that Admiral Somerville should be reluctant to act until every alternative has been explored.'

The two men were seated in a small office in Admiralty Arch, for Churchill had chosen to stroll across Horse Guards Parade from his underground bunker in Whitehall to savour the warm summer's day. The office had an uninterrupted view of Buckingham Palace at the other end of the Mall. Now the building, with the royal standard flying above it to show that the royal family were in residence, sparkled in the sunshine, a reminder to the Prime Minister of everything he held dear.

Before becoming Prime Minister on 10 May 1940, less than two months earlier, Churchill had been First Lord of the Admiralty, the Royal Navy's political chief, as he had been during the Great War of 1914–18. So he knew the Royal Navy as a mother knows her child. It was the country's senior service and its centuries of duty and loyalty to the Crown had been unwavering.

But Churchill knew it also possessed a stubborn streak of independence. The War Office and the Air Ministry were merely administrative organizations; the Admiralty was an operational headquarters with the power to command and direct great fleets and great actions. Upon its decisions the fate of the nation could hang, and it guarded this independence with the jealousy of a lover. It did not take kindly to political intervention, from whatever source.

He could, the Prime Minister thought, take the bull by the horns. As a forthright individual, he always favoured this option: the bull, in his experience, when shaken hard, often turned out to be only a cow. But he knew Pound was a hard man, a bull to be reckoned with, and being the consummate politician he was, the Prime Minister instinctively knew that on this occasion confrontation was not the answer.

'Look, Dudley,' he said quietly. 'I do understand your problem and I do appreciate your loyalty to Somerville.'

'I support my admirals because I believe in them, Prime Minister,' Pound replied stiffly, even more wary of Churchill when he adopted a conciliatory mood, 'not because it is my duty to do so, though it is that, too. It is my profound belief that Somerville is right. We must give the French Navy every chance before we resort to force.'

'Let us hope they take it,' Churchill replied gruffly. 'We cannot allow the French fleet to fall into German hands, and our resolve to fight on cannot be seen to falter.'

He leant forward and studied the chart of the western Mediterranean that lay between them. 'You say the bulk of the French fleet lies at Oran.'

His stubby forefinger pointed to a large bay some two hundred miles west of Algiers, on the North African coast, and three hundred miles east of Gibraltar.

'There and at Mers-el-Kebir on the opposite side of the bay.'

'And Somerville has the fire-power?'

'He flies his flag aboard the *Nelson*, Prime Minister.'

No more needed be said on that point: HMS *Nelson* was among the most powerful battleships in the world.

'Then we can only await the outcome of the negotiations.'

Churchill stood up and gazed out of the window towards the Palace. For once the burden of decision weighed heavily upon him. It was an odious task that he had to perform, but perform it he must if he was not to lose an even more important battle: the one for the minds of the American people. If the Americans were convinced that Britain would fight on alone, and showed it by going to the extreme of destroying the fleet of a conquered ally, then sooner or later they would join them. Such an alliance would be unbeatable.

There was a knock on the door. 'Come,' said Pound.

A lieutenant commander entered. 'A signal from Admiral Somerville, sir.'

Pound took the slip of paper, read it and wrote a reply

on the signal pad that the officer was carrying. 'With all dispatch,' he said to the officer as he returned the pad. The officer left.

Churchill turned from the window. 'Well?'

'Admiral Gensoul still refuses,' said Pound quietly. He folded the signal and threw it on the table.

'We have given him enough time, God knows,' said the Prime Minister, slumping back into his chair. 'And we have given him enough choices. He can join us, he can choose disarmament in a British or West Indian port, or he can scuttle. What *does* he intend to do?'

'Fight,' said Pound, 'isn't that what you would do when threatened?'

The jaw of the bulldog face jutted out. 'We cannot afford to waste any more time.'

'I have suggested to Somerville that he send a personal emissary who knows Gensoul well.'

'Will Gensoul receive him?'

Pound sighed. 'I doubt it. But we must try.'

Churchill stood up again and paced the floor. It was always the waiting that was so trying, knowing that the flow of events was out of your hands.

Five minutes passed and neither man had spoken, when the silence was broken by another knock on the door. On Pound's command the same officer entered. 'Yes, Bill? Problem?'

'Gibraltar have just signalled to say they have intercepted a signal from the Minister of Marine, Admiral Darlan, to Admiral Gensoul, sir. It was *en clair*.'

The effect on the two men was electrifying. Governments *always* transmitted signals in code, *never* in plain language. It could mean only one thing: the French wanted the British to know what the signal contained.

'What did it say?' Pound asked, though he already knew what the purport would be.

'"French squadron dispatched Toulon 1100,"' the officer read carefully, '"will be transferred to your command 1500 today."' The officer hesitated. 'Our cipher people decided not to translate the last phrase, sir.'

'What does it say?'

'*Vive la France.*'

The silence was profound. Then Pound said quietly: 'Thank you, Bill. Wait outside, would you.'

Churchill sat down. 'I'm sorry, Dudley, so desperately sorry.'

Pound shook his head. 'We've done all we can, Prime Minister. Somerville must not be allowed to be caught between the two forces. We both know that.'

There was nothing more to be said. The Admiral stood up, walked to the door and opened it. 'Come in, Bill.'

The officer entered. Later he was to say that he had never seen two such powerful men so obviously gripped by emotions they found hard to control.

'Top-priority signal to Admiral Somerville,' Pound dictated, not trusting the trembling in his hands to write the words himself. 'French squadron sailed Toulon 1100 today. Imperative that you act immediately.' He hesitated and then added: 'God bless you all.'

The afternoon sun was down below the roofs of Whitehall when the two men received Somerville's reply: 'French Fleet at Oran engaged at 1754 today. *Bretagne* blown up, *Dunkerque* sunk, other units severely damaged. Some have escaped and will be hunted down. Estimated loss of French lives: 1200.'

2

Admiral Sir Roger Keyes glanced across at the captain of the commando ship *Glengyle*. There was a hint of a twinkle in his eye. 'Well, Dick. What do you think?'

Captain Richard Broakes knitted his fingers together on top of the table and considered them carefully. He was a grave, donnish figure, with a high-domed forehead which was now wrinkled with perplexity.

Keyes knew his friend was considered by many of his peers to be not only over the hill but well down the other side. However, the Admiral viewed his old colleague differently. He remembered him as a dashing young destroyer captain when he, Keyes, had commanded the Dover Patrol, which had wreaked such havoc among the German Navy between 1914 and 1918. It was a different war they were fighting now, of course, but not *that* different.

Not liking the proposition that had been put to him, Broakes unwove his fingers and placed his hands apart, palms down on the table. The mahogany surface had been buffed by generations of men who knew that when the Royal Navy said clean it meant clean, and the four gold rings on Broakes's sleeves glittered back at him from its burnished depths.

Not a spot, not a blemish – just like Broakes's naval record.

Keyes knew what the gesture meant and Broakes knew he knew. But there were others sitting round the table who would not. So Broakes looked at the Admiral and said quietly but firmly: 'Rubbish, sir. Absolute rubbish. Not possible.'

Keyes swung round in his chair and glowered under his bushy, grey eyebrows at the large, khaki-clad individual with the battered face standing at ease in front of the table.

'Look, Pountney,' he said, not unkindly. 'With Dunkirk this country has just suffered one of its greatest defeats in its long history. If it hadn't been for the Navy . . .'

'And the Royal Air Force, Admiral,' the Air Vice-Marshal at the end of the table interjected.

'And the Air Force,' the Admiral added imperturbably. 'If it hadn't been for the Navy and the Air Force the entire British Expeditionary Force would still be in Dunkirk in one big POW camp. And we would have no army to face Mr Hitler's storm troopers when they arrive on our shores.'

'If they arrive,' the Air Vice-Marshal interceded again. 'They're going to have to defeat us in the air first.'

'*When* they arrive,' the Admiral said firmly. 'They'll come all right. Much as I hate to say it, Pountney, we are all thinking about how we are going to defend this fair isle from the German legions, and what with. There are hardly enough rifles to go around, much less automatic weapons. And you bowl in and suggest we go on the attack. Doesn't make sense, does it, laddie?'

Although their interviewee was standing at ease, there was about him a tenseness, an alertness, that transmitted itself to the high-ranking officers around the table. He was like a coiled spring.

'With respect, sir,' said Roger 'Jumbo' Pountney, former big-game hunter, one-time middleweight boxing champion, now an HO (Hostilities Only) officer in the King's Royal Rifle Corps, 'attack is often the best form of defence.'

Keyes glowered at the young man for a moment, as if demanding that he should retract such an absurd statement. Then he relaxed, leant back in his chair and nodded his pleasure.

'I thought you might say that, Pountney. That's exactly why Mr Churchill has appointed me Director of Combined Operations. It is our job to take the offensive, come what may. We did it at Oran and we've got to keep doing it wherever and whenever we can.'

In the pause that followed this pronouncement Pountney felt the headiness of success beginning to envelop him. So it was going to be all right, despite what everyone had said. This board of old geezers was, after all, big enough and bold enough to see the potential of his scheme to use canoes launched from submarines to attack enemy shipping. And there was plenty of that on the other side of the Channel at the moment, for the German preparations for the invasion were well advanced.

As the pause continued, Pountney brimmed with excitement and gratitude towards the Admiral. Keyes was a genius, of course; the offensive spirit personified. You had only to read about the Zeebrugge raid of April '18 to know that. The old boy might be over seventy now, but he knew when to give the next generation their head.

That innate caution that keeps only the best big-game hunters alive stopped Pountney from opening his mouth and reeling off details of the idea that had been maturing within him for months.

The grandfather clock at the far end of the room filled the hot, silent afternoon as it laboriously marshalled its mechanism to strike four o'clock.

Time for tea, thought Pountney feverishly, but would there be honey?

Keyes waited for the clock to stop whirring and striking, then laid down the pencil he had been toying with.

There was something about this deliberate gesture that alerted Pountney. It alerted him just as a snapping twig had that time in the Serengeti when the old lioness had broken cover: a yellow streak, a bolt out of the blue.

Now Pountney tensed, suddenly expecting trouble, just as he had tensed on that peaceful, beautiful day in the Kenyan bush; but now, as then, he was not exactly sure what the trouble would be or from what direction it would come. In the Serengeti he had instantly snapped the safety-catch off his .475 Mannlicher and raised the rifle's polished butt to his shoulder; now he could only grip his hands behind his back and wait.

The old lioness had come, it seemed, from nowhere, charging with a snarl that had turned his blood to ice. Now Keyes did rather the same by leaning forward and surprising even those around the table with the vehemence of his words.

'But lookee, Lieutenant Pountney, I'm not going to waste my precious time and my even more precious resources on any old crackpot scheme that some foolhardy, hare-brained youth has dreamt up in his cups but not thought through. I hope that is plainly understood by you and all your "act first, think afterwards" friends.'

Pountney swallowed his disappointment. Silly old farts, the lot of them, he railed inwardly. They were all fighting the last war, if not the one before that.

They didn't understand that it was a different world now.

He pictured again as he stood stolidly silent the piles of dead civilians in the Norwegian streets and the obscene, swaggering arrogance of the German SS *Untersturmführer* he had captured, and felt his teeth gritting. It was a very different world. He remembered the recent statement in the House of Commons by a Government minister that a certain German target had not been bombed because it was private property, and felt a derisive laugh swell within him. There would be no gentlemanly tactics this time round, no chivalrous conduct. This war wasn't going to be won on the playing fields of Eton. It was going to be a bloody, no-holds-barred affair.

As well as seeing the enemy in action in Norway, Pountney also knew from what had happened when the German Panzers had swept into Holland, Belgium and France in May: this time round they were fighting common killers, Swastika-toting criminals who murdered civilians and unarmed prisoners of war without a second thought.

The clock intruded on the silence, ticking the moments away with a steady, maddening rhythm, and Pountney felt an overwhelming impulse to tell this old fossil where to get off. But again his highly developed instinct for self-preservation reined him back and he swallowed the protest Keyes had been deliberately trying to provoke. When it didn't come, the Admiral smiled slightly. He had been right, he told himself with the satisfaction that the elderly gain from a correct judgement: the lad had restraint and discipline as well as plenty up top.

So far so good.

Keyes said crisply: 'However, I don't put your idea in

that category, Pountney. In fact, I quite like it and I can see that you have given it mature consideration. But I must have proof. From the proposition you have put to us, you obviously understand that, and I must say that makes me feel inclined to listen to you further. But you do understand that even if you succeed in the little stunt you propose, the odds against you getting the go-ahead are high? Very high?'

A surge of excitement passed through Pountney like an electric current, just as it had when he had calmly stood his ground in the Serengeti. Then he had deliberately avoided squeezing the Mannlicher's double-pressure trigger until the lioness had been so close that he swore he had smelt her feral heat. He was, he knew, a gambler at heart.

'Yes, sir. I understand.'

'Very well. Let battle commence. We meet again at nine tomorrow morning. Thank you, gentlemen. It's time for tea.'

Pountney swore under his breath. The wind had switched from its prevailing direction, the south-west, to the south-east, so that the water in Dover harbour no longer had the protection of the long, curved sweep of the granite breakwater. Instead, the freshening July breeze blew steadily and directly through the harbour entrance, out of which the tide was ebbing strongly. The effect of wind against tide ruffled the normally flat-calm surface into a chop that occasionally glittered white out of the darkness. It wasn't much, but propelling a canoe through any kind of a sea was an extra chore Pountney could have done without.

He grasped his companion's elbow and whispered in

his ear: 'Which direction do you reckon the shore patrol will come from?'

Lieutenant Philip Ayton, Royal Marines, as fair-haired and as slight as Pountney was dark and broad-shouldered, pointed to the right.

Ayton had met Pountney when the young Royal Marine officer, as part of the Marine detachment aboard the cruiser *Sheffield*, had been sent ashore to bolster Norwegian Army units around Namsos. Later, in the heat of battle, Ayton and some of his men had become separated from the rest. So they had joined one of the Army's Independent Companies – the forerunners of the Commandos that Keyes was now forming – which had counted Pountney among its number. Shortly afterwards Ayton had met Pountney in a snow-filled ditch which had been under fire from a German machine-gun nest. There it had been Ayton's cool restraint, showing maturity beyond his years, which had, in Pountney's mind, undoubtedly saved both their lives. He had never told Ayton that – Pountney wasn't a man who praised others easily – but he had noted it with approval.

Normally Pountney considered all Royal Marines constipated with tradition and incapable of innovative thinking, but he liked the younger man's sense of humour, admired his icy calm under fire, and they soon found that they shared a passionate interest in canoeing. Pountney also noticed that, though Ayton was slightly built, he was tough and resilient, had an inexhaustible supply of energy and was possessed of a quick, intuitive intelligence.

For Ayton, 'Jumbo' Pountney was the elder brother he'd never had, who, he hoped, would lead him into some interesting scrapes – and perhaps out again if necessary, though Ayton had few qualms about his own ability to extract himself from danger if the need arose. The Marines had a long tradition of being able to look after themselves, and were trained to give no quarter and expect none.

Not every Marine would have had the initiative – or the determination – but on the return of the defeated British forces from Norway Ayton had badgered and argued until he had wangled a secondment to the new Commando force.

The present escapade seemed rather a lark to Ayton, though Pountney had impressed upon his companion that he would be as dead from a British bullet as he would be from a German one. Invasion was expected at any time and they had been told that the shore patrol would fire on sight if it caught anyone in the prohibited area they had entered. The patrol's motto, Pountney knew – because it had been his business to find out all about the patrol – was to shoot first and ask questions afterwards.

But Pountney's special training with the Independent Companies, the two bleak months in Norway and the initial training course they had both recently attended at the School of Special Warfare at Inverailort, had taught them how to move unseen and unheard at night. Besides, the shore patrol was mostly composed of elderly men with even more elderly rifles. They just added a certain piquancy to the adventure, but no real danger.

That would come once they were on the water, for the harbour patrol boats were efficiently manned and their crews were alert and well armed. Some of them even possessed the much-prized Thompson sub-machine-gun, an American automatic weapon that fired heavy .45-calibre slugs. At short range it could do an awful lot of damage to a man's health. In July 1940 it was as rare as hen's teeth and even the Independent Companies had been issued with only a handful. If the harbour patrol had these weapons they would know how to use them. On the whole, Pountney and Ayton had agreed, it was best to avoid the harbour patrol, though one of Pountney's earlier plans had been to capture one of the boats and come alongside the *Glengyle* in it.

Then there would be the ship's own patrol system. Unlike the shore and harbour patrols, those aboard the *Glengyle* were expecting a raid, and the crew might well have a cutter in the water as well as a standing patrol on deck. Because the ship's company had been alerted, they might not shoot the intruders. But the shame of being captured by a bunch of matelots was, the two commandos agreed, worse than being shot.

'It's due any minute,' Ayton whispered.

'We'll let it pass, then launch the canoe.'

The two men eased themselves down among the rocks. They were both dressed in khaki overalls and brown plimsolls, and their faces were blackened with cork. They wore woollen hats and each carried a sheath knife on a leather belt around his waist. Stowed in the canoe were wire-cutters, two hip-flasks of whisky, a torch, night-glasses and a can of water. The most important item of all – a piece of white classroom chalk – Pountney carried in the pocket of his overalls.

Ayton heard the patrol first, and touched Pountney's arm. It was just the faintest of scrunching sounds as the men plodded along the beach on the fringe of the ebbing water. The murmur of subdued talk was carried to them by the freshening breeze. Metal clinked on metal, boots scraped on rock, and the two commandos saw the glow of a cigarette furtively cupped in the hand, before the patrol, four shadowy figures, sloped along in front of them and passed out of sight to their left.

'Fucking shower,' Ayton whispered cheerfully.

'Let's get going,' Pountney snapped. Sometimes Ayton was just a bit too relaxed. The shore patrol was no concern of theirs.

They lifted the canoe carefully from its hiding-place among the rocks and carried it down to the water's edge, crouching to keep their profiles low. Pountney climbed in first, then held the canoe steady with his double paddle as Ayton slid in behind him.

It was a civilian canoe with a wooden frame which had a piece of rather tired, crinkled canvas stretched over it. There was one open cockpit but no seats. They both sat on a wooden grating that covered the bottom and Ayton immediately felt water seeping through his overalls.

'It's leaking,' he said in disgust.

'Tough,' Pountney answered brusquely. 'It's all I could find at short notice in the Sea Scouts' shed.'

Shit, thought Ayton, the war's going to be won in a fifteen-foot canoe, *circa* 1912, which leaks like a sieve and is owned by the Dover Sea Scouts.

Old it was, but the canoe moved sweetly enough across the water, slicing through the wavelets without fuss. The leak, if it was a leak, seemed to get no worse. If I get away with just a wet arse, Ayton thought, it will have been an evening well spent.

Pountney had planned their approach in a series of grandmother's footsteps. He was not going to attempt to reach the *Glengyle* directly, because it lay a long way out in the harbour. Instead, they moved in its general direction by paddling from one moored ship to another, for Dover was full of all sorts of ships, many of them merchantmen which had escaped in the nick of time from countries recently overrun by the German armies.

At each ship the two men rested for a while by sheltering under the bow and hanging on to the chain that secured the vessel to its mooring buoy. They took long draughts from their hip-flasks and eased their aching legs and shoulders. Paddling in such a position put an enormous strain on the upper torso and Pountney made a mental note to ask the 'sawbones' – the surgeon commander at Dover Command, who had taken an interest in Pountney's ideas – how best to alleviate this stress.

Each time, before moving on, they scoured the dark waters around them with their night-glasses to make sure they did not run across the harbour patrol. They did see it once, a dark, moving shadow between two anchored destroyers, but it was a long way away and not heading in their direction.

After they had been on the water for about half an hour the rain clouds above them broke up and in the clear patches of night sky the stars glittered brightly. Pountney turned to Ayton, pointed skywards, then raised his thumb. Ayton nodded and grinned. Good visibility was just another piece that needed to fit neatly into the jigsaw of their operational plan – well, not plan exactly, Pountney thought: gamble was nearer the mark.

Eventually, after nearly an hour, they reached the ship nearest to the *Glengyle*. An old tramp steamer in ballast, its rusting hull was so high out of the water that the two men were able to cling on to part of the barnacle-encrusted rudder while they got their bearings. The *Glengyle*, lying on the tramp steamer's starboard quarter, was a large ship, a former cross-Channel steamer now converted to take a number of small raiding craft, and these hung from special davits on both sides of the boat deck. Some were used in the harbour, for commando exercises or for ferrying the crew, and these were secured to a boat boom which stuck out horizontally from the *Glengyle*'s side to keep them from bumping the hull.

The two men took it in turn to study the ship's outline with the night-glasses. The twin Oerlikons on the foredeck were plainly visible, their long barrels pointing skywards. They were dual-purpose guns firing 20mm shells. Of Swedish manufacture, they had been purchased in large quantities by both the Germans and the British and had proved to be extremely accurate and reliable. There was another pair in the stern and on either side of the bridge anti-aircraft quick-firing pom-pom guns had been fitted.

To complete its armament, the *Glengyle* had just astern of its squat, single funnel an anti-aircraft device that fired rockets from a simple tube. Pountney had seen it in action in a Norwegian fiord where the ship had been anchored and knew it to be quite useless against the low-flying German aircraft which had swept down to strafe and bomb it. The appearance of the rocket blasting its way skywards might have distracted the pilots, he imagined, but they were certainly never in any danger of being hit. His original aim had been to remove this useless piece of apparatus as proof that he had been aboard, but that was before he had found that the only canoe he could get was small, old, leaky and very fragile. He had to face the fact that, though he had planned in great detail how to get up to and then on to the *Glengyle*, he had not thought what he would do once he was aboard.

As if sensing what his companion was thinking, Ayton whispered, 'What now, Jumbo?' in Pountney's ear.

'How far away do you reckon she is?'

'Two cables,' said Ayton. 'Four hundred yards,' he added, in case Pountney was not familiar with naval terminology.

Pountney grunted. Ten minutes' paddling, ten minutes' exposure to those guarding the ship. It was a long time, but at least there was no cutter patrolling around the *Glengyle*. The donnish captain must really feel as confident as he had sounded earlier in the day.

Pountney glanced at his watch. They hadn't much time. 'We'll move into a position so that we approach her bows on,' he said.

'The tide's almost finished ebbing,' Ayton reminded him. 'She'll start swinging towards us soon.'

'Can't wait that long. You know how punctual our Luftwaffe friends are.'

They pushed off from the tramp steamer's rudder, paddled gently along the vessel's rusting sides, skirted the mooring buoy and, feeling naked and vulnerable, headed into open water. They paddled for two or three minutes, then turned to starboard. The *Glengyle* now lay directly ahead of the canoe, its bows pointing towards it.

By lying motionless and keeping their upper bodies bent forward, Pountney knew they would either be virtually invisible to anyone looking in their direction or they would be thought to be a piece of flotsam that had drifted into the harbour. After the mayhem of Dunkirk, he thought grimly, there were plenty of bits of wreckage floating up and down the Channel, and those aboard the *Glengyle* had no idea that a canoe was going to be used by the raiders. It would probably not occur to anyone that such a flimsy craft could be employed seriously or that its occupants would be crazy enough to use it to try to avoid the harbour patrol. Broakes had only been called into the meeting to hear that his vessel would be attacked, not how it was to be done.

'Hope Jerry is his usual prompt self,' Ayton whispered. 'I make it 0130 exactly.'

'Perhaps Goering's given them a night off,' said Pountney, but even as he spoke the air-raid siren on Dover Castle began to crank itself up before beginning its undulating, penetrating whine. It rose and fell, a banshee warning of death and destruction to come, and moments later fingers of searchlights began to stab the sky, criss-crossing one another as they sought out the intruders. Then the two men heard the first throb of an aircraft's engines and, almost simultaneously, the 4.7-inch anti-aircraft battery on the cliff at the far end of the port opened fire. It sounded like a series of old tin doors being continually banged shut in the wind.

'Let's go,' said Pountney. They dug their paddles into the water and spurred the ancient canoe forward. As they paddled they could hear the sound of the aircraft engines increase, then the crump of the first bomb falling. By the time they had reached the *Glengyle* the raid was in full swing. Tracer criss-crossed the sky, sparkling red and white, and the Oerlikons aboard the commando ship coughed out their 20mm shells at the dark shadows sweeping overhead. They made a terrible racket.

Suddenly, out of nowhere, the distinctive outline of a Dornier swept towards the *Glengyle* almost at water level and machine-gun bullets whined and skipped around the canoeists. Then abruptly it roared skywards and swung out to sea.

'Shit,' said Pountney. 'Too close for comfort.'

They had gambled on the nightly German 'tip-and-run' air raid on Dover as cover for their own attack, but

Pountney had not reckoned with the *Glengyle* being one of the Luftwaffe's targets.

The canoe was now under the bows of the commando ship and they could feel the hull vibrating as the Oerlikons pumped their shells into the night sky. As the canoe moved slowly down the ship's side Pountney fumbled for the chalk. He held up his hand palm forward to indicate to Ayton to stop the canoe and then he chalked, well above the water-line so that it would not be washed off, a large cross on the ship's side.

The first explosive device had been fixed.

He raised his hand again, this time making a forward motion, and Ayton eased the canoe towards the commando ship's stern.

Right by where he reckoned the engine-rooms were situated, Pountney made another cross and, for good measure, wrote 'bang' in equally large letters. Then he raised his hand again and this time indicated with a circular motion of his forefinger that Ayton should turn the canoe around.

Now came the really tricky bit.

Pountney turned and leant back so that he could whisper in his companion's ear: 'They might be keeping an eye on the boat boom. I'm going up the mooring chain.'

Ayton nodded. Suddenly, as if someone had blown a whistle for half-time, all the guns in Dover stopped firing at the same moment. The canoe was now facing towards the town and the two men could see an ominous glow of flames where a bomb had fallen on a row of terraced houses near the docks.

Above them someone began heaving empty shell cases over the side and shouting for more ammunition. Ayton glanced at the luminous dial of his watch, then bent forward. 'Second round should start in two minutes,' he whispered. Pountney nodded and took a swig from his hip-flask.

The second wave of German bombers came from a different direction, showing, Pountney thought, at least a degree of imagination. But the defenders knew this little trick and were quickly in action. The canoeists watched one bomber caught, like a fly in a web, by three searchlights and a fourth quickly joined in. However it ducked and weaved, the searchlights moved with it and then the puffs of exploding shells from the heavy anti-aircraft battery on the cliff surrounded it.

One moment the bomber was there, a black beetle surrounded by light; the next there was a flash of flame and it was gone. Inwardly Pountney cheered. Somehow it was a good omen for his own mission.

As they moved the canoe towards the *Glengyle*'s mooring buoy, the ship's armament opened up again. Ayton held on to the large, can-shaped steel buoy with one hand and steadied the canoe as Pountney cautiously lifted himself out of its cockpit, grasped the steel chain and hauled himself on to the buoy. For a moment he crouched there, taking in his surroundings, then began slowly, steadily ascending the massive chain that held the commando ship to the buoy.

The chain sagged slightly under Pountney's weight and the buoy dipped and swung. Using the links as footholds, he managed to stay balanced until he was almost two-thirds of the way up the chain. But it then became too steep and for the last third he had to haul himself up arm over arm.

The hawse pipe was not big enough to allow him to squeeze through it, but he was over the bulwark in one quick movement and crouched down behind the anchor winch which dominated the forecastle. The deck vibrated under him as the twin Oerlikons a few yards from him began pounding out their shells again. He could see the sun crew gathered round the mounting, their white anti-flash masks standing out plainly in the semi-darkness. The noise was appalling. He might be seen, but he certainly wasn't going to be heard.

He dodged from the anchor winch to another piece of machinery and considered what to do. He could chalk another cross, but it could easily be obliterated. He really needed to take back something tangible, something that was identifiable with the ship. Bent double, he moved cautiously aft towards the Oerlikons, which were still pumping out their shells, while at the same time watching for any movement further aft. Suddenly his foot hit something soft and he crouched down and examined it. It was just what he needed. He stuffed it down his overalls, ran doubled back to the ship's bows and slid down the mooring chain so fast he felt his hands and thighs burning painfully. He lowered himself into the canoe and took up his paddle.

'Go like shit,' he shouted to Ayton above the hammering of the Oerlikons. 'We're in business.'

Keyes shuffled the papers in front of him and looked over his spectacles at the captain of the *Glengyle* seated at the other end of the table. 'Why don't you kick off, Dick?'

Broakes cleared his throat and opened in front of him a large, black book. 'This is the deck log for the last twenty-four hours,' he said. 'After our meeting yesterday I informed my executive officer that someone might try and board the ship during the course of the night. He therefore doubled the sentries and asked if I required a standing patrol to be mounted in a cutter around the ship. I said I considered this unnecessary, but that a lookout should be detailed for the bridge with specific instructions to watch for any unusual movements in the harbour.'

Broakes glanced down at the black book and began reading from it. ' "At 0128 he reported what looked like a piece of wreckage directly ahead but neither he nor the officer of the watch could discern what it was. Two minutes later the nightly German 'tip-and-run' raid began. The for'ard Oerlikon opened fire at 0135, the after Oerlikon at 0136. The for'ard Oerlikon fired 172 rounds, the after Oerlikon 194. Both guns ceased firing at 0156. The pom-pom crews were closed up but did not open fire. No damage reported, except for superficial damage caused by machine-gun bullets from a low-flying Dornier. These chipped . . ." '

'Quite, quite,' Keyes interrupted gently, not wanting a list of where the paintwork of the captain's precious ship had been damaged. 'What about Lieutenant Pountney? When did he arrive and what did you do about him?'

Broakes looked up, took off his glasses and wiped them, then looked down at the book again. A moment later he shut it and said to Keyes: 'No intruders were reported in the deck log. I also checked this myself with the officers of the watch this morning before I left the ship.'

'I see. And could he have come and gone without your guards knowing?'

'Impossible, sir. Except during the raid, when all hands were needed at action stations, there were guards the length of the ship and a roving one as well.'

Keyes sighed. It seemed a disappointing end to a

creditable idea. 'Let's ask Lieutenant Pountney what happened to him,' he said, and nodded to the Marine standing by the door to open it.

Pountney entered and saluted smartly, and was told to stand at ease. No one noticed that he was carrying a small kitbag, which he placed unobtrusively behind him.

'How did it go, Pountney?' asked the Director of Combined Operations.

'Very well, thank you, sir.'

'A success, then?'

'I would judge it a total success, sir.'

There was a murmur of surprise around the table. Keyes cleared his throat. He obviously found the situation highly amusing.

'But Captain Broakes says there was no intrusion. His deck log does not record one, and therefore it couldn't have happened.'

'If Captain Broakes would care to send someone over the starboard side of his ship, sir, they will find two chalked crosses on the hull. One near the bows, the other where the engine-rooms are.'

'We found those,' admitted Broakes. 'But how do we know it was Lieutenant Pountney who put them there?'

'Well, Pountney?'

'I wrote this word near one of the crosses, sir.'

Pountney handed Keyes a piece of paper.

The Admiral unfolded it and smiled. 'Very appropriate, I'm sure. There was a word by one of the crosses, Dick?'

'There was, sir.'

'And what was it?'

' "Bang".'

A ripple of laughter went round the table.

'Well, that seems to settle that point,' said Keyes. 'But you told us, young man, that you would get aboard the *Glengyle* unseen and unheard, and that was the crucial part of the raid. I assume that Captain Broakes is correct in saying that no one boarded his ship last night?'

Pountney stiffened. 'No, sir. He is not.'

Again, there was a murmur of surprise.

'He is not correct?'

'No, sir. I climbed up the mooring chain and went aboard over the bows.'

Captain Broakes leant forward. 'At what time was this?'

'Immediately the air raid started, sir.'

'You used the air raid as cover?' Keyes said sharply.

Pountney nodded. 'If the weather's clear Jerry comes every night around that time. He's very punctual.'

'Good,' said Keyes, 'very good.'

Broakes's smile softened his severe features. 'Quite an accomplishment under the circumstances. I congratulate you, Lieutenant.

'Thank you, sir.'

There was a pause before Broakes added: 'But how do we know? If no one aboard saw you, what proof have we?'

'That's right,' Keyes said. 'Did you use your chalk on board?'

Pountney shook his head.

'Pity,' said Keyes. 'No absolute proof then.'

'Was nothing reported missing aboard the *Glengyle*, sir?' Pountney asked.

Keyes looked enquiringly at Broakes, who shook his head.

'It should have been,' said Pountney. He bent and shook open the bag he had brought with him.

'May I, sir?'

Keyes nodded and Pountney placed a large, sleeve-shaped canvas cover on the table. Keyes turned it over and exposed the word 'Glengyle' stamped along one side of it.

'An Oerlikon muzzle cover?'

'Yes, sir.'

Keyes passed the canvas cover down the table to Broakes, who looked at it and turned it over, then shook his head in disbelief.

Keyes stood up and extended his hand. 'Congratulations. How many men do you want?'

'A dozen to start with, sir.'

'You shall have them. I'm seconding you immediately to No. 8 Commando, which is now training on the Isle of Arran. Good luck.'

3

'Periscope depth, Number One.'

David Woods's two wavy gold stripes on his sleeves showed he was an officer in the Royal Naval Volunteer Reserve, the 'wavy navy'. Inevitably, he was known to his many friends as 'Timber' and he sported a luxurious beard and moustache, both of which were, like his hair, tinged with red. They hid the youthfulness of his face, but his eyes were no longer young; they had a strained, alert look which conveyed, better than any words, the burden of responsibility which lay upon him as the submarine's captain, and his constant proximity to death.

'Aye, aye, sir.'

The First Lieutenant of the two-hundred-foot S-class submarine *Sentinel* turned to the two coxswains who controlled the vessel's external planes. 'Take her to thirty feet,' he ordered.

The planesmen sat on the port side of the submarine's control room in front of two large depth gauges. They watched these as they swung the wheels which altered the angle of the planes. The gauges' needles, which had been rock-steady on eighty feet since the submarine had dived at dawn that morning, began to rise steadily, though all those in the control room could feel was a slight tilt of the floor beneath them.

No one and nothing broke the silence until the First Lieutenant said sharply: 'Thirty feet, sir.'

'Up main periscope.'

The engine-room artificer sitting at the control room's vent-and-blow panel moved a lever and the larger of the two bronze columns which ran through the control room and up through the submarine's pressure hull began to rise smoothly and silently. As soon as the end of the periscope, with its two rubber eyepieces, emerged from its well in the bottom of the hull, Woods moved towards it. While it was still moving he crouched down and snapped open the periscope's two control handles, and by the time the column came to rest at shoulder height he already had his eyes glued to the eyepieces. Bending slightly, he moved the periscope expertly through a complete circle, his body moving with it.

'Where should we be, Pilot?'

The navigator, a chubby-faced sub-lieutenant in the Royal Navy, looked up from the chart spread out on the chart table in front of him. 'Four miles south-south-east of the port of Rhodes, sir. We should be two miles offshore. The chart shows a windmill a mile inland.'

There was a pause as Woods scanned the shoreline: 'More like three miles.'

He gave the right handle of the periscope half a turn away from him, as if he was changing gear on a motorcycle. It was now in high magnification, which gave a narrower but more powerful picture.

'Yes, I see it. Good. Well done. Down periscope.'

The end of the bronze column slid silently back into its well. He turned to the elder of the two men watching him. 'We've got you here, Jumbo. What next?'

'We must find the best beach to land on, Timber. The

nearest to Maritsa,' said Pountney without hesitation, 'and then tonight we land.'

Together they bent over the chart table with the navigator. Pountney pointed out Maritsa airfield in the north-west of the island.

'I can see only three possible landing places,' Woods said, pointing them out, 'and one of those looks rather close to an inhabited area to be of much use.'

Pountney studied the chart. Most of the coastline of Rhodes was rocky. Isolated beaches in the area where they wanted to land were not going to be easy to find.

'Perhaps. Let's have a look at it anyway. You agree, Phil?'

Ayton nodded immediately. Where they landed was Pountney's decision, not his. He had learnt from their training in Scotland that the older man's knack in finding the right place to land in a canoe – or 'folbot' as their precarious, fragile means of transport was now officially called – was uncanny. Ayton's area of expertise was making up the various explosive charges he had been trained to use and laying them to make sure they did maximum damage.

Having worked together on Arran for the past nine months, the two men knew each other's strengths and weaknesses, understood every expression, every innuendo. They could anticipate each other's moves with uncanny accuracy and a flick of the fingers or the movement of the head was instantly and correctly interpreted.

After acclimatization and further training on the Bitter Lakes at Kabrit, Pountney, now a captain, and his men had been attached to the First Submarine Flotilla at Alexandria and renamed No. 1 Special Boat Section. But, apart from a beach reconnaissance on another part of Rhodes which Pountney had made with a friend of his, Lieutenant commander Tony Eden, this was their first operation since the Section had been shipped to Egypt as part of a commando force, called Layforce after its commander, Major-General Bob Laycock.

Much to Pountney's delight, the Section's unofficial secondment to the Royal Navy had put it outside direct Army control and out of the grasp of the empire-building General Headquarters staffs in Cairo. This suited everyone – except the empire builders. The unit's new name sounded suitably anonymous, but Laycock warned Pountney to guard his independence 'like a virgin guards her virtue' as the 'desk wallahs' in Cairo and Whitehall hated the newly formed independent special forces.

'They're trained to think for themselves and they pinch all the best men. Both are unforgivable crimes in the mind of any Army bureaucrat.'

Enemy airfields were the SBS's top-priority targets, for Malta was already under siege from the air. Destroying aircraft on the ground would help lessen the increasingly heavy odds against the convoys dispatched from Gibraltar and Alexandria being sent to sustain the island.

'We'll take her back down to eighty feet, Number One.'

The First Lieutenant, or Jimmy as he was always known by the crew, repeated the order to the planesmen. The planesmen spun their wheels to adjust the submarine's two sets of planes and the *Sentinel* slipped quietly back into the depths.

'Eighty feet, sir.'

'Group down,' Woods said into the voice pipe which connected him to the engine-room.

'Course, Pilot?'

'Three-five-five degrees, sir, up to the cape,' the navigator answered unhesitatingly. 'Then one-eight-five degrees once we've rounded it.'

'Very good. Three-five-five it is.'

'Steer three-five-five, sir,' the helmsman repeated from his corner of the control room. He pronounced the numbers 'three ... fife ... fife' and did so clearly and distinctly to make quite certain he had heard them correctly. He eased his wheel, watching the gyro compass spinning slowly in front of him.

'Distance to the first beach, Pilot?'

'About twenty-five miles, sir.'

'Three hours' running. Very good. Let me know when we get there, Number One.'

The submarine arrived off the first beach just before noon and Woods ordered it to periscope depth. Now the full heat of the spring day made the air shimmer in the lens of the periscope, distorting distances and blurring landmarks. The water was glassy calm, but Woods brought the submarine as close to the shore as he dared. After making sure there were no ships in the area, he handed over the periscope to Pountney.

'A steep shingle beach,' Pountney told Ayton, who was standing beside him. Ayton was close enough to Pountney to notice how the prisms in the periscope were concentrating the light into a pinpoint which pierced the pupils of Pountney's eyes. 'There's a road behind. And a building ... Looks like a hotel. Very grand. Oy, oy, what have we here? Krauts. Lots of them. Must be an officers' mess of some sort. Have a look.'

He unbent and stood back, allowing Ayton to take his position. Ayton had never looked through a periscope before, though Woods had taught them both how to alter the magnification and angle of the lens. He was surprised how wide the angle of vision was. He changed the magnification to high and the figures on the hotel lawn sprang at him, astonishingly close. He could even make out some of the details of their uniforms. Most of them looked like Luftwaffe officers, probably off-duty pilots from Maritsa airfield.

He turned the left handle half a turn away from him to change the angle of the lens. Now he was looking at the hills that lay blue-grey in the distance, then at the sky directly above the submarine.

'What do you think?'

Ayton's eyes were still glued to this fascinating toy. He swivelled the periscope back until it was again focusing on the hotel's crowded lawn.

'Bit close to those Krauts,' he said doubtfully. He stepped back and Woods ordered the periscope to be housed back in its well.

'That's what I like about it,' growled Pountney. 'They won't be expecting anybody to come through their back door. We might even have some explosive left over to leave them a welcoming early-morning call.'

'If you think it's OK, let's do it,' said Ayton immediately. It seemed an unnecessary risk to him, but Pountney appeared to positively enjoy taking unnecessary risks.

Pountney rubbed his chin. He knew what Ayton was thinking. He said to Woods: 'We'll have a dekko at the others before we finally decide.'

Once more the submarine dived back to eighty feet. This was the minimum depth for safety in the clear blue of the Aegean Sea. Any less and the submarine might not avoid detection from the air, even though it was painted the cobalt colour of the surrounding water.

The electric motors hummed quietly. The air in the pressurized hull was heavy now from the lack of oxygen and Ayton could feel beads of sweat forming on his forehead.

After twenty minutes Woods ordered the submarine back to periscope depth. They were now much closer to Maritsa airfield, and the danger of being spotted from low-flying aircraft made him particularly cautious. He scanned the sky above the horizon intently, before turning to peer at the shoreline.

Pountney concealed his impatience by pretending to study the chart, but Ayton could feel that he was bursting to get going.

Eventually Woods straightened up and called Pountney over to the periscope. Eagerly, Pountney clasped the handles and adjusted the height until he could stand easily on the circumference of the periscope well.

After a moment he stepped back. 'No bloody good at all,' he said with disgust. 'Are you sure we're in the right place?'

The young navigator looked reproachful. 'Quite sure.'

'See what you think, Phil.'

Ayton adjusted the periscope height and looked into the eyepieces. He saw at once that what the chart had shown as a beach was not one at all. It was a rocky outcrop over which the waves were breaking and swirling with a force that would have made landing in the fragile folbot impossible.

'Hopeless,' he agreed.

Then, reluctant to lose touch with the outside world, he swung the periscope round to the north before racking the lens angle upwards with the handle to look above the headland.

33

Beyond the curve of the land, just above the horizon, he saw three indistinct dots. At first his brain did not register what they were, as they seemed not to be moving. But when he changed the periscope to high magnification they leapt out at him. He stumbled back and felt Woods brush past.

'Aircraft,' he said as the latter seized the handles. 'Three, I think.'

'I've got them,' said Woods. 'Impossible to tell at this distance, but they're probably Capronis. Well spotted.'

He snapped the handles closed. 'Down periscope. One hundred feet, Number One. But don't take her down too fast. We don't want any disturbance on the surface.'

The First Lieutenant issued his orders. The planesmen spun their wheels. All was quiet, but there was a tension in the control room that hadn't been there before. Everyone knew that the Italian Caproni bomber was also used as an anti-submarine patrol aircraft, and that in this role it carried depth-charges as well as bombs.

The moments ticked by.

'One hundred feet, sir,' the First Lieutenant said quietly.

'Turn on the echo-sounder, Pilot,' Woods ordered the navigator. 'What depth have we under us?'

'Fifty feet, sir.'

'Take her down to the seabed, Number One. We'll lie there for a while.'

Again the planesmen spun their wheels. Woods cut the speed back further until they all felt the hull bump and jar on the sea bottom. Then he said quietly: 'Stop engines.'

Neither Pountney nor Ayton knew what to expect and Woods, busy issuing his orders, was far too occupied to tell them. But the navigator, seeing Ayton's expression, said cheerfully: 'They won't see us this deep. Especially as we're lying doggo.'

Pountney glanced at his watch. Woods caught the movement and said: 'I know. Time's short. Can't be helped.'

The minutes passed and the air seemed to get thicker and hotter, making any movement tiring. Ayton felt a trickle of sweat on his face. Pountney fidgeted with his watch, but forced himself not to look at its dial. He knew Woods would surface when he thought it was safe and not before. He was beginning to learn that, as in all areas of combat, there was a lot of hanging around in submarine operations. It didn't suit Pountney. One thing he hated was hanging around.

After half an hour Woods ordered the submarine to 'group down' and steer for the third beach. 'Let's hope it's going to be suitable,' he said to the SBS officers. 'Thanks to those Wop bombers there's not going to be time to recce any others. Remember, we're going to have to recharge our battery before we land you.'

Pountney didn't argue with that. The SBS men hadn't been aboard the *Sentinel* long, but it had been long enough for them to have learnt the vital necessity of conserving the power of the submarine's fifty-ton battery, which drove the electric engines when the submarine was submerged, and of ensuring that it remained as fully charged as possible. They knew that the order 'group down' meant that the battery cells were put in series instead of parallel, to save precious juice, and that the battery could only be charged by the submarine's diesel engines, which could only be used on the surface. At full speed on the electric motors, the battery lasted only an hour. In that time the submarine could cover about eight miles. At slow speed, say two knots, the battery could last a day or more. A dead battery meant a dead crew; it was as simple as that.

Twenty minutes later they were off the third beach. Its pebbles, bleached white by the sun, glittered and sparkled in the periscope. It was long and narrow and shelved only gradually. It was perfect to land on, but when Pountney surveyed it he could not see any way off it.

'Well?' said Woods. There was a note of irritation in his voice.

Pountney stood back and shook his head. 'It'll have to be the first beach or nothing.'

'Then you'd better have another look at it,' said Woods. 'But it'll be midnight before I can land you there.'

'The Krauts in the hotel should all be tucked up in bed by that time,' said Pountney. He exchanged glances with Ayton, who shrugged.

Woods ordered the submarine to submerge to eighty feet. By the time they reached the first beach again and returned to periscope depth, the sun was setting behind them. The light was quite different now. It threw a yellowish, mellow glow over the beach and the hotel, and the flat surface of the sea had turned a fiery orange red.

Several German officers were having a last bathe of the day. Ayton watched them with the main periscope on high magnification. They seemed so close he could almost touch them; they certainly appeared close enough to shoot, and he felt a tremor of cold hatred pass through him.

Both SBS men scanned the beach again from end to end with meticulous care. Their lives were going to depend on reaching it, crossing it and moving off it without being detected. It was something they had practised time and again on Arran in all sorts of weather and against all kinds of simulated opposition. But no exercise, no training, however thorough, could fully prepare them for what they were about to do.

The submarine turned seawards, and dived. Woods kept her at eighty feet and, five miles offshore, ordered: 'Surfacing stations.'

The order was repeated through the submarine, and brought more seamen into the control room. In one corner the hydrophone operator, his earphones on his head, listened intently for the sound of any surface ship. The minutes passed, then Woods ordered: 'Darken ship.'

The control room's lights dimmed until only a glimmer illuminated the depth gauges and the steering compass.

'It's to get our eyes used to night vision,' the navigator told Ayton. 'Your eyes use an entirely different set of muscles to see in the dark. It takes fifteen minutes for them to dilate to maximum efficiency.'

The hydrophone operator took off his earphones. 'No HE, sir.'

'Good.'

'Hydrophone effect,' the navigator said when Ayton gave him a puzzled look. 'It's the noise the propellers of a surface ship make. The hydrophone can pick them up from a distance of some miles.'

'Up periscope.'

'The Captain won't be able to see much,' the navigator confided, 'but at least he can check we're not surfacing next to a Jerry patrol boat. They sometimes lie quiet on the surface waiting for a sub to surface. It's one of their tricks.'

'Stand by to surface.'

In the dim light Ayton could see one of the crew step up to the conning tower's lower hatch, slide aside its heavy metal clips and open it upwards until it clipped into the side of the tower.

'Ready to surface, sir,' the First Lieutenant reported.

'Down periscope,' ordered Woods. 'Surface.'

He began climbing the steel ladder up the interior of the conning tower, followed by the two surface lookouts.

'Twenty-five feet, sir,' the First Lieutenant called up to him; then: 'Twenty feet.'

Suddenly a roaring noise filled the control room. Ayton jumped. The navigator chuckled. 'Just compressed air expelling water from the ballast tanks,' he said reassuringly.

'Fifteen feet,' shouted the First Lieutenant.

'Ten feet.'

Woods opened the upper hatch and a gale of stale air swept up the conning tower as if someone had turned on a huge vacuum cleaner. The two lookouts mounted the ladder and disappeared from view. Ayton said he thought air would rush into the submarine, not out of it.

'There are always small leaks in the system of compressed-air pipes,' the navigator explained. 'So air pressure builds up when we've been submerged for any length of time.'

The roar of the compressed air stopped as suddenly as it had begun and now sweet, fresh air did flow down the conning tower into the control room. Ayton felt the submarine roll gently under his feet. They were on the surface.

'We'll keep going on our electric motors until the lookouts are sure Jerry's not lurking somewhere,' said the navigator.

'When they're certain everything's all right, we'll start the diesel motors, but not until then.'

Ayton stepped forward from the chart table and looked up the conning tower. Way up at the other end of the steel tunnel he could see the night sky. A star swung to and fro across the opening of the top hatch.

'Start main engines,' Woods boomed into the voice pipe from the bridge. The engine telegraphs clanged as the order was transmitted to the engine-room aft. There was a pause, then the hum of the electric engines ceased and the heavier throb of the diesels started. These could drive the submarine on the surface at nearly fifteen knots. They were the only way the battery which powered the electric engines could be recharged at sea.

'Captain says you can go on the bridge if you like,' the First Lieutenant said to the SBS men. 'Careful how you go. The ladder's a bit slippery from condensation.'

Woods greeted them with a cursory nod, then returned to scanning the black horizon with his night-glasses. Positioned back-to-back at the rear of the bridge, the two lookouts, dressed in the submarine service's ubiquitous dress, white roll-neck jerseys, were doing the same. Above the bridge the radar aerial had been extended and was rotating slowly.

The submarine surged through the flat-calm water, occasionally throwing up a white crest from its bow. To keep its profile as low as possible, Woods had ordered the internal trimming tanks to be filled just enough to keep the decks almost awash.

Ayton glanced around him. Immediately behind the bridge was a bandstand with a single Oerlikon 20mm gun on it and in front of the bridge was the submarine's main surface armament, a three-inch gun, its barrel glistening in the dark. Above the bridge, supported by the periscope standard, was the jumping wire, which stretched from stem to stern. This allowed the *Sentinel* to sneak under submarine nets without becoming entangled, though Woods had told Ayton that no submarine commander in his right mind ever went near submarine nets.

Astern of the submarine, Rhodes had already been swallowed up in the night, but ahead Ayton could just make out, etched across the sky, the mountainous mainland of Greece.

Woods stooped down to the voice pipe and ordered an alteration of course. Being low in the water, the submarine was slow to answer the helm, but eventually swung round so that the Greek mainland was now more to starboard.

'We'll run towards Simi for a while,' Woods said without taking his eyes away from his binoculars.

'How long will it take to charge the battery?' Pountney asked.

'Too long if we stay under way,' said Woods. 'But I'm going to stop. That way the engines will give the battery a stronger boost. We'll have you ashore by midnight.'

'The electric motors can be reversed and used as dynamos,' the First Lieutenant explained to the baffled SBS men when they went below. 'But the diesels aren't powerful enough to drive the propellers *and* make the dynamos give a high charge to the battery. To do that you have to disengage the propellers.'

'We'll have to lay up during the day and make the attack tomorrow night,' Pountney said to Ayton as they made their final preparations, 'Timber wasn't too pleased when I told him that meant a twenty-four-hour delay for him.'

'The Navy's job is to sink enemy ships,' Ayton reasoned. 'No submariner wants to hang around in risky waters like these just for the sake of a couple of cloak-and-dagger boys.'

'Crap!' said Pountney with his usual vehemence. 'I know you bootnecks are part of the Navy and think the sun shines out of its arse. But if the Navy wants to stop its Malta convoys from being bombed it's going to have to rely on the likes of us.'

They rested while the *Sentinel's* diesels throbbed gently, pushing power into the battery. They woke when they heard orders being given for the submarine to submerge and the navigator put his head round the dividing curtain. 'The Captain says he will be in position to drop you in half an hour. He can take you to within half a mile of the beach as the seabed's pretty steep-to there.'

'Excellent,' said Pountney, brightening up. 'Please thank him.'

The navigator grinned. 'Thank me, instead. I think he wanted to drop you here.'

His head disappeared, to be replaced by that of one of the seamen carrying two steaming cups of cocoa. Pountney levered out his hip-flask from his trousers, and poured some rum into his.

As they sipped the warm, sweet, gluey mixture – known as 'ki' in the Navy – they checked each item of equipment again. There were packets of plastic explosive, boxes of primers, detonators and time-fuses, sets of magnets, adhesive tape, cordtex, a dozen clam mines and six Gammon grenades. These were all carefully packed into one of the bergen rucksacks, ready to be primed – submarines were too valuable to risk doing this on board.

The other bergen contained 'K' rations, spare ammunition clips, binoculars, first-aid equipment, morphine syringes, Benzedrine tablets, wire-cutters, a torch, a small stove and two ponchos in which they could wrap themselves for sleeping or use as a tent cover for shelter or to camouflage a hide-out. The two men wore black, oiled sweaters with sniper's netting tied round their necks like scarves, black woollen hats and lace-up rope-soled shoes which would not slip on the submarine's deck or on rocks. They each carried in a shoulder holster a Welrod pistol with a built-in silencer. This 22-calibre weapon had been developed for one of the British secret services and had proved very effective at close range. Both men also carried a Fairbairn-Sykes commando knife in a sheath strapped to their legs.

They had debated whether to bring heavier weapons, such as tommy-guns, but had decided against it. 'Speed is what matters,' Pountney had said. 'Don't let's clutter ourselves up with anything unnecessary.'

But now he said: 'I wish I'd brought my carbine. I feel bloody naked without it.'

Ayton grinned. Without his favourite weapon – an American lightweight automatic .300 carbine with a folding stock – Pountney seemed like a blind man without his white stick.

'You'll survive,' the younger man retorted. 'If the alarm is raised while we're still inside the perimeter we'd be hopelessly outgunned whatever we were armed with.'

'Yeah, but I might shoot a few of the buggers before they plugged me,' said Pountney, making Ayton think, not for the first time, how pugnacious a personality he was for the creator of a unit whose members depended on subterfuge and cunning for their survival.

'I sometimes think you're fighting the wrong war,

Jumbo,' he said. ' "Up and at 'em" must be your family motto.'

'No, it's "High living and low thinking",' retorted Pountney, then drained the last drop of ki from his cup and chased it down with a final swig of rum from his flask. 'And the trouble with you bloody bootnecks is that you're constipated with tradition.'

Pountney was always airing his jaundiced views about the Royal Marines, a corps he said was pickled in the aspic of centuries-old customs. By now it was an old joke between them, and caused no animosity.

'Come on, we'd better black up,' said Ayton, pulling out of his pocket a tin of camouflage cream. This he placed on the wardroom table and opened. As they began smearing their faces and hands, orders rang out in the control room as the submarine prepared to surface, and a few minutes later the two men felt the deck lurch slightly beneath their feet as the vessel rose from the depths.

The First Lieutenant put his head round the curtain. 'Five minutes to go, chaps. The Captain requests your presence on the bridge.'

They handed the bergens to each other as they climbed up the conning tower's ladder. Once on the bridge they saw that Woods was keeping the hull down until they were ready to disembark. He was, as ever, scanning the darkness intently with his binoculars. But this time he let them drop when the SBS men joined him, so that he could point out to them two leading marks. From these they could take compass bearings for a rendezvous with the submarine when they returned from the operation.

'The hotel is an obvious one and over on your right is a very distinctive tower. Can you see it above the skyline?'

Pountney nodded.

'Right. We're nine hundred yards off the beach. These are the reciprocal bearings of the hotel and the tower.'

He handed Pountney a slip of paper. 'This is the rendezvous. Agreed?'

'Good,' said Pountney. 'Excellent, in fact. Couldn't be better for us.'

'I'm going to surface fully now. You'll be as quick as you can, won't you?'

He shook the men's hands with a warmth which was in marked contrast to his usual aloofness. 'Good luck to you both. See you in forty-eight hours.'

He turned away and said into the voice pipe: 'Finish blowing numbers one and three ballast tanks.'

The order, taken by the helmsman, echoed back at him: 'Aye, aye, sir. Finish blowing numbers one and three ballast tanks.'

Compressed air bubbled around the sides of the submarine as it expelled what water remained in the two tanks, and gradually the hull eased itself to the surface, water streaming off its forecasing. Followed by the two seamen who would help them launch the canoe, the two SBS men climbed down the outside of the bridge using the steps inset into it, and walked cautiously along the forecasing with their bergens slung over their shoulders. Every so often a wave slopped across the hull, for Woods was still keeping the *Sentinel* as low in the water as he could by not totally emptying the other ballast tanks.

Ayton noted with approval that the two seamen wore thick socks over their feet to avoid slipping on the wet steel of the forecasing and that when they opened the torpedo hatch they loosened its butterfly nuts with a wooden mallet to deaden the noise. Any excessive sound on such a quiet night could easily carry to the shore. The seamen swung open the hatch, carefully hauled out the folbot, which had been handed up to them from below, and laid it on the forecasing before closing the hatch and resecuring the butterfly nuts with soft blows of the mallet.

The eighteen-foot Cockle MkII**, its official designation, was a development of the civilian canoe the two men had used to raid the *Glengyle* the previous year. It had a wooden frame covered with a toughened, waterproof canvas skin painted a dull khaki. The canoe, which had proper buoyancy and a watertight cockpit for each of the paddlers to sit in, was designed to fit down an S-class submarine's torpedo hatch. For this purpose, the lateral struts of its wooden frame amidships could be adjusted to narrow its beam by the required number of inches.

Pountney and Ayton worked quickly and with practised ease. They straightened the lateral struts, put one of the bergens into the bows and the other into the stern, then checked that all the equipment was in place. The next manoeuvre, launching the canoe, they knew from experience was the trickiest part of the operation, for it would be easy to capsize the fragile craft while lowering it over the submarine's bulbous ballast tanks, and even easier to capsize it when lowering themselves into the cockpits.

But the two seamen helping them knew their job, and after the canoe had been put into the water, one held it by its bow rope while the other steadied the hull to allow each canoeist to slide slowly and cautiously into position. Once seated, the SBS men clipped the waterproof coverings around their waists and unfastened the double paddles from the canoe's deck.

'Ready, sir?' asked the seaman holding the bow rope, peering down anxiously at them.

'Ready,' Pountney confirmed.

The seaman undid the rope from the bow, tied it into a neat coil and handed it to him. Pountney put the coil into the bows and told the seaman holding the canoe amidships to let go. This man then gave the side of the folbot a firm shove to get it clear of the casing.

The fragile craft swung away as both SBS men dug deep into the water with their double paddles, and moments later a thousand tons of submarine slipped back into the depths, leaving a widening circle of ripples. Operation Angelo was under way.

4

They aimed for the right-hand side of the beach, the opposite end from the blacked-out hotel. It was much darker at sea level than it had been on the *Sentinel*'s bridge, as if the starlight could not penetrate that close to the earth's surface. They seemed to be paddling into a black abyss and if Pountney hadn't checked the P8 compass fitted in front of him they could have been heading directly out to sea for all he knew.

Slowly the land began to take shape ahead of them, and soon they heard the grinding roar of the waves breaking on the beach and then sucking the sand and pebbles back with them. The sound told Pountney immediately that, though the sea was calm, there was probably a strong lateral current which they would have to take into account when landing.

All of a sudden the motion of the water became more turbulent and both paddlers worked hard to keep the folbot heading directly for the beach. A small wave slopped over the bows, then a bigger one hit the sides, pushing the craft sideways. They dug deep with their paddles to counter the spin. Spray flew into their faces. The sound of breaking waves became a roar as the folbot was swept towards land as if some invisible hand had picked it up and propelled it forwards.

Ayton shipped his paddle and secured it to the deck. Then he unsnapped the waterproof cover around his waist and, lifting his legs clear, swung them sideways and lowered them into the water, at the same time bending backwards to keep the canoe on an even keel. Pountney, aware of what his partner was doing, automatically leant the other way as Ayton launched himself into the water by pushing with his hands. He had timed it right, for the water was waist deep. He grabbed the stern to steady the folbot as Pountney made his own exit from the front cockpit. They towed the folbot through the breaking waves, keeping as low a profile as possible, ran it clear of the water's edge, then threw themselves on to the sand. They had not seen any patrols during the day, but they had no means of knowing if there were any at night.

They lay on the sand, searching the darkness. Nothing stirred except the cicadas which chirruped away in the bushes behind the beach. After a few minutes they rose cautiously and, half crouching, ran with the folbot to the jumble of rocks that marked the end of the beach. They slid the craft into a crevice before returning to the beach to erase their footsteps with a special rake they carried. This done, they returned to the folbot, took out the two bergens, climbed the rocks, crossed the road behind the beach and sheltered behind a drystone wall.

'So far so good,' whispered Pountney. Ayton could hear the suppressed excitement in his voice. 'We'll head inland and find a place to lie up during the day.'

'Good,' said Ayton crisply. He felt icy calm now.

'It'll be just a lot of Wops guarding the airfield. We'll run circles round 'em.'

'Perhaps,' said Ayton. Sometimes, he thought, Pountney's persistent optimism could be counter-productive.

They slung the bergens on to their backs. Pountney took out his pocket compass, set the correct bearing which would take them into the mountains near Maritsa, and set off at a steady pace with Ayton ten yards behind him.

At first they had to cross drystone walls and skirt the occasional farmhouse, but soon any signs of habitation disappeared. The ground underfoot gradually became rougher and more uneven, and then began to rise quite steeply. After two hours they rested in an outcrop of rocks. Ahead and above them the mountain ridge cut a clear line across the night sky. Looking back the way they had come, they could see the coastline below them and the sea a black mass beyond it.

They opened two cans of self-heating soup, Pountney lacing his liberally with rum from his hip-flask. When they had finished them they buried the cans, and while Pountney checked the route with his compass Ayton studied the map with a shaded torch.

'If we're where I think we are,' he said, 'I reckon we're about ten miles from the airstrip.'

'We'll cover that before dawn, no problem,' Pountney replied. 'So we should have plenty of time to find a hide-out for the day. Might even be able to recce the airstrip quickly.'

But the gradient became steeper than ever and in the dark they had difficulty clawing their way up. Soon they were forced to abandon a direct route to the ridge and take a zigzag one instead. Eventually they stumbled across a rough path, spotted here and there with mule dung, and followed it upwards. It petered out near a ruined building tucked under the ridge. They climbed the last hundred yards to the crest over large rocks, to find themselves looking down on a flat coastal plain. Pountney scanned the area with his binoculars, but everything was too shrouded in mist and darkness for him to be able to see the airfield. They rested for ten minutes before beginning the descent. This proved even more difficult than the ascent, for the ground was a scree of loose rocks on which they slithered and slipped. The noise they made echoed alarmingly off the mountainside, but they comforted themselves with the fact that they were miles from any habitation.

The ground levelled out after a while and when it began to steepen again the scree was replaced by rocky outcrops, clumps of coarse grass, bare earth and the occasional sparsely leafed bush or tree. They half slithered, half climbed down, hanging on to what they could, tired now from the weight of their bergens and concerned that it would soon be light. At last they were able to walk without difficulty, though the ground was strewn with loose stones and rocks, so that they stumbled frequently. They were both well aware that a turned ankle would be fatal to the operation.

Glancing back, Ayton saw the first glimmer of light above the ridge. At the same moment Pountney said: 'There it is.'

Just discernible in the pre-dawn gloom below them were the two parallel lines of the runway, much lighter against the dark background of the plain. Ayton could just make out the curves and humps of a line of hangars. Ten minutes later they came to a crumbling stone hut. Its corrugated-iron roof had slipped so that one edge of it lay propped on a nearby rock. The only sign of previous habitation was an iron stove which lay rusting on its side.

'This'll do,' said Pountney, sliding his bergen off his back. They cleared the rubble from the compacted earth floor and spread out their ponchos, ate one of the 'K' ration meals, and took liberal swigs from their hip-flasks.

'I'll stand sentry first,' said Pountney, and as Ayton slept he watched the morning sun climb steadily above the mountain ridge. The heat shimmered off the rocks, blurring the air and distorting the landscape. It grew in intensity all morning until Pountney had to seek the shelter of what shade the corrugated-iron roof could provide.

At midday he shook Ayton, and together they brewed some tea on the tiny collapsible solid-fuel stove they had brought with them.

Ayton felt refreshed and more cheerful. Pountney lay down on his poncho, pulled his bergen under his head, told Ayton to wake him at four, then fell asleep immediately.

The heat intensified and the hum of the cicadas grew more persistent. The roof was now too hot to touch and too hot to shelter under. Ayton took Pountney's binoculars and climbed a nearby tree. This shaded him from the sun and, as he had hoped, exposed him to a faint, cooling breeze that carried with it the scent of thyme. He settled back in a fork near the top of the tree and began scanning the area with the binoculars. From his vantage point he could just see parts of the airstrip, which he judged to be about two miles away. His view included a stretch of the perimeter fence which he studied intently. This seemed to consist of ordinary linked-wire netting topped by a triple row of barbed wire angled outwards at forty-five degrees. It did not look particularly formidable, though Ayton supposed there was an outside chance that it might be electrified. It would certainly be protected by anti-personnel mines or booby-traps unless the Italians were even more incompetent than they were reputed to be. He knew that there would be patrols. There might also be dogs, though he fervently hoped not, for he liked dogs and had a healthy respect for their abilities. Throwing a dog off your scent once it had got on to you was not easy, as he had learnt during his training in Scotland. A trained Alsatian could scent a man at a hundred yards in optimum conditions.

He moved the binoculars to study the one hangar he could see, but it was closed and there was no sign of life around it. As he switched to another building he could not immediately identify, he heard the throb of aero engines to his left, and turned. They looked like triple-engined Savoia-Marchettis, the type they had been told were stationed at Maritsa, but their outlines shimmered so much in the heat that it was difficult to be sure.

He watched the three bombers circle the airfield and land. Shortly afterwards another three appeared from the same direction, and touched down. Then another came in, lower than the rest, and Ayton could see that it was in trouble as it swung groggily in the sky. But, to Ayton's disappointment, the pilot managed to land it.

The sound of the engines revving up came to him clearly as they taxied off the runway. Then there was silence again except for the constant hum of the cicadas. Ayton waited an hour before returning to the hut to wake Pountney.

'Seven of them, you say?'

'Well, six and a half. The damaged one looked on its last legs.'

'I expect they've been bombing some convoy to bits or attacking Crete. The bastards.'

British forces had just withdrawn to Crete from Greece, which the Germans had invaded the previous month, and were now bracing themselves for a German attack on the island.

'If the perimeter fence is the walk-over you say it is, we won't have any trouble getting into the place.'

'Do you want to recce it beforehand?'

Pountney shook his head. 'I'll just take a shufti from your tree.'

Pountney moved off with the binoculars and Ayton began unpacking the bergens. He was delighted to see they had been given the latest type of plastic explosive. The earlier version, known as Nobel 808, had an almond smell which always gave him a severe headache, however carefully he handled it. The new stuff, known to everyone simply as PE, was much more malleable and hardly smelt at all. It looked like a block of butter but had the consistency of plasticine.

The ten rolls of PE were wrapped in waxed paper. Ayton laid them in a row on the floor of the hut. Each weighed 224g, half of which was enough to destroy any aircraft. Then he took out the clam mines – small explosive devices designed to be attached to their targets with magnets – and the empty sacks of the Gammon grenades, and laid them to one side.

The clams could be useful if there were any trucks or small armoured vehicles on the airfield worth destroying, but they wouldn't need the Gammons unless they were discovered and had to fight their way out. He'd never used them, but he'd been told they were just the job against armoured cars and light tanks, especially the Italian ones, whose armoured plate was paper-thin.

Next he took from the bergens the primers and detonators and pencil fuses for the explosive charges he wanted to make up, and finally he placed on a nearby chunk of masonry the lengths of cordtex he had brought with him, just in case Pountney decided it was worth laying a series of charges which would explode simultaneously. Then he took out his pocket knife and began to cut the rolls of PE in half. He had just finished doing this and begun taping the magnets to the charges, when Pountney returned.

'It all seems so quiet down there,' he said. 'You'd have thought we'd have seen perimeter patrols or at least some trucks going in and out.'

'Too bloody hot for them, I expect,' said Ayton. He finished taping the magnets and opened the box containing the primers. These were cork-shaped pieces of explosive with a hole drilled in the middle to take the detonator. He took care to keep wiping away the sweat trickling from his brow. Though the primers were covered with a damp-proof coating, any liquid that came into contact with them could prevent them from working properly.

Ayton began working the primers into the charges. This was simpler than it had been in the Scottish climate, because the heat made the PE easy to mould. He inserted a primer at each end of the charge, for everything had to be duplicated to cut the risk of equipment failure.

Pountney watched Ayton's meticulous preparations restlessly, his mind churning over every possible thing that could go wrong. 'This place is hundreds of miles from the nearest British base,' he said, almost thinking aloud. 'It's way beyond the range of any British bomber base. So they can't be expecting an attack from the air, much less one from the land.'

'That's what the SBS is all about, Jumbo. Surprise. In and out before anyone's had time to say as much as fucking hello or goodbye. I just hope the others have as good a chance as we've got.'

Pountney grunted his agreement. He'd been wondering how the others had been getting on. The complete Special Boat Section of twelve men had been committed to Operation Angelo, the aim of which was to destroy as many enemy aircraft on the ground as possible so as to lessen the air attacks on the vital Malta convoys. The target airfields were scattered across the Axis-occupied parts of the eastern and central Mediterranean and no fewer than six submarines had been committed to help carry out the raids as part of their routine patrols.

'If the LRDG can do it, so can we,' Pountney said.

The Long Range Desert Group had become past masters at raiding aerodromes behind enemy lines in Libya with their heavily armed jeeps and trucks, and had a proven record of success. But the SBS still had to prove it could be done from the sea, and Pountney knew the future of his unit hung on the success or failure of Angelo. If it failed to produce the goods, the SBS might not have a second chance, and Pountney knew he could then very well be returned to the humdrum existence of an infantry officer, a fate which he had worked strenuously and consistently to avoid.

'We can do it,' Ayton said quietly.

He finished inserting the primers into the plastic explosive and began inserting a detonator through the hole of each primer, making sure that it was the open end of the detonator which was sticking out. He handled each detonator with great care for, unlike PE, which could be hit by a bullet without exploding, the half which was inserted into the primer was made with a very sensitive explosive. To protect it from dampness, each detonator had been packed in sawdust, and Ayton was careful to tap off every trace before inserting the detonator in the primer. It was a long, slow business which needed patience – which was why it was Ayton's job not Pountney's.

'You're bloody methodical, aren't you, Phil?' Pountney remarked. Part of him admired this trait in his companion, but a larger part was irritated by it. He knew well enough that the greatest care always had to be taken in preparing explosive charges, but he couldn't for the life of him see why Ayton had to remove every speck of sawdust before inserting a detonator, or why the charges were laid out as if they were on parade. It was, he supposed, simply part of a Marine's training. The Marines didn't just clean the caps of their boots until they could see their immaculately shaved faces in them; they also polished the leather sole under the boot as well. And then they put Brasso on the studs.

'Better safe than sorry,' Ayton replied. He was aware of the triteness of the remark, but as a result of his training, and from stories he had heard from those who had returned from operations, he knew how unreliable explosive charges could be, especially those detonated by time-fuses. It seemed pointless for him and Pountney to expose themselves to such danger, only to be thwarted in their aim by a badly assembled charge which either failed to detonate or, worse, detonated prematurely, perhaps killing the man who had laid it.

After inserting primers and detonators into each roll of PE – firing systems were always duplicated in case one failed – Ayton checked and double-checked each one to make sure that they were clean, secure and dry before starting on the trickiest part of the assembly.

Pountney watched Ayton irritably for a while before turning away and leaving the hut. He glanced at his watch and then at the late-afternoon sky. The sun was sinking now, but was still strong enough to force him to shade his eyes as he scanned the open country ahead. He wanted to move up to the airfield while it was still light, so that they could recce the place properly and then break through the perimeter as soon as it got dark. If they didn't they would be behind schedule, because they were going to need the best part of the night to return the way they had come and rendezvous with the submarine before dawn.

'How long, Phil?' he asked impatiently when he returned to the hut.

'Give me a quarter of an hour,' Ayton muttered.

He removed from the bergen the two cigar-shaped containers in which the pencil fuses were packed. As their name implied, these were about the shape and length of a pencil. At one end of each fuse was a copper tube, at the other a sprung-steel connector with a percussion cap inside it. In the middle was a spring-loaded striker held off the percussion cap by a thin wire.

Ayton looked through the inspection hole in each fuse to make sure that the wire was not broken or obstructed in any way. If he was in any doubt he put the suspect fuse aside. He connected the fuses by pushing their connectors into the open end of the detonators. When the time came, all that he and Pountney would have to do was to crush the fuse's copper end between forefinger and thumb and remove the coloured safety strip which prevented the striker from being accidentally released. Crushing the copper end broke an ampoule of acid which ate through the wire at a predetermined rate. In theory it was all very simple; in practice it didn't always work out that way.

When he had finished with the charges, Ayton prepared a detonator and pencil fuse for each of the clam mines. These were small Bakelite containers, filled with explosive, which already had magnets and primers fitted to them. It was exacting work in the intense heat of the late afternoon, but Ayton worked steadily, making sure that each fuse fitted securely into its detonator.

Pountney was standing over him again and Ayton could feel his impatience. Pountney stooped and picked up one of the faulty fuses and examined it.

'Green. How long a delay is that?'

'Nine hours.' Ayton hated being interrupted, but tried not to sound irritable.

'That's much too long, Phil. It will be daylight by then and they're bound to be spotted before they explode.'

A slight frown wrinkled Ayton's forehead. It told anyone who knew him that he was annoyed, but he worked on in silence for a moment before saying quietly: 'Nine hours is an estimate, Jumbo. You know that as well as I do. How hot do you think it is now? Eighty?'

'At least,' said Pountney. 'Nearer ninety, I'd say.'

'And how much does it drop during the night?'

Pountney shrugged at such minutiae. 'Haven't a clue. Quite a bit, I suppose.'

'Yeah, but not by all that much, and metal aircraft are bound to retain some of that heat, aren't they?'

'You're probably right,' replied Pountney. He knew what Ayton was driving at. Even so, nine hours! He'd have used six-hour fuses and to hell with it.

'As you know, these fuses are made on the assumption that they will be activated at seventy degrees,' said Ayton patiently. 'Any colder and they take longer to work; any hotter and they take a shorter time. I reckon these could go off after eight hours, perhaps seven or even six and a half. I don't know about you, but I want to be safe and sound aboard the sub before those charges go off, because they'll wake the whole bloody island. By my reckoning it's going to be a close-run thing.'

Pountney put the dud fuse back where Ayton had placed it, and nodded. 'I suppose you're right,' he said grudgingly.

'I know I am,' Ayton replied with a grin. He began carefully packing the charges back into the bergens, putting five in each, then divided up the clam mines so that they each had half a dozen. Ayton kept the empty Gammon grenades and what remained of the PE in his bergen, for if the Gammons were needed it would be he who made them up.

Sitting in the last rays of the dying sun, they ate a quick meal of cold tinned stew and washed it down with rum. Then, working methodically and from force of habit, they erased all signs of their presence in the hut and collected together in one of the ponchos everything they didn't need for the raid. They hid the bundle in a crevice between two rocks, and covered it with earth and stones. That done, they blackened each other's faces with camouflage cream, carefully checked their Welrods, transferred two spare ammunition clips to the pockets of their parachute smocks, synchronized their watches and made sure, by jumping up and down, that no rattle or clink would betray their presence.

'Let's go,' said Pountney, and led the way down the slope towards the airfield. By now the sun had turned a golden red and was dipping below the horizon. Once they heard a donkey bray, but otherwise the countryside seemed uninhabited. The last of the mountainside petered out, giving way to sparse grass and scattered bushes and olive trees. As the men walked, grasshoppers bounced off the parched yellow stalks of the grass and the cicadas kept up their persistent noise.

They came to a road, dusty and unmetalled, which they recced carefully. Tyre marks showed that it was used frequently by military-type transport as well as local mules and donkeys, and they guessed it must lead to the airfield. They crossed it quickly and to their relief the bushes and trees immediately became bigger and more luxuriant. This extra cover allowed them to move more quickly and to approach the airfield's perimeter fence without difficulty. It looked no more formidable close to than it had at a distance.

They followed the fence round to the left until they came to the main gate. Even here there did not seem to be much activity. The opening was protected by a barrier which could be lifted by pivoting it upwards. Beside it lounged two Italian soldiers, their rifles slung across their shoulders. One was twiddling his moustache, the other leant against the barrier cleaning his fingernails with a piece of stick. Beyond them the last rays of the sun glittered along the row of hangars.

Pountney gripped Ayton's elbow. 'Do you see what I see?' he whispered into the younger officer's ear.

Ayton nodded. He saw all right, and the prospect sent a shiver of excitement through him. For beyond the hangars, on a large concrete apron, stood row upon row of triple-engined bombers. 'Savoia-Marchettis,' Ayton murmured.

'How many of them, do you reckon?'

Ayton counted quickly. 'Fifteen, perhaps twenty. I can't see them all.'

'We'll need to use the clams then.'

They moved on round until they were behind and then

beyond the row of hangars. This gave them a clear view of how the airfield was laid out. In the middle, between the two parallel runways, stood the control tower, a squat, brick-built building with the Italian flag flying on top of it. On the far side were rows of small wooden accommodation huts and a long, low building which looked like a mess hall. Bordering the far side of the large apron on which the aircraft were parked were three large workshops, from one of which came the sound of engines being tested.

'Have we got enough explosive to do those workshops a mischief?' Pountney murmured to his companion.

'I reckon,' said Ayton quietly, 'but the only pencils left are the dodgy ones.'

'Do the best you can.'

Pountney kept watch while Ayton shrugged off his bergen and in the dying light began working on one large charge. In case one of the pencil fuses failed, Ayton used two of them, linking each to a separate primer and detonator.

So far there had been no sign of any guards apart from the two at the main gate, but as the sun disappeared behind the line of trees at the far end of the airfield, four figures appeared from one of the hangars and straggled off round the inside of the perimeter fence. Two of them, Pountney saw at once, had the antiquated 6.5mm Carcano rifle with which all second-grade Italian troops were armed. The other two carried sub-machine-guns, probably Berettas, though Pountney couldn't be sure. He noted the time, then studied the patrol through his binoculars until it disappeared round a bend in the perimeter wire. Shaking his head in wonderment, he said softly to Ayton: 'Looks as if they've eaten too much spaghetti. What a shower!

I reckon we won't have much trouble keeping out of their way.'

Ayton grunted.

It was pitch-dark by the time Ayton had assembled the larger charge. By then the workshops had closed down for the night and the men working in them had walked across the airfield to the wooden huts. The two SBS men agreed that they had to assume there was a guard of some sort on the aircraft, even though they had not seen one.

'We'll wait until the patrol comes round again,' Pountney murmured, 'and then we'll go through the fence behind the hangars.' Ayton nodded and they settled back to wait. It seemed to take the patrol an age to reappear. Once it was past them the two men slid towards the perimeter fence.

The ground around this had been cleared for a width of about thirty feet, and they knew at once that it was almost certainly mined. Ayton drew his commando knife from its sheath, dropped to his hands and knees and with its point began prodding the earth in front and to either side of him very gently and very slowly.

Almost immediately he hit something hard and unyielding. He put the knife down and began, with great care, scraping away the soil with his fingers until the top of a small steel canister appeared. Slowly he dug around this with the knife until he could lift it out of the ground, making sure as he did so that he did not touch the two whiskers of steel wire that protruded from its top. These were, he assumed, the trigger mechanism. He handed it to Pountney and they wriggled their way back to shelter.

'An S-mine,' whispered Pountney and Ayton felt his mouth go dry. He had heard about the *Springenmine*, which the Germans had just started using around Tobruk.

If you trod on one of the whiskers the canister discharged a smaller, shrapnel-filled one which exploded at chest height, to fatal effect.

Pountney carefully handed the device back and Ayton gently unscrewed it and rendered it harmless by removing the detonator. They found four more S-mines before they got close enough to the perimeter fence to cut a way through it with the wire-cutters and by the time they reached the back of one of the hangars both men were bathed in sweat.

They drew their Welrods and carefully worked their way down the back of the hangars until they were opposite the parked aircraft. They crouched down, weapons at the ready, and scanned every inch of the concrete apron, particularly those parts in deep shadow.

Satisfied that there was no guard on the aircraft, Pountney cupped his hand and whispered into Ayton's ear: 'We'll let the patrol pass through.'

They settled down to wait. Twenty minutes later they heard the murmur of conversation as the patrol straggled on to the apron. The Italians passed by the hangars and disappeared into the dark. Nothing else stirred. Five minutes later Pountney stood up, put his pistol back in its holster and indicated to Ayton that he should follow him. They slipped silently along the side of one hangar and across to the stationary aircraft. Pountney took the first row, Ayton the second.

The best place to fix the charges was underneath the fuselage, where the wing joined it, but in case the magnets did not hold the charge they also used tape. Once the charge was fixed, the end of the pencil fuse was squeezed to release the acid, and the safety tag was removed to allow the pin to hit the percussion cap. They worked quickly and efficiently, both looking every now and again at their watches. When they had used all the charges they fixed the small clam mines to unobtrusive parts of the remaining aircraft. On its own the lighter clam might not destroy an aircraft but it could certainly damage its vital parts and, with any luck, set it on fire.

When they had finished, they had just ten minutes to spare before the patrol was due to arrive back on the apron. They moved silently across the apron to the biggest workshop. Pountney eased back the door and they slipped through it. The place smelt of oil and petrol, and men's sweat, and was in total darkness except for a dim bulb burning at the far end, which cast a pale circle of light. Moving among the lathes and work tables, they tried to find the best target on which to lay the big charge. They approached the light, but paused outside the area it illuminated.

'That'll do,' said Pountney quietly, pointing at a large, complicated piece of machinery which looked as if it was used to rebore aero engines. Ayton nodded and was moving forward, one hand in the bergen to extract the charge, when a man dressed in overalls came round the corner of the piece of machinery and stepped out in front of them. He looked as surprised as Ayton felt.

'*Cosa vuole*?' he asked. He was tall and dark, no longer young. He appeared perplexed at finding them there, not angry or frightened. The fear only came in the split second before he died, as he saw the glint of light on the barrel of Pountney's Welrod. The pistol made a sound like a bottle being uncorked and the man sank to his knees soundlessly, then slowly rolled over on to his back. His eyes, wide open and blank, stared up at them reproachfully.

'Fix that bloody charge, and let's get out of here,' Pountney hissed.

He dragged the body to one side and covered it with a tarpaulin. Ayton moved round the machine. He remembered the sabotage instructor's advice: find a cast-iron part, not steel. Steel could be mended by welding; cast iron shattered beyond repair. He ran his hand over one component of the machine. It was rough, a sure sign it was cast iron. He extracted the charge, squeezed the ends of both pencil fuses, then placed the charge on top of the casting. Minutes later they were out of the compound and making for the mountain ridge which towered in the distance.

No longer carrying the heavy explosives, they made good time back to the ruined hut to retrieve the poncho and its contents.

'I'll make up some Gammons,' Ayton said. 'Just in case we run into trouble.'

'Good idea,' agreed Pountney, still hoping to give the guests of the beach hotel an early-morning surprise. 'I'll look around to find something to fill them with. Anti-personnel shrapnel?'

Ayton nodded. 'We're more likely to meet a patrol than an armoured vehicle.'

That was the advantage of the Gammon grenade: it could be made up to suit the circumstances.

While Pountney collected bits of metal, nail ends and small stones to use as 'shrapnel', Ayton quickly moulded three lumps of PE into the prescribed beehive shape and made holes in the top of each for the primer cups. Then he inserted the special No. 8 detonators into the cups and screwed them on to the percussion fuse attached to the cloth bags. Holding the bags clear, he inserted the primer cups into the holes in the lumps of explosive, drew the bags over them, filled what space remained with the shrapnel and tied the bags tight. Once assembled, the grenades could be quickly activated.

They glanced behind them just once as they climbed up to the ridge. The airfield was shrouded in darkness. On the ridge they paused to eat some rations before clambering down the other side. They found the donkey track and an hour before dawn were back on the beach, where they retrieved the folbot. Pountney gave the darkened hotel a regretful backward glance as they moved quietly out on to the water, but he knew it would be foolhardy to attempt an attack on it.

He paddled while Ayton took a series of bearings with his pocket compass on the two landmarks. They were weary now and the rendezvous seemed much further out than a thousand yards. The coastline receded behind them and in the half-light Ayton found it difficult to see either the hotel or the tower. He wondered if exhaustion was playing tricks with his eyesight, and shook his head and tried to focus his eyes, peering over the rim of the pocket compass. But try as he might, all signs of the land had gone. He swore under his breath when he realized what had happened. Pountney glanced back.

'Mist,' said Ayton. 'Fucking mist. I can't see a thing.'

'We can't be far away now,' said Pountney. 'We'll stay on the same course. We're bound to see the sub when it surfaces.'

He bent to his paddles while Ayton took the torch from his bergen, made sure the blue filter was in place and began flashing 'L' in Morse code. Dot ... dash ... dot ... The torch blinked into the darkness, but there was no reply, no movement, no light – nothing.

Was there a current? Ayton had no idea. Pountney paddled slowly and methodically, then rested.

'It must be about here,' he said.

The sea mist boiled and swirled gently all around them. The water was oily-still. Ayton glanced at his watch.

'It should have surfaced by now.'

'It'll come. Try signalling again.'

But it didn't come. They circled to keep warm. The visibility was over two hundred yards, they reckoned, but they now had no idea how close they were to the rendezvous or how accurately the submarine would be able to navigate to it.

'What now?' said Ayton after another ten minutes.

'The Gammons,' said Pountney. 'They'll pick up the explosion on their asdic. They'll know it's us.'

'Christ. I hope so,' Ayton sighed. 'They'll certainly hear the explosions ashore.'

He took out one of the grenades, unscrewed the black Bakelite cap which protected the percussion fuse, taking care that the white tape wound around the fuse did not unwind prematurely. With the grenade in his right hand and the bag filled with explosive resting in his palm, and his thumb and forefinger firmly grasping the end of the tape, he used an action similar to throwing a ball to hurl the device as far as he could. He saw the white tape unfurling. When it had completely unravelled it would pull out the safety pin and the grenade would explode on hitting the water.

'You must be a cricketer,' said Pountney as they both instinctively turned away. The Gammon went off with a terrible thump, making the folbot rock and skip.

They waited several minutes in silence, then Pountney said calmly: 'And the next.'

Ayton could feel the sweat pricking the palms of his hands, but his fingers were steady as he worked quickly to unscrew the cap of a second grenade. This time he rose slightly from the craft and managed to throw the bomb farther than the first.

'Good one,' said Pountney. He seemed to be enjoying himself.

They watched the grenade arc through the mist. The tape unravelled, but when the device hit the water it sank without exploding.

'Shit,' Ayton growled.

'Try again.'

'It's the last one.'

'Third time lucky.'

Ayton's fingers were trembling as he removed the cap, but he steadied himself before hurling the grenade as high and as far as he could. The blast as it hit the water and exploded reverberated back to them.

'That'll bring them up,' said Pountney.

But once the water had settled again, nothing broke the glassy surface. Ashore a searchlight came on and began to sweep the night sky.

'They must think they're being bombed,' said Pountney.

A second searchlight sent up a finger of light, but after roving aimlessly above them it went out and the other died shortly afterwards. Ayton began to suggest that they had better start paddling towards Cyprus, when Pountney cut him short.

'There it is,' he said, and dug his paddle into the water, swinging the canoe away from the shore. Ayton could not see the submarine at first, and thought Pountney might be hallucinating – a common enough occurrence among canoeists on such operations. But then he saw a conning tower surging out of the water and he plied his paddles with a strength he didn't know he had. As they approached, the submarine rose higher, and when they reached its side they scrambled aboard with the help of willing hands.

'No time to stow the folbot, sir,' one of the seamen said. 'The Captain said to sink it.'

One slash of Pountney's knife sent the folbot plunging to the bottom.

The SBS men ran up the forecasing and more hands helped them over the bridge coaming.

'Straight below, you two. Well done!' said 'Timber' Woods.

As they half slid, half clambered down the conning tower's ladder the klaxon wailed its warning that the submarine was about to dive.

'One clip on,' Woods shouted down calmly as he closed the upper hatch. 'Both clips on.'

'Open main vents,' the First Lieutenant snapped, after slapping the two SBS men on the back.

Woods appeared in the control room, and a seaman moved forward to shut the lower hatch. 'Take her to sixty feet, Number One, he ordered, and turned to Ayton and Pountney to shake their hands warmly. 'Thought we'd lost you there for a moment,' he said. 'Luckily we've got a first-rate asdic operator who managed to get a distance and bearing on those grenades you used.' His eyes, red-rimmed and hollow, looked at them intently. 'Everything go as planned?'

'Like clockwork,' Pountney answered. 'But we've got to think of a better way of arranging a rendezvous. The present method isn't half bad for my nerves.'

5

'Oh, Christ! Not you two again.'

Woods was leaning over the edge of his bridge as Pountney and Ayton stepped from the gangplank on to the *Sentinel's* forecasing.

The submarine's new base at Malta, the home of the already famous Tenth Submarine Flotilla, was the Lazaretto, a building constructed of crumbling yellow stone. At one time it had been a hospital for the Grand Knights of Malta and was built on Manoel Island, which lay between Sliema and Lazaretto Creeks, close to Grand Harbour.

All around them the SBS men could see the scars of the aerial siege that the island was undergoing. In Sliema Creek the masts and upper superstructure of a bombed merchant ship stuck out of the water and in the distance palls of smoke still hung over Valletta itself from the latest air raid. Even as the two men came aboard, the ominous, undulating wail of the air-raid siren started up for the umpteenth time that day.

The grin of welcome on Timber Woods's bearded face belied his first words as Pountney and Ayton mounted the conning tower. He shook their hands and then pointed to a mound of equipment that had just preceded them. 'What's this garbage then? I can't have my ship cluttered up with a lot of experimental rubbish.'

'RG equipment,' Pountney answered. 'Infrared lamps.'

He showed Woods the Aldis-type lamp, designed to send a beam of invisible infrared light from the submarine. The beam, he explained, could be picked up on the screen of a small receiver the size of a box camera, which the SBS team carried with them.

Woods shrugged. 'Better than hand-grenades, I suppose.'

On the supporting standard of the *Sentinel*'s main periscope an outsize Jolly Roger fluttered in the breeze: the flag flown in harbour by all British submarines to broadcast their successes against the enemy. Below the crossbones was sewn a single commando dagger commemorating the submarine's role in the attack on Maritsa airfield the previous month. On the left were three white bars, signifying that the *Sentinel* had so far torpedoed three enemy ships; on the right was a single star which showed that it had also sunk one with its gun.

'I see you've been busy since we last graced the *Sentinel* with our presence, Timber,' Pountney said with sincere admiration, knowing his friend was fast becoming an ace submarine commander, the stuff legends were made of.

'Had some luck,' Woods admitted, tugging at his beard, a sign that he was embarrassed. He turned to Ayton. 'Keeping him in order, Phil?' he asked, to change the subject.

'Some hope,' Ayton replied cheerfully. 'Just wait and hear what he's let us in for now.'

As they went below to the wardroom the anti-aircraft batteries on the far side of Valletta opened up with a concerted thunderous roar. Woods opened the 'medicine cabinet' and took down a bottle of gin and a smaller, dark-brown bottle. The cabinet was open in harbour but always locked at sea, with its key safely clipped on to the Captain's key ring. Glasses and a carafe of water were asked for and produced.

'Well, where is it this time?' Woods asked as he shook a few drops of a dark liquid into the glasses, then twirled the glasses expertly in his hand to distribute the Angostura bitters.

'Sicily,' said Pountney.

'I know that much,' Woods retorted. The eastern side of the island was his new 'billet', his patrol area. 'But whereabouts?'

He measured the gin exactly by closing his forefinger and index finger together and putting them alongside each glass. Satisfied, he topped up the measures with half the amount of water and stirred each glass with a teaspoon before passing them to his guests.

'North of Catania. There's a big airfield just to the south of where we're planning to land. Apparently the Krauts have just reinforced it with another squadron of Stukas.'

Woods raised his glass: 'To Admiral Nelson, God bless him.'

They all stood and touched glasses.

'Admiral Nelson,' the two SBS men repeated solemnly.

The Senior Service had its fair share of eccentrics and Woods was one of them. The Marines were part of the Royal Navy, so Ayton was used to toasting the great admiral. Pountney, however, had objected the first time, but his objection had been quickly overruled by Woods's dictum 'no toast, no gin'. The submariner knew that such rituals helped to relieve the tension they all felt before an operation.

Outside they heard the thud of the first bombs falling.

'So, it's another airfield raid?' said Woods.

Pountney shook his head. 'Not this time.'

'There are so many airfields near Catania,' explained Ayton, 'that the powers that be think it's a better use of resources to choke off vital supplies to them than to try and attack each one.'

Woods nodded and refilled their glasses. 'Makes sense.'

'Anyway,' said Pountney, 'since Angelo every Axis airfield in the Med has been put on the alert for commando attacks.'

'So what's the drill?'

Pountney pulled out a large-scale map of Sicily from one of his many pockets and spread it on the wardroom table. The sound of exploding bombs drew gradually closer. The anti-aircraft guns on Fort Manoel, behind the Lazaretto, began firing and were joined by the high-angle 5.5-inch guns of a cruiser anchored nearby. The racket was terrible, but Pountney did not even pause. With his forefinger he traced a coastal railway line running south from Messina through Catania to Syracuse and on to Ragusa. 'They ship everything across the Straits of Messina and then load it on to supply trains. Food, ammunition, fuel, bombs, spare parts – the lot.'

Ayton glanced across at Woods. 'Do you go into the Straits, Timber? Sounds as if you would find some prime targets.'

Woods snorted derisively. 'Know anything about the Straits of Messina, Phil?'

Ayton shook his head.

'No submarine can operate there: the current's too strong. It's like a mill-race at times.'

A near miss exploded in the water close to the Lazaretto, shaking the moored submarine from stem to stern. A second hit the island somewhere and debris clanged against the side of the vessel. The three men waited tensely, but the next exploded farther away, while the fourth was just a distant thud. But the guns continued their clamour in an attempt to divert the next bomber swooping on the creek.

'That's why we're being used, I reckon,' said Pountney calmly. 'It's the only way we can get at those bastards bombing the hell out of this island.'

'What about our boys in blue?' asked Woods.

'Sicily's well beyond the range of any of our bomber bases,' Pountney explained. 'And as you well know, Timber, your aircraft carriers are having their work cut out protecting the convoys trying to get through to here. So it's down to us.'

Suddenly the raid was over as quickly as it had begun, for the guns stopped firing and moments later the even wail of the all-clear siren drifted across the creek.

'There's a railway line running along the northern side of Sicily, too,' said Woods, scrutinizing the map of the roughly triangular island.

'The sub which patrols there is landing one of our teams near that line at about the same time as you'll be landing us.'

'The *Salmon*, that would be. Good man, Sandy Hargreaves – he'll not let you down.'

The duty steward put his head through the curtains. 'You'll be eating lunch ashore, sir?' he asked pointedly.

Woods glanced at the other two. 'Base received a few boxes of rations yesterday, so we might as well see what we can scrounge.'

They climbed on to the bridge and paused to watch the highly decorated *dghaisas* moving like coloured beetles across the creek. The craft were not rowed in the normal way: the oarsmen stood and pushed the oars, like gondoliers.

The SBS men watched as the *dghaisas* gathered in one area of the creek.

'That's where the bomb must have dropped into the water just now,' Woods told them. 'They're hoping some stunned fish might have floated to the surface. If we don't get some food in soon the islanders are going to start dying like flies.'

Lunch was a meagre meal, interrupted by another air raid. The Lazaretto trembled as the bombs cascaded down. Dust settled on the soup and the leaden heat of the afternoon added to the atmosphere of foreboding. A surgeon commander sitting with them described with the detached interest of his profession the outbreak of scabies among the civilian population – the first signs, he said, of serious malnutrition.

Yet another raid was developing when the *Salmon* and the *Sentinel* sailed together at dusk. Once north of the island they went their separate ways, the first heading north-west through the Sicilian Channel, the second north-east across the sixty-mile stretch of water between Malta and Sicily known as the Malta Channel. In the *Sentinel*'s wardroom the two SBS men were served breakfast – mealtimes in submarines were often reversed – and Pountney ripped open the envelope containing his orders.

The orders were, the two of them agreed after they had

studied them, sketchy in the extreme. But the urgency of the situation came through the terse paragraphs plainly enough. A vital Malta convoy from Gibraltar would pass through the Sicilian Straits in three days' time and the massed strength of enemy aircraft on Sicily had to be depleted before then. The orders did little more than give the map coordinates of the raiders' landing beach near Taormina, stating that it had been chosen because at that point the railway ran close to the coast through a series of tunnels. These burrowed their way under the hilly foothills of Mount Etna, which in that area reached the eastern shoreline.

Aerial reconnaissance photographs were included in the sealed envelope, but added little to the written orders. The verticals were taken from too great a height for either Pountney or Ayton to make much sense of them – though they showed the tunnels clearly, as they did the winding railway line itself – and the obliques of the landing beach were blurred and indistinct. There had been no time for the interpretation unit to look at the photographs.

'We'll just have to take pot luck,' said Pountney cheerfully. He always preferred too few orders to ones which detailed every move he had to make. Using your initiative, that's what the SBS was all about. To the more thoughtful Ayton, the mission they had been given appeared a one-way operation. But he knew now, as he could not have done before visiting Malta, just how vital it was going to be.

They made their way to the torpedo compartment to have a final check on the folbot and their equipment, then returned to the wardroom, unfolded the cots from the bulkhead and turned in.

* * *

By dawn, a pale-pink strip on the starboard bow, Catania was abeam but beyond the horizon. The navigator had just taken a star sight with his sextant to confirm the submarine's position, and Woods was preparing to dive, when one of the lookouts shouted with ill-concealed excitement: 'Masts on the port bow, sir.'

Woods swung his binoculars. 'Where?'

'Bearing red twenty, sir.'

All sightings were given in degrees relative to the submarine's bows, red for port, green for starboard, but sometimes the lookouts forgot to do this in the excitement of spotting a possible target. Woods could see the masts now, needle-fine above the horizon. It was either two separate ships close together or one large one. Whatever it was, the hull, or hulls, were still below the horizon, but the masts could plainly be seen against the lightening sky. Everyone on the bridge studied them closely through binoculars, and it was some minutes before the lookout broke the silence.

'A schooner, I'd say, sir. Under power.'

Woods grunted by way of agreeing. The Italians sometimes sent large trading schooners across to Tripoli with supplies.

'She'll cross our bows, sir. Moving at about six knots, I'd say.'

Woods made up his mind. 'Starboard five,' he said down the voice pipe; and then: 'Wheel amidships.'

The two vessels, now on converging courses, began to close with each other. Woods pressed the klaxon button and the lookouts tumbled below. He followed, sliding expertly down the ladder, and on reaching the control room gave orders for the submarine to dive to periscope depth.

As it was flat-calm on the surface, he ordered the attack periscope to be raised. This was smaller than the main periscope – it tapered to only two inches in diameter – and created hardly any wake, making it almost impossible for any surface lookout to spot it. But its light transmission was poor compared with the main periscope and it was some time before Woods could positively identify the vessel by the large Italian naval ensign flying from the backstay of the mainmast. It was quite large, about 180 feet in length, but not, Woods decided, worth wasting a torpedo on, even if he had been able to judge an attack correctly in the half-light of the morning.

He waited until the schooner was almost within gun range before ordering the *Sentinel* to surface. Once on the bridge, he could see that the schooner was maintaining its course and speed.

'Close up, gun crews,' he ordered down the voice pipe.

Seamen tumbled out on to the forecasing and began preparing the three-inch gun for action. On the bandstand behind the bridge the Oerlikon gunners did the same. Moments later the gunnery control officer joined Woods on the bridge. In the wardroom the two SBS men were woken by the ammunition rating, who made ready to feed shells up to the gun crew through a hatch in the wardroom deckhead.

On the bridge Woods and the gunnery control officer studied the schooner through their binoculars. Coming, as the submarine was, out of the remains of the night, the schooner had not yet seen it.

'Range and speed?' Woods asked.

'Four thousands yards. Around six knots,' replied the gunnery control officer.

'What do you make of her?'

'She doesn't look armed, sir. I suppose we ought to have a quick look at her.'

'I agree.'

Intelligence was badly needed and small vessels like this often carried important papers or personnel.

'Stand by, boarding party,' Woods said into the voice pipe.

'Stand by, boarding party,' the First Lieutenant called out from the control room.

'That's us,' said Pountney, emerging from the wardroom with Ayton close behind him. The SBS now regularly formed part of a submarine's boarding party, but the First Lieutenant looked at the two SBS men doubtfully. 'Can't afford to lose you two if there's any trouble. You've got your own fish to fry.'

Pountney brushed aside his protest. 'Nonsense,' he said brusquely. 'We need some fresh air. Better than staying cooped up down here all day.'

Pountney's patience aboard a submarine was always on a short fuse. The confined space and the heavy, stale atmosphere made him pine for action, any action.

Still the schooner stood on, rolling awkwardly in the swell as its diesels powered it through the water. Those aboard it, thought Woods, were either asleep or blind. The barrel of the three-inch gun was tracking the schooner's progress as it moved across the *Sentinel*'s bow.

For a minute or more Woods studied the target with his binoculars. He could now see the schooner had a wireless, because a wire ran up the mast from a small cabin aft of the main one, and he pointed this out to the gunnery control officer.

'Take that after cabin out first,' the gunnery control officer shouted down to the crew. 'Range four thousand yards and closing. Speed six knots. Stand by to fire.'

The seconds ticked by. Anxiously, the gunnery control officer glanced across at Woods, who responded with a nod.

'Fire!'

The crack of the shell reverberated throughout the submarine and a whiff of cordite blew across the bridge. The shell went slightly high and fell beyond the schooner, which now swerved violently away from its attacks.

'Fire!'

The second shell ripped the wireless cabin apart.

'Now one across her bows,' said Woods.

A great plume of water rose in front of the schooner, which continued to turn to port. A cloud of exhaust fumes from its counter told those on the *Sentinel*'s bridge that it was putting on speed.

'Up two hundred. Fire!'

The next shell fell farther ahead of the schooner.

'He must have the message by now,' said Woods. 'Or is he trying to make a run for it?'

The next shell made up the schooner captain's mind for him. He swung his ship back on to its original course and came to a halt. A lifeboat was lowered from davits into the sea, and figures, some of them in uniform, could be seen scampering along the deck.

'Boarding party on deck, Number One,' Woods said into the voice pipe. The submarine's rubber dinghy was brought up, inflated and fitted with its outboard engine. The First Lieutenant, who was in charge of the boarding party, hurriedly strapped on his revolver, then issued Pountney and Ayton and two seamen with Lanchester carbines, the Royal Navy's standard small-arms weapon. A third seaman, also armed with a revolver, took charge of the outboard engine.

While the boarding party was being prepared the submarine continued to close with the schooner until it lay abeam of the stationary Italian vessel, both its guns trained on it. Covered as it was by the submarine's main armament, the schooner was not about to go anywhere, and the lifeboat bobbing alongside its dirty white wooden hull remained empty.

As the dinghy approached, a rope ladder was thrown over the schooner's side. Pountney and Ayton were the first up it, their Lanchesters at the ready, but the crew, an ill-assorted bunch, made no attempt to resist. The SBS men first made for the wrecked wireless cabin to make sure that the shell had destroyed the wireless. The cabin was a gruesome spectacle, as the remains of the operator were splattered all over its smouldering walls.

'Get everyone on deck,' the First Lieutenant ordered. 'I want the whole ship searched from stem to stern.'

There were a number of unarmed Italian air crew on board, but no one could explain what they were doing there. The one member of the crew who spoke some broken English just kept shrugging his shoulders. The schooner's cargo was hardly more interesting than its human one: it consisted entirely of pasta.

Ayton, who had been given the task of laying the scuttling charge, went below to find a good position for it. He found one aft of the main saloon. He knelt down, lifted the wooden sole to get at the bilges, and began preparing the charge. He was about to insert the detonator into the primer when he heard a sound in front of him. He looked up and automatically dropped a hand to the handle of his knife.

Standing about ten feet away from him was a German *Feldwebel*, a non-commissioned officer, in desert uniform. On his head he wore a cap bearing the death's-head insignia above its peak. Ayton had not seen this since Norway, but he knew immediately that it meant the wearer was a member of the SS, Hitler's elite guard. He tightened his grip on the hilt of his knife and began carefully to work it out of its sheath.

The German had a holstered revolver at his hip, but his hands were nowhere near it. '*Was machst du denn hier?*' he asked sleepily, rubbing his eyes.

Ayton made no reply, but beckoned the man as if to show him something, and as the *Feldwebel* stepped forward and crouched down inquisitively Ayton drew his knife. The movement alerted the German and Ayton saw first the puzzlement and then the fear in his eyes.

Ayton drove the knife upwards between the SS man's fourth and fifth ribs, and into his heart. The man sagged forward so that Ayton had to hold the body back with his left hand to prevent it toppling on to him. Then, in one swift movement, he withdrew the knife, pushed the dead German backwards, stood up, wiped the blade on the man's shirt and thrust it back in its sheath. Then he grasped the man under his armpits and hauled him into the cabin where he had been sleeping moments before, and shut the door.

When he had finished preparing the charge, Ayton took the SS cap back on deck and threw it into the dinghy.

'A little souvenir,' he said.

By now the schooner's crew and passengers had all

taken to the boats or had scrambled on to life-rafts. Pountney turned the cap over curiously. 'Where did you get this?'

'Just someone I bumped into,' Ayton replied. 'We were acquainted only very briefly. He must have been missed during the search.'

Pountney grinned up at him. 'One of Captain Fairbairn's little tricks?'

Fairbairn, an ex-Shanghai policemen, had been their instructor in the use of the knife that he and another instructor, a Captain Sykes, had invented for the commandos.

'Worked a dream,' Ayton replied.

As they reached the submarine's bridge, where Woods was waiting for them impatiently, the scuttling charge exploded with a dull thud. The schooner shuddered and began to settle in the water. Decks awash, it was still wallowing in the slight, glassy swell when Woods gave the order to dive.

All day the submarine ran submerged at one hundred feet, coming up to periscope depth in the late afternoon so that the SBS men could study the coastline where they were to land after dark. The sun was over the land and blazed through the eyepieces as Pountney swept the coast with the main periscope in low power. Then he ratched the periscope up to high power and the beach leapt out at him, long and narrow and filled with barbed wire and other defences.

'Nobody said anything to us about the beaches being fortified,' he said when they went to the ward-room to study the reconnaissance photographs one last time and to look for any indication that the beach was mined.

'Well, they wouldn't, would they?' Ayton replied bitterly. It was an unfair comment, he knew. An expert would have picked out the defences on the photographs, but no one else, apart from an agent on the ground, could possibly have known that they were there. And there were no agents on the ground – at least none who were able to make contact.

After dark the submarine partially surfaced and Woods and the SBS officers climbed on to the bridge. In the distance the conical mound of Etna stuck up into the night sky, a reassuring landmark from which to take a compass bearing. It was a clear, calm night, intensely dark but with a brisk inshore breeze which would carry the slightest sound to the shore.

'Best if I piggyback you in,' said Woods, 'No problems then about noise. There's plenty of water under my keel.'

Ayton glanced at Pountney, who shrugged. 'Why not. Just don't submerge too quickly and take us with you.'

Woods ordered the submarine to surface completely and the canoe and the explosives were brought on to the forecasing. The folbot was packed and the SBS men then stepped into it as the submarine crept in towards the shore, moving so slowly it created no wake.

'One hundred and fifty feet, sir,' the navigator said into the voice pipe, relaying the reading on the echo-sounder. Woods tapped the lookouts on the shoulder and indicated that they should go below. 'One hundred feet . . . eighty feet . . . sixty feet.'

'Dive, dive, dive,' Woods barked into the voice pipe.

He gave one last look at the folbot sitting transversely on the forecasing, then climbed down the ladder.

In the control room the First Lieutenant ordered the

inner ballast tanks to be blown first and told the planesmen to submerge the submarine at a shallow angle. The bow dipped, and the folbot floated off the forecasing. Free of the submarine, the SBS men paddled hard to avoid being caught in the suction it produced as it continued to submerge.

The onshore breeze helped propel them in, but closer to the beach the swell turned to surf, which they could hear crashing on to the sand. The heavily laden folbot became progressively more difficult to contol, and fifty yards from the beach they decided to tow it in by swimming the rest of the way. It was better to arrive soaking wet than to risk capsizing the folbot.

The surf tumbled them ashore, then tried to suck them back out to sea, but they pushed the folbot clear of the water and lay beside it, winded by the force of the waves. As they strained to see if there was any movement, Ayton remembered a remark made by another SBS man, Eric Newby. A windswept enemy beach at night was, he had said, the loneliest place in the world.

He was right.

They lay flat on the sand watching and listening. It was now that any SBS team was at its most vulnerable. If they had been spotted, they didn't stand a chance. The only temporary retreat would be the open sea, where they could be picked off at leisure.

But all they could hear was the wind sighing through the coils of barbed wire which ran the length of the beach twenty yards in front of them. After waiting a few minutes they took out their knives and, dragging the folbot along between them, carefully probed the sand ahead for mines. When they reached the coils of barbed wire Pountney used cutters, while Ayton unfolded the spade. By the time Pountney had cleared a path, Ayton had buried the folbot upside down and eliminated any trace of the landing.

They crawled through the gap in the wire, dragging the bergens carrying the explosive behind them. Once through, they closed the gap and noted its position. The back of the beach was only a short distance away. Pountney ran towards it with both bergens while Ayton again covered their tracks. There had been no mines in front of the wire, so it was unlikely that there would be any behind it, but fear and tension brought sweat trickling down their faces as they crossed the sand.

A line of trees separated the back of the beach from a narrow road, beyond which was the railway line. At this point the line ran through a shallow cutting, but to the left, after about two hundred yards, it disappeared into a tunnel.

They crouched in the undergrowth and listened. Above them the wind sighed through the trees. Behind them the surf sucked and boomed on the beach and the cicadas sang around them in the broad swathe of bushes and coarse grass which divided the road from the railway line.

Pountney glanced at his watch. They were already behind schedule; they would have to get on with it. He was about to cross the road when he heard subdued laughter to their right. He motioned Ayton back, but then both men froze as boots clattered on stones. Male laughter – coarse and throaty mingled with female giggles. Pountney swore under his breath. They must have landed on a lovers' haunt.

From the shadows falling across the road emerged two figures: a soldier with his rifle slung across his shoulder, and a girl clinging to his arm and looking up at him. Sweet whispers of Italian floated through the night air. The SBS men watched the couple approach, and with their hands on their knives, waited for them to pass by.

Instead, the soldier stopped and said something. The girl giggled and shook her head. The soldier dropped his hand on to the girl's breast and she stood on tiptoe and kissed him. As the soldier took the girl by the hand and turned towards the beach, Ayton and Pountney instinctively leant farther back into the shadows. The girl resisted, then relented, and the couple sauntered between the SBS men crouching in the undergrowth.

Once on the beach, the soldier wasted no time. He tossed aside his rifle, took off his shirt, laid it on the sand and lowered the girl on top of it. He sat beside her, pulling off his boots and trousers as she tucked up her skirt.

Pountney began easing his knife out of its sheath. He knew he was going to have to kill them, because they could not afford to waste any more time. There were, he thought grimly, worse ways to die than in the middle of a screw.

He waited his moment.

Ayton watched the couple, his knife in his hand. The girl opened her legs and Ayton felt a surge of desire. He hadn't been with a woman for a month. It felt like years.

The soldier lowered himself on to the girl. Pountney weighed his knife in his hand and took a cautious step forward.

Young and inexperienced, the soldier climaxed immediately with a cry and a grunt.

Pountney hesitated.

The soldier rolled off the girl laughing, and picked up his trousers. The girl laughed too, then sat up, threw back her hair and scrambled to her feet. She smoothed her skirt down across her thighs and, stooping slightly so that her long black hair shaded her face, brushed the sand away from her bare legs in an infinitely graceful motion.

Pountney crouched down as the soldier snatched up his shirt, shook it and slung it with his rifle over his shoulders. The young man took the girl's hand and whispered something in her ear. She giggled and they crossed the line of trees and continued down the road.

'Talk about a quickie,' Ayton murmured when he rejoined Pountney. They crossed the road, their rubber-soled boots making no noise on the broken surface, and walked quickly through the tall, coarse grass and stunted bushes which separated it from the railway. They climbed over the two strands of wire fence, and jumped down from the cutting on to the single track.

'At least we won't have to worry which is the right one,' said Pountney.

Ayton looked along the line, crouched down and tapped his knuckles on the reinforced cement in which the wooden sleepers were embedded. He supposed this was a precaution to prevent movement of the rails in an area where landslides were common.

'This is no good,' he said quietly.

'What do you mean, "no good"?' Pountney hissed. To create the maximum damage, Ayton explained patiently, the charge had to be laid under a rail. That way, if the pressure switch was fixed to the rail the right distance from the charge, the engine fell into the hole the explosion created. And that caused problems to those trying to clear up the mess.

Pountney looked along the track to where it disappeared

into the black cavern of the mountainside. 'What about the tunnel? Got enough explosives?'

'Probably not. But it's better than nothing.'

They followed the line until they came to the tunnel. At the entrance Ayton made up three charges: a small one to derail the train, and two bigger ones to destroy the tunnel and seal in the train with fallen masonry.

They walked cautiously into the tunnel, which smelt of damp and urine, walking between the rails and treading on the sleepers to avoid making any unnecessary noise. Once Pountney tripped and the sound of boot on rail echoed around them. Every few yards they stopped and listened. The tunnel curved slightly and the entrance behind them disappeared. It was intensely dark.

'Christ! This must be far enough,' Pountney whispered into Ayton's ear. He shaded the beam of the torch with his hand while Ayton crouched and fitted the charge to the rail. He placed the pressure device, called a fog signal, close to the charge, hoping that when the train triggered the charge it might cause another, bigger explosion in the engine itself. The two bigger charges he fitted with sympathetic fuses which would, with luck, be triggered by the tremors caused by the destruction of the engine in the confined space of the tunnel. He taped the first to the side of the tunnel twenty feet in front of the fog signal. Then they walked back to the entrance and he taped the second one some ten feet inside it.

He was repacking the bergens when Pountney tapped him on the shoulder and put his finger to his lips. Ayton paused. Pountney put his ear to the rail and indicated that Ayton should do the same. They could hear a faint, spasmodic, but quite distinct ringing.

'A train?' Ayton whispered.

Pountney shook his head. 'Something's hitting the line.'

They looked into the blackness of the tunnel. The faint beam of a torch, held by someone beyond the bend in the tunnel, flickered up and down.

'A patrol,' Pountney whispered. 'Let's get the fuck out of it.'

They scrambled out of the cutting, crossed the road and crouched in the undergrowth. A few minutes later a patrol of five men emerged from the tunnel, trudging along between the rails. From the shape of the hats they wore the SBS men knew they were *carabinieri*, armed Italian police.

When they had passed, Pountney signalled to Ayton to return to the beach while he covered the retreating patrol with his tommy-gun. The patrol didn't pause and three minutes later it had disappeared from view.

Ayton worked feverishly to open up the gap in the wire. Once through it, he retrieved the spade from under its shallow layer of sand and began digging up the folbot.

Pountney waited until the footsteps of the patrol had died away and looked at his watch. They were hopelessly behind schedule: the submarine had been due to pick them up half an hour ago. He ran down to the beach to join Ayton. It was, despite the brightness of the stars, still very dark. But first light was not far away, and in the Mediterranean it came very quickly.

The surf had subsided and they launched the folbot without trouble, leaving the beach with quick, powerful strokes. After taking their bearings, Pountney brought out the infrared receiver from its waterproof pocket beside the front cockpit and held it up at head height.

The screen was speckled with green pinpricks – the

infrared light from the stars – but as Pountney swung it slowly in an arc, a large green spot appeared. 'Turn to starboard,' he said to Ayton. 'More, more . . . that's it.'

Now the hidden beam lay dead ahead. Pountney noted the bearing on the P8 compass, then they both bent to their paddles, thrusting with what remained of their strength. Ahead of them the first glimmer of dawn began to tinge the sky, but at sea level it was still pitch-dark.

Ayton felt exhaustion seeping through him. He could tell from Pountney's flagging strokes that his strength was running out too. The *Sentinel* was probably gone by now. With dawn spreading rapidly across the sky, Timber could hardly risk staying on the surface. His mind wandered to the possibility of finding their own way back to Malta: a hopeless proposition. But he knew neither of them would ever admit defeat, never willingly surrender.

If a windswept beach was the loneliest place in the world, an empty sea was the most forbidding.

'There she is!' Pountney cried.

Ayton peered into the darkness, but saw nothing. Beads of sweat ran into his eyes and he rubbed them with his forearm.

'Where?'

'There.' Pountney pointed with his paddle.

As much as Ayton stared, for him nothing broke the line of the horizon and everything below it was inky black.

Then suddenly he saw it. It was the conning tower, a blacker shadow on the black sea. He gleefully thumped Pountney on the back.

'It's there!'

'I told you it fucking was, you dimwit Marine.'

They redoubled their efforts and as they drew slowly, agonizingly slowly, closer, the *Sentinel* rose from the sea like some huge whale, compressed air frothing round its hull. Men clambered down from the conning tower and ran along the forecasing. Eager hands grasped the folbot and hauled the two men out of their cockpits and on to the submarine.

There, they stumbled along the slippery forecasing and climbed on to the bridge, where Woods was waiting for them. 'You've taken your time,' he said.

6

The General was tall, lean and bald, with a clipped moustache which glistened with sweat. He had been a general for so long the red tabs on his khaki bush shirt were a faded pink.

Looking at his campaign ribbons, headed by the vertical red-blue-red of the DSO, Pountney decided that the man must have been in the Army since the year dot, yet there was a vigour about him that he liked.

The General waved the SBS officer to a seat while he paced about his office like a caged bear. Cairo was sweltering and a large fan turning slowly in the centre of the ceiling seemed to do no more than slightly rearrange the foetid air.

Pountney waited apprehensively. He didn't mind action. In fact, he rather enjoyed the heat of battle. It brought out the best in him, he always thought; made the old grey matter work much faster. What he couldn't abide, what he had spent his whole adult life avoiding, was the methodical, humdrum, everyday existence of the civil servant, the paper shuffler. He couldn't abide such types – and he knew they couldn't abide him, if only because they couldn't pigeon-hole him. But in the man now prowling around him he thought he might have met his match.

'The fact is, the War Office don't like it,' the General

said eventually, expanding on his theme. 'Nobody has acted up to now, because no one took your unit seriously. I hope you don't mind me being frank.'

'Not at all, sir,' said Pountney politely.

'Everyone thought you were just another of Keyes's foibles. Lot of people not too keen on Combined Ops out here, you know. They don't like having their best men volunteering for the Commandos.'

'Is that so, sir?'

The General wiped a handkerchief over his thinning hairline, then shot Pountney a glance. 'You wouldn't think of resigning, would you? I'd guarantee you promotion to major and post you anywhere you liked.'

'I could hardly do that, sir,' said Pountney gently.

The Army man shook his head sadly. 'No. No, of course you couldn't.'

He brightened. 'Well, you certainly shook the Wops up last week. No casualties, I hope.'

'Unfortunately, sir, the *Salmon*, the submarine carrying the other SBS team, was sunk soon after she reached her billet. So they never got ashore.'

The General shook his head again. 'I'm sorry to hear that, very sorry. Such highly trained men, too. We can't afford such losses.'

There was a moment's pause before the General continued. 'And what was the final score with Angelo?'

'As you know, sir, we sent out six patrols in total. Two weren't able to be landed for operational reasons, but the other four reached their targets, and all returned.'

'Splendid. Splendid. And the damage?'

'Air reconnaissance reported a number of wrecked aircraft at both Maritsa and Lombardo, sir. And then there was the ammunition train we managed to bag on Sicily last week.'

The General's eyes gleamed. 'Excellent, Pountney, excellent.' He slapped his thigh enthusiastically before the realities of the situation closed in on him again. He sat down heavily behind his large teak desk. This time he wiped his moustache. His eyes, a light, watery blue, bulged unnaturally under his bushy eyebrows.

'Well, what are we going to do with you, Pountney? After your successes I can't possibly disband you, or Mr Churchill will be sending the Commander-in-Chief one of his memos.'

Pountney nodded sympathetically. He had heard about the Prime Minister's memos. They usually began: 'Pray let me know this day, on one side of a sheet of paper, why . . .' The Great Man didn't like desk-bound generals any more than Pountney did – though, to be fair, Pountney thought, the one he was now talking to obviously loathed that fate himself.

'Let us get on with it, sir,' Pountney said immediately. 'The Navy likes us and we like the Navy.'

The General shook his head doubtfully. 'But the War Office thinks it's all so *irregular*, Pountney. We simply can't have a dozen men wandering around on their own. Not attached to any formation, not responsible to any hierarchy.'

'I do report directly to General Laycock, sir,' Pountney reminded him.

'Yes, yes, I know all that, but you're not on any proper Army establishment. You don't even have your own cap badge or insignia.'

'We have our own motto, sir.'

'You have? And what is that?'

'*Excreta Tauri Astutos Frustrantur.*'

'Eh?'

'Latin, sir.'

The General snorted. 'I gathered that, Pountney.'

'A classics don at Oxford composed it for me, sir. It means "Bullshit Baffles Brains".'

The General's eyebrows beetled together, and for a moment Pountney thought his motto would not be well received.

But the General roared with laughter. 'Very good, Pountney. Very good indeed. So that's what you think of us desk-bound warriors.'

He leant back in his chair and the smile slowly faded from his face. 'Well, I'll tell you what I'll do. I'm being posted in a couple of weeks. They don't want old fogies like me at the sharp end any longer. I'm going to put the War Office's query at the bottom of my pending tray, where it can pend until my successor gets round to it. God knows when that will be.'

'Thank you, sir.'

'Anyway, if this chap Rommel continues to advance in the desert at the rate he's doing he'll be here by the end of next month. That will solve your problem, as they'll burn all the records before he arrives.'

He got up to indicate that the interview was over. Pountney jumped from his chair, came to attention and gave as smart a salute as he had mustered in years.

As Pountney turned to go, the General said: 'Good luck to you, Pountney. You're going to need it.'

As he shut the door behind him, the SBS man knew that the General had been wishing him luck with fighting Whitehall and its red tape – not the enemy.

7

Pountney felt his tread lighten as he left the GHQ building where the General had his office. Somehow he had got away with it; quite how, he was not sure. He made his way through the crowded, clamouring streets of Cairo to the coolness of the bar at Shepheard's Hotel, where Ayton was waiting for him.

'Whisky and soda,' Pountney said in answer to Ayton's question, and added unnecessarily: 'a very large one.'

'Well?' queried Ayton when he had given the order to the waiter.

'We're all right for the moment,' said Pountney. 'The old codger wasn't a bad sort for a pen-pusher. He promised to "lose" the file. He thinks Rommel will be here by the end of next month anyway, which will make everything pretty irrelevant.'

'Jesus,' said Ayton, although the news didn't come as that much of a surprise: there was already an air of unease about Cairo.

They fell silent as the waiter approached, balancing a tray: no one talked shop in front of the waiters. He arranged a coaster before each of them, placed a bowl of nuts between them and then, with the flourish of a conjuror producing a rabbit, put two large glasses of whisky and a soda siphon on the table. Ayton gave him a note and waved away the change.

'Jesus,' he said again when the waiter had gone. 'How serious is it, do you think?'

Pountney shrugged. He couldn't see what all the fuss was about himself. 'Haven't a clue. But I have a feeling that's what Bob Laycock wants to see us about.'

Laycock, besides being a charismatic commando leader, was a man who knew how to make himself comfortable – always the sign of a veteran campaigner. He had installed himself in a luxury villa a stone's throw from the hotel, and after draining their glasses Ayton and Pountney walked round to it.

The commando guards snapped to attention as the SBS men passed through the gate. Laycock's aide, a young lieutenant in the Household Cavalry, greeted them at the front door, and led the way to Laycock's office.

The General waved them into two chairs in front of his desk and offered them his silver cigarette box. 'Egyptian on the right, Virginia on the left. A dicky-bird tells me you had a positive interview with General Marker,' he said to Pountney, 'and that you've managed to maintain your independence for the moment.'

As an officer in the Royal Horse Guards, part of the Household Cavalry, Laycock knew everything and everyone. The rumour was that those waiters who declined to spy for the Germans worked for him instead. Pountney related what had been said at the interview.

'Doesn't surprise me,' Laycock commented when Pountney had finished. 'The War Office loathes the word "commando". Smacks of irregular warfare. Blimps in Whitehall don't like that. If it wasn't for the Prime Minister we would have all been disbanded long ago.'

Laycock shook his head in wonderment at the vagaries of officialdom. As part of the political wrangling in high places his force had been transmuted first into lettered battalions and then into something called the Middle East Commando – all part of the military bureaucracy's attempt to try to gain control of Laycock's group before dismembering it.

Stubbing out his cigarette with a brusqueness which showed his disgust, Laycock added: 'Well, I didn't disturb your few days' well-deserved leave to talk about my problems when there are rather larger ones in the offing.'

'Then it's true what they're saying about Rommel, sir?' Pountney asked.

Laycock nodded. 'He's just captured Sollum and now has forward units at the Halfaya Pass. These could cross the Egyptian border any day now.'

Pountney and Ayton looked at each other. Both whiffed the scent of action to come.

'His lines of supply and communications must be stretched to the limit, then,' Pountney said.

'Exactly,' agreed Laycock. 'You see the bright side of everything, don't you, Roger? Every mile he advances is a mile more for his transport to travel to keep him supplied with fuel and ammunition.'

'Vulnerable, that coastal road,' Pountney mused.

'Exceptionally so.'

Ayton watched his superiors in silence. He could see that both men were savouring the possibilities spread out before them. The poor old regular infantry and armour might be getting a bashing in the desert, but for the elite such as them it represented an exceptional opportunity for raiding.

'So,' said Pountney, leaning forward eagerly, 'a series of raids from the sea. Is that the idea, sir?'

Laycock chuckled. 'It certainly is. Cut Rommel off from his supplies and it's like choking a man to death.'

Pountney sprang from his chair and strode over to a large-scale map pinned to the wall behind Laycock.

'I'd suggest here and here, sir.'

Laycock swung round in his chair.

'The coastal road runs next to the sea at both points,' Pountney remarked, 'and we'd bag God knows how much transport in the loop of road between them.'

'Exactly.'

'We'd need some support, sir.'

'We, Roger?'

Pountney's brow furrowed. 'I assumed you would be asking the SBS to mount these raids, sir.'

Laycock shook his head. 'Then you've assumed wrongly, I'm afraid. The Middle East Commando will be mounting them. It will be in support of a general offensive by our troops to stop Rommel in his tracks.'

Pountney looked crestfallen. 'Yes, sir.'

'I honestly don't think the SBS has the capability to undertake such large-scale operations, do you?'

Laycock was right, of course. Pountney nodded and returned to his seat, knowing now that he and Ayton had just been called in to be kept briefed and perhaps to tender some advice if it was solicited. But with luck they might be given a minor role to play.

'However,' said Laycock, 'I have something much more interesting for you two to consider.' He leant forward. 'You well know the Italians were on the run in Libya until Rommel showed up in February. They'd all be in the bag by now if it hadn't been for him.'

'And his Afrika Korps, sir,' Pountney added.

'Ah, but our intelligence people say that, though the Afrika Korps have first-class troops, there aren't that many of them. Not enough to have made such a huge difference to the situation.'

'You're saying that's down to Rommel, sir?'

Laycock nodded. 'I am. The man's a genius, in my opinion. Quite brilliant. He runs rings round us. So much so that it's getting harder to convince the ordinary Tommy that he can be beaten.'

That was the Cairo gossip. Rommel was unstoppable. Nonsense, of course, but even the Egyptians in the street had begun to sense the growing sense of panic and were becoming openly hostile to the British military in their midst.

'And that, gentlemen, is a very serious situation indeed.'

Laycock paused, grim-faced.

Pountney immediately saw what he was driving at. 'So Rommel's the crux of it, sir? Get rid of him and we solve the problem?'

'Exactly, Roger.'

Ayton now spoke for the first time. 'Do we know where Rommel is, sir?'

Laycock unlocked a drawer of his desk and withdrew a map, which he unfurled and spread out on his desk. The SBS men could see that it was a large-scale map of part of the Libyan coastline.

'Luckily, we do,' Laycock said. 'We have had a man working on the problem for some time. He speaks Arabic and Italian fluently and has the confidence of the local people. He was infiltrated into the area by submarine a month ago and the Long Range Desert Group picked him up last week. He says Rommel's HQ is here, at Beda Littoria, some fifteen miles inland from the coast on the Via Balbia – the main road we'll be cutting further east.'

The SBS men studied the map in silence. From its contours it looked like wild and hilly countryside.

'Where is Beda Littoria exactly, sir?' Ayton asked.

'Between Benghazi and Tobruk. It's about two hundred miles behind enemy lines, though it might be three hundred by tomorrow at the rate Rommel is advancing.'

Pountney felt a pulse of excitement run through him. This was exactly what he had envisaged to be the purpose of the SBS: small-scale raiding from the sea of vital targets behind enemy lines.

'When do we move, sir?' he asked.

'As soon as possible. Unfortunately, we're hamstrung to a certain extent by the lack of available submarines. However, with some arm-twisting the Admiral has let us have two.'

'Two folbot teams to a submarine,' Pountney mused. 'That's eight men.'

'If you can't do it with eight men I don't suppose you could do it with eighteen or eighty.'

'No problem, sir.'

Ayton was wondering how they would return – no use expecting precious submarines to be deployed in an area thoroughly alerted by the assassination of the Germans' top general – when Laycock answered his query by saying: 'The LRDG will bring you back. They know every inch of the desert. Drive around it as if it was Piccadilly Circus.'

He drew out another, smaller-scale, map and spread it over the large-scale one, and with a pencil traced a route which led straight inland from Beda Littoria into the desert. When he reached a small circle marked 'Gialo Oasis' he tapped it and said: 'That'll be your rendezvous with the Group.'

Pountney looked at the scale of the map, then measured the distance between Beda Littoria and the oasis with his eye. Laycock grinned at him when he heard his sharp, involuntary intake of breath. 'Nice little walk for you, Roger.'

Pountney's expression remained unchanged, however, and he answered: 'Well, at least Jerry won't bother to chase us out there, sir.'

'Don't worry,' said Laycock reassuringly. 'We're not expecting you to walk it. Our man is being delivered back into the area soon. He'll meet you on the beach, and after the operation he'll be waiting for you with a truck. His name's Tommy, by the way. Don't bother to ask him what his real name is. All I can tell you is that he is one of our most trusted and valuable agents.'

'Who would you pick to come with us, Phil?' Pountney said as they left the villa.

'Daly and Bob Harmon, for certain,' Ayton replied briskly. 'They proved themselves at Lombardo. Kelly and Davidson had bad luck, but Davidson certainly deserves another go.'

Pountney nodded. Kelly was still recovering from a bullet in the shoulder, so another partner would have to be found for Davidson. 'I agree. Who else?'

'Bailey and Tim Robertson perhaps?' said Ayton with less certainty.

'Not Maitland?'

Maitland was their latest recruit, a raw-boned Glaswegian who rarely spoke.

'He's a first-rate canoeist,' Ayton conceded, 'but he's not really had time to prove himself, has he?'

On the train back to Alexandria they continued to argue about who to pick. By the time they had boarded the depot ship they had decided to allow Maitland his chance in partnership with the experienced and reliable Lieutenant Tim Robertson. This meant that Bailey, a cheerful cockney corporal with nerves of steel, would partner the quieter, more introverted Davidson.

Davidson was a sergeant in the Royal Marines who, since his parents had been killed in an air raid on Liverpool, seemed to regard the war as a personal vendetta against the Axis forces in general and the Germans in particular. Such fanaticism had its drawbacks, but Pountney knew Davidson also happened to be a crack shot. Watching him handle a weapon was like seeing an art connoisseur inspect some rare treasure. If he didn't get carried away by his personal hatreds, Davidson was going to be an invaluable member of the unit and was potentially officer material.

The chosen party had only a few days in which to train and be briefed. Then one morning Laycock came on board and the officers chosen for the raid were summoned to the final briefing. He explained again what had to be done and why, then wished them luck. When he had left, Pountney spread out, alongside the large-scale map of the area, the air reconnaissance photographs of Beda Littoria that Laycock had brought with him.

The beach on which they would land looked straight-forward. They could tell from the way the waves broke at regular intervals that its gradient was neither too shallow nor too steep. The Mediterranean was virtually tideless, but that did not prevent quite strong local currents and eddies forming close to the shore.

However, from the angle at which the wave pattern approached the shore, there appeared to be no rip tide or inshore current of any great strength. The reason why the pattern did not run parallel with the shore was simply that the prevailing wind at that time of year, the Levanter, was blowing from the east and set the waves at a slight angle to the coastline. The coastal area itself looked flat and bare, and devoid of any easy landmarks, either natural or man-made, so the navigators of the submarines might find it difficult to pinpoint the landing area exactly.

Next the raiders examined the route inland to Beda Littoria. From the map contours it was clear that most of the hills were to the west and east, and Pountney surmised that the area through which they would have to pass would be mostly gently undulating sand-dunes. The map indicated that there was a track of some sort to Beda Littoria from the coastal area, but on the reconnaissance photographs it seemed to peter out before reaching the coast.

Well, that was Tommy's problem, whoever Tommy was, and Pountney just hoped that the mysterious agent knew what he was doing. Trudging over dunes would be tiring and slow, and even the most knowledgeable guides got lost in the desert. But in any case, he told himself, there was nothing he could do about that. He had other matters to worry about. Nevertheless, experience told him that such imponderables as he had already found meant a generous time factor would have to be built into the operation.

Lastly there was Beda Littoria itself. The photo reconnaissance unit had done a fine job by taking not only verticals of Rommel's headquarters, and the compound around it, but also a number of low-level obliques, before, doubtless, anti-aircraft fire had driven off the fast-flying Mosquito fighter-bombers which flew these missions.

The verticals showed the layout of the small town very well and enabled Pountney to work out the best approach to Rommel's headquarters. The *Rommel-Haus*, as the local Arabs apparently called it, was situated in a compound situated at the edge of the town and was surrounded by smaller buildings. Pountney could see that the best way of getting to it was to skirt the town and approach from inland, where the ring of surrounding buildings were most sparsely scattered.

But it was the low-level obliques that drew the party's undivided attention, for they could see from them that the building was three storeys high while the surroundings ones were all single-storey. Less surprisingly, its roof was covered with various wireless antennae and dotted here and there were trees and bushes, ideal terrain for arriving unannounced at someone's doorstep.

Besides the photographs and maps, Laycock had also brought a very rough sketch of the interior of the *Rommel-Haus*. He had handed it over with the warning that it must be treated with caution. 'The locals are eager to help,' he had said, 'but their intelligence can't be graded higher than C3.'

The sketch showed the position of the wireless room on the ground floor as well as of the sentries, and Laycock seemed to think that these details were probably accurate. He had also brought a pre-war photograph of Rommel, from which the man's pugnacious, square-jawed features stared out at them. There was no humour in the face and the mouth, thin-lipped, was set in a grim, downward line.

The group passed around the sketch and photograph, then returned to the oblique photographs. Most unusual of all there appeared to be no perimeter fence, but when one of the party mentioned this, Pountney simply said: 'Remember, this building's two hundred miles behind the lines. Why should they have a fence? The Houses of Parliament don't have one and they're a lot nearer the Germans than we are to Beda Littoria.'

When the final plan had been formulated Pountney asked in the captains and navigators of the two T-class submarines which had been detailed to take the raiding party to its destination, and explained his mission. The navigators had brought charts of the area. These confirmed that there was no natural hazard which would stop a landing taking place and that the submarines would be able to approach within eight hundred yards of the beach.

At dawn the next morning, with the greater part of No. 1 Special Boat Section aboard, both submarines sailed from Alexandria harbour and dived to eighty feet.

8

'Bloody glad I'm not going to have to pick you lot up again.'

The captain of the T-class submarine *Turbulent*, a lieutenant commander in the Royal Navy, was a jovial, red-faced character who looked as if he would be more at home on a farm than on the bridge of one of His Majesty's submarines, and indeed he was known to all and sundry – out of his hearing – as Farmer Giles.

'I can't see one good landmark to take a bearing on, much less two,' he said as he scanned the shoreline again with his binoculars, propping his elbows on the side of the bridge to steady them. Then he took them off from round his neck and handed them to Pountney. 'See what you make of it.'

They were still some distance from the Libyan coast, but its outline against the night sky looked uniformly flat and featureless.

'Are you sure we're in the right place?' asked Pountney.

'No,' the *Turbulent's* captain answered cheerfully. 'Never sure of anything in this game. But my pilot's first-rate and I guarantee we're not far from it.'

The submarine crept forward towards the shore. The Captain, an old hand at clandestine operations, had employed a different technique to Woods: he preferred to surface well offshore before ordering the folbots on deck. These had been secured by long painters to the upper superstructure of the bridge, and the *Turbulent* had then been trimmed down until only the conning tower remained above the water, with the folbots tethered alongside it. Pountney saw the advantage of this method: there was no need to worry about making a noise and the folbots could be brought up from below without hurrying. This lessened the possibility of the enemy being alerted to the presence of the submarine and of the folbots being damaged because the crew were rushing to complete the job. On the other hand, two perfectly good folbots could be lost if the submarine had to crash-dive. Also, if there was any sea running, the small, fragile craft could get swamped. But the surface now was flat-calm, for the Levanter had temporarily blown itself out.

'Can you go as close as eight hundred yards?' Pountney asked, handing back the binoculars.

Farmer Giles looked up at the night sky, which was blanketed by cloud. 'No moon. Plenty of water under us. I'd say we can take you in to within five hundred. That close enough for you?'

The man might look like an easygoing rustic, but he must have nerves of steel to agree to go that close in, Pountney thought.

'You bet,' he said appreciatively.

Attached to the canoes were inflatable rubber floats on which some of their gear was secured, so it was essential to get as near to the shore as possible.

'But my crew haven't had any practice in crash-diving stern first,' Farmer Giles added, 'so I'm going to have to keep my bows pointing seaward.'

'Fair enough.'

'Which means I can't use my main gun to cover you if anything goes wrong and you have to re-embark.'

'I'll take that risk,' Pountney said.

He had, he believed, got the better of the bargain. Farmer Giles returned to scanning the shore. The minutes passed, but there was no signal from the shore. Then, just as Pountney was resigning himself to the fact that they must be in the wrong place, or that 'Tommy' had not made the rendezvous, from the black ribbon of coastline there came two quick winks, pinpricks of light, followed by a longer one.

At first Pountney thought he must have been imagining it, but then it came again and Farmer Giles said: 'That's a "V" all right. Ready to go in?'

'Yes,' said Pountney. 'It must be him.' But he felt far from convinced.

Farmer Giles altered course towards the flashing signal and when the operator of the echo-sounder reported through the voice pipe that they had a hundred feet of water under them, he ordered the submarine to make a 180-degree turn. For the last few hundred yards it moved slowly astern under its electric engines – a submarine's diesel engines could not be reversed – before he ordered the internal trimming tanks to be blown.

The blinking of the torch was much stronger now. The huge, bulbous carcass of the submarine rose slowly from the water as it forged slowly astern. Compressed air bubbled round its hull, and the folbots, each with its inflatable supply bag, bobbed and jostled by the conning tower. Farmer Giles ordered the engines to be put into neutral, and when it seemed that the submarine had stopped he threw a white wood chip into the water. It bobbed alongside, then slowly floated slowly seawards, showing that the submarine was going astern.

'Slow ahead, both engines,' he said into the voice pipe, then almost immediately: 'Out both engines' clutches.'

He waited for a moment and then threw in a second chip. This time the piece of wood remained stationary by the bridge.

'Ready when you are,' he said to Pountney. Ayton and the two crewmen of the second folbot were already poised at the bottom of the conning tower's ladder and on Pountney's orders were on deck in a moment. A seaman followed them to release the painters.

Pountney shook Farmer Giles's hand, scrambled down the ladder on to the forecasing and lowered himself into his canoe, which Ayton was keeping steady with the outboard blade of his paddle.

'Cast off,' Pountney said quietly, and the seaman undid the painter and handed it to him.

A few brisk strokes and they were clear of the submarine, which immediately began to trim down. The inflatable bag bounced and yawed behind them, but they hardly noticed the slight drag it caused as they paddled steadily towards the shore. They could not see Tommy's signal now. Perhaps they were too low in the water, Pountney told himself, but there remained the ever-present nagging doubt that he was leading his men into a trap.

On their right they could just see the dim outline of the second folbot. Five minutes later they heard the surf breaking ahead and braced themselves for a rough landing. But the waves were modest in height and had not been whipped up by the wind, and Pountney even managed to catch one as it broke, which allowed him to surf the folbot right into the beach. He wished that it was always that simple, and out of the corner of his eye he saw that the other folbot was not having such an easy time.

He and Ayton scrambled out and dragged the folbot and its supply bag clear of the water before lying flat on the sand, their tommy-guns at the ready. To their right they saw the second folbot broach to, dumping its crew unceremoniously into shallow water, but they too quickly wriggled free and dragged the folbot away from the breaking waves.

Carefully, Pountney and Ayton scanned the beach for any movement and listened over the slop of the breaking waves for any unusual sound. But the beach resembled the desert: it looked and felt not just empty but as if they were the first humans ever to have visited it. There was no sign of their guide.

Ahead of them the beach appeared to give way to dunes, and after a final look round Pountney signalled to Ayton to make for these. The other pair followed and all four men sprinted inland, leaving the folbots on the beach.

The sand was soft, covered here and there by sparse gorse and clumps of grass. The group flung themselves down under the skyline of the nearest dune, then Pountney moved cautiously forward on his stomach until he could see beyond it. As he did so, the Levanter piped up suddenly from the east. It sighed eerily through the gorse and the spindly leaves of the high clumps of coarse grass, blowing eddies of sand off the ridge of the dune into his face.

Inland, other dunes undulated away into the black horizon. It seemed as if the party had arrived on another planet, so utterly barren did it look. Then, out of the dark, as if from nowhere, a figure appeared. Pountney covered him with his tommy-gun, and when the man, who was dressed in flowing Arab robes, was almost upon him, said the password softly. The figure swung round, gave the answering password, then strode forward, his hand extended.

'I'm Tommy. Glad you made it,' he said.

While they waited for the second party to arrive, they brought their folbots up to the dunes. Then they brewed tea, ate stew out of self-heating tins and checked every item of equipment for their trek inland. They also cleaned their weapons with scrupulous care, knowing that just one grain of sand could cause the firing mechanism to malfunction.

Pountney had told each man to tape a second magazine to the one already clipped on to his tommy-gun, so that when the first was expended it could be unclipped and flipped over, and the second quickly snapped into the breech. He had tried it out on a firing range after their visit to Maritsa. It had brought down on him the wrath of the Guards weapons instructor at the range, who was horrified at such irregularity. But it had worked perfectly, and he knew that the success of the present operation depended on such innovation as well as meticulous attention to detail.

Tommy watched their preparations in silence, his face shrouded in his Arab head-dress. When the second submarine was due, Pountney began flashing the letter 'V' at regular intervals. They never saw the submarine, but an hour later the other half of the party came surfing out of the dark. The crews sprinted up the beach with their folbots and equipment, and while Ayton returned there to erase any signs of the landings, got themselves ready to move. Pits were dug in the dunes for the folbots so that no trace remained of them. Then Tommy, holding a luminous hand compass, led the way inland, striking off in a direction which Pountney presumed would take them as quickly as possible to the path he had seen on the map. For a while they marched in single file to make it easier for the last man to erase their footsteps, but before long this became unnecessary, for the dunes gave way to hard, rocky, windswept ground.

It was surprisingly cold and the Levanter cut through their clothing. Pountney had just begun to think that the recce photographs must have been correct, and that the path had somehow been obliterated, when the edge of the escarpment along which they were marching ended abruptly and they stumbled right on to it. The first glimmer of dawn was now lightening the sky, so they dispersed among the gorse bushes to hide until dark.

In the light of day Tommy had the appearance of an Arab, but his English accent was impeccable, and Pountney soon found they had friends in common. Nevertheless, he had no idea of Tommy's real name and, as Laycock had ordered, made no attempt to find out.

'Are you sure Rommel's at his HQ?' he asked.

Tommy shook his head. 'It's impossible to know for sure. He comes and goes so much. But every indication is that he is there now. My local contacts say they saw him two days ago.'

Pountney refrained from saying that the Arabs were not the most reliable source of intelligence for fear he might offend his guide. But Tommy read his thoughts. He shrugged and said: 'I know. The Arabs look at things differently. Two days might mean two weeks. But Cairo must think it worth trying, otherwise you and I wouldn't be here, would we?'

'I think it's a last throw of the dice myself,' said

Pountney. 'Many people think that if we don't stop Rommel now he'll be in Cairo in six weeks.'

They dozed fitfully during the day and made as good a meal as they could in the evening twilight. Then they blacked their faces, primed their No. 36 grenades and made a final check of their weapons. At nine o'clock they moved off in single file behind their guide. Tommy reckoned they were now about ten miles from Beda Littoria, or just over three hours' march at a steady pace along the rock-strewn path.

Shortly after midnight the first bungalows on the out-skirts of the town appeared on the skyline. Tommy waved the others down to one side of the path into a dried-up wadi, and Pountney and Ayton then went forward with him to make a final reconnaissance. Tommy led them round the edge of the outlying bungalows before striking up a small, unmetalled road towards the town's centre.

The whole place was deserted and in complete darkness. Occasionally a dog barked, but otherwise only the moan of the wind around the eaves of the modern, single-storey buildings could be heard.

They passed through the only Arab-looking part of the town, the souk, or marketplace, and paused while a convoy of trucks rumbled down the Via Balbia, which ran through the central square. Then, when they had nearly reached the far side of the town, Tommy indicated a nearby building. 'Go down the side of that bungalow,' he whispered, 'and you'll come to open ground. There's plenty of cover, though. On the right you'll see the vehicle compound and, beyond the trees, the *Rommel-Haus*. You can't mistake it. I'll bring the rest of the party to this spot now, and have the truck here waiting for you. Good luck.'

He disappeared into the night, the sharp wind billowing his Arab robe around him.

'Fucking Lawrence of Arabia,' said Ayton quietly. 'I hope he bloody well knows what he's doing.' He felt uneasy about putting his life in the hands of such a mysterious character. Ayton hated mysteries.

'He knows,' said Pountney. 'Let's go.' He led the way down the side of the bungalow, his tommy-gun at the ready. He had crept forward only a few yards when he saw that their guide's description was not entirely accurate. There was, as he had said, a large patch of open ground. But between where they were crouching and the *Rommel-Haus*, which stood out white and square-shaped like a blockhouse in the distance, there was a broad swathe of rocky ground which offered no cover whatsoever.

Pountney swore under his breath. They would have to find another approach. They skirted the vehicle compound, which was lined with staff cars, some of them half-tracks, and one of the absurd Italian CV3 tanks whose reputation lived up to its nickname of 'tin coffin'. Ayton looked at these tempting unguarded targets as they walked by silently and wished he had some clams with him.

Beyond the compound the undergrowth was thicker, so that they could work their way towards the *Rommel-Haus* without undue risk of being seen by the guards who they knew must be somewhere around. Tommy had told them that his Arab informants had said there were two outside the entrance and another two patrolling the immediate grounds. They weren't Germans, apparently, but Italian Blackshirts, Mussolini's fascist militia who fought along-side regular Italian Army units in the desert. They were fanatical in their devotion to their fat Duce, but not noted for their skill on the battlefield, and the SBS men were sure they would not cause them any problem.

They inched as close to the *Rommel-Haus* as they dared and could now see the two sentries by the entrance. One sat on a chair, his rifle across his knees, the other leant against the wall, apparently half asleep, his rifle propped beside him. Their nonchalance made Pountney uneasy. If Major-General Erwin Rommel, the charismatic, hard-nosed commander of the German 7th Panzer Division, which had swept all before it in France the previous year, was in residence, would they be quite so lax?

Then he saw what he guessed must be the sergeant of the guard come out of the main door, and the man's high-pitched, indignant voice could be heard berating the guards, who immediately sprang to attention. When the Italian had gone back into the building, the two SBS men moved on around it. They noticed that all the windows, except those on the top floor, were protected by steel shutters. None of Tommy's Arab informants knew where Rommel's private suite was situated. It made sense to Pountney that it should be at the top of the house, well away from the General's headquarters staff and the map and wireless rooms, which Tommy had said were all on the ground floor. The shuttered windows meant that the only possible way of forcing their way in was through the guarded entrance. But Pountney had expected this, and the sloppiness of the sentries only confirmed his conviction that they would succeed.

Warily, the two men moved from one piece of cover to the next as they looked for the patrol which they knew must be somewhere in the area. It was Ayton who saw them first. He squeezed Pountney's shoulder and pointed. The two enemy soldiers were walking side by side across the open ground, heading directly towards them. Pountney nodded once to indicate that he had seen them. He pointed to Ayton to stay where he was and take the man on the right while he moved across to another patch of gorse so that he could deal with the other one.

Ayton drew out his knife and weighed it in his hand. The manner in which he had dispatched the SS *Feldwebel* on the Italian schooner had reaffirmed his confidence in Fairbairn's methods of teaching. Besides showing his pupils exactly where to place the knife to kill a man immediately, Fairbairn had taught them how to fight with a knife in close combat by slashing at vital parts of the body. He had also shown them how to kill a man quite silently, by wrapping an arm around the target's throat from behind and driving the knife between the collar-bone and the neck. This severed the subclavian artery and the victim choked to death on his own blood in seconds. It was this method that Ayton chose to use.

The two soldiers loomed larger in the dark now, and the SBS men could hear that they were talking in an undertone. Both had their rifles slung over their shoulders, the thumbs of their right hands stuck under the slings to relieve the pressure on their shoulders.

Walking a yard or so apart, they passed inches from the two waiting men. Ayton caught a whiff of cheap aftershave which overlaid a more pervasive smell of sweat and tobacco. Pountney struck first, but Ayton's target was too slow to react and the SBS man strangled the man's cry into a gurgle with the crook of his arm around his windpipe. Then he thrust a knee into the base of the Italian's spine, at the same time snapping his head back with his forearm with every ounce of strength he could muster. He heard the man's neck crack, then the body went limp. He bent down and felt the jugular vein. Finding no pulse, he rolled him aside and looked around for Pountney. Kneeling, the older man was wiping his knife on the back of his victim, who was lying face down.

'Now what?' Ayton whispered. He wondered how they were going to get safely across the open ground to collect the rest of the party. As Pountney straightened up, Ayton could see the grin on his face.

'We'll pretend to be the patrol, of course,' Pountney said. He tugged the rifle from under the dead man, took the black beret off his head and stuck it on his own. Ayton did the same. They hid their tommy-guns under their clothing and strolled out casually from the undergrowth, imitating as closely as they could the shambling steps of the guards.

It seemed to take an age to cross the open ground, but once they reached the other side, where the undergrowth hid them from view, they were able to divest themselves of the rifles and berets, then hurry to the rendezvous.

The other six men were all sitting on their haunches, their backs against the wall of the bungalow, their weapons cradled in their arms.

'Thought you'd copped it,' Bob Harmon whispered cheerfully.

Pountney didn't answer, but began to lead the way back through the undergrowth, past the vehicle compound and up to the edge of the *Rommel-Haus*. The sentries outside the front door were quickly and soundlessly dispatched by Bailey and Davidson; then Harmon, who spoke good German, knocked on the door and demanded to be let in. A German officer opened it. He stood at the entrance, silhouetted by a dim light glowing in the hall behind him. As he stood barring the door, asking what Harmon wanted, Pountney stepped forward and rammed a pistol in his ribs. Harmon warned the *Hauptmann* not to speak, but the German grabbed the muzzle of Pountney's pistol, forced it away from his stomach and began shouting for help. Pountney kicked him in the knee and as the man's hands dropped down he shot him in the chest. The *Hauptmann* slid to the floor, but behind him there was a commotion as other Germans jostled by the door, which led to the room on the right. Pountney lifted his weapon and fired a burst at them. One fell and the others scrambled back into the room and shut the door. Harmon stepped forward with two hand-grenades, opened the door, rolled in the grenades and shut it again.

The double explosion shook the house and the SBS men heard muffled screams. There was a pause, then another German officer, his uniform in tatters, staggered out of the door. Pountney, who had moved into the house, fired a short burst and the man rolled over and lay still. Davidson stepped past him, kicked the door wide open and loosed several equally short bursts. The room was so full of smoke that it was difficult to see across it, but Pountney noticed the outline of a man rising from one corner. He shouted a warning, but Davidson either ignored it or did not hear it. A single shot rang out and Davidson fell soundlessly to the floor.

Pountney threw himself sideways and slammed the door shut, then moved into the hall, followed by Ayton and Corporal Daly. They sprayed the area with fire before running for the flight of stone stairs on their right, which led to the upper floors. As they did so, a *Hauptmann* flourishing a Schmeisser came running down the stairs while another officer, armed with a Luger pistol, leant over the banisters shouting instructions.

Before Ayton could get a bead on the German with the sub-machine-gun, a burst from the weapon caught Daly and twisted him round, and the heavy 9mm bullets threw him against the wall. Daly slid to the ground and Ayton saw blood gush from his mouth. The German turned the muzzle towards Ayton, who fired at the same moment. The bullets whined over Ayton's head. Then the *Hauptmann*'s knees buckled and the weapon clattered noisily down the stone stairs, followed closely by the man's body.

The German with the Luger was still leaning over the balustrade, and now holding the pistol in both hands to steady his aim. He fired and Pountney felt the bullet pluck his arm as he swung his tommy-gun upwards and pressed the trigger. The Luger clattered on to the stairs as the man staggered forwards, slumped over the balustrade, then slowly toppled over the top, to hit the hall floor with a terrible, bone-breaking thump.

'Come on!' shouted Pountney.

If Rommel had been asleep he wouldn't be now, but he had no way of escape. Pountney ran for the stairs, leapt over the dead German at the bottom of them and started ascending, two stairs at a time. He flung open the door of a room on the first floor from which were coming the strains of a Viennese waltz. The room, comfortably furnished with a rug and several sofas, was brightly lit, and in one corner a gramophone was playing the music he heard. Pountney saw the startled face of a German officer peering at him from behind one of the sofas. It certainly wasn't Rommel. The SBS man pulled out the pin of a hand-grenade, rolled it in, shouted '*Gute nacht*' and slammed the door.

Behind Pountney, Harmon fired a burst into the other first-floor room, and someone inside began cursing and shouting in German. The hand-grenade went off and the waltz turned to a screech before fading away.

By now Pountney was halfway up the next flight of stairs, with Ayton close on his heels. The top floor also had two doors. Pountney tried one, but it wouldn't open. He stood back, and in one movement blasted off the lock, kicked open the door and flung himself into the room.

The other door was ajar. Ayton kicked it open and raked the area in front of him with fire. The room was full of stacked furniture, but otherwise unoccupied. Ayton cursed and turned. As he did so, he heard three separate bursts of automatic fire from the other room. He ran across and dived through the door, his weapon at the ready. He found himself in a kind of ante-room.

'Here, Phil,' Pountney called from an inner room. Ayton went through and found him ransacking an empty bedroom lit by a single standard lamp. To the right was a bathroom. Its door stood wide open and Ayton could see the line of gouges across the tiled wall where Pountney had sprayed the room with bullets.

'No one here,' said Pountney in disgust.

On a highly polished coffee-table stood, in a large onyx frame, a photograph of Rommel's smiling wife and solemn, bespectacled son. Several silver-backed monogrammed hairbrushes were neatly lined up on the top of a dressing-table and a pair of gilded slippers stuck out from under the bed. The bed was narrow and covered with a grey blanket of the type familiar to all British service personnel. Perhaps they *were* British, Ayton thought.

'Fuck all,' Pountney cursed, wrenching open drawers in a fury as if expecting to find Rommel in one of them.

'Come on,' urged Ayton. 'Let's get out of here. You're not going to find the Afrika Korps' operational plans rolled up in his pyjamas.'

Smoke, mixed with the stench of gunpowder, drifted up the stairwell as they ran back down to the ground floor. It hung in the hall, thick and acrid. The dead *Hauptmann* proved to be only wounded and was groaning loudly. Daly had been taken outside, and Harmon had his tommy-gun levelled at the closed doors. He looked up questioningly; Pountney shook his head.

'There's still some of them in there,' Harmon said, nodding at the nearest door. 'I've laid charges in the wireless room. They'll go off any moment.'

'Let's get the hell out of here, then,' said Pountney. 'How's Daly?'

'Dead,' Harmon replied.

'And Davidson?'

'He's dead, too.'

Pountney swore. Vendettas didn't work in wartime. War was impersonal. It needed a cool head – and luck. Especially luck.

Minutes later they had laid Daly and Davidson out under the front wall of the house and covered their bodies with a gas cape. Raindrops began to spatter the cape as Pountney bent over the dead SBS men and ripped off their identity tags. As he did so the charges in the wireless room exploded, shaking the house to its foundations. It seemed a suitable farewell.

Robertson emerged from the darkness to report that, as Pountney had ordered, the telephone wires had been cut before Pountney had entered the *Rommel-Haus* and that two Germans – who had come running from a nearby bungalow when the shooting had started – had both been shot.

Pountney led the way back. He noticed that there were several lights on in the town now, and from the vehicle compound he heard the engine of one of the half-tracks cough into life.

They ran across the open ground well apart in case they came under fire. Opposite the bungalow from which they had started out an Italian three-ton truck was parked by the side of the road. Tommy was standing by it; he was in army uniform now and carried a Sten gun. He waved them over urgently.

Pountney glanced back and saw the *Rommel-Haus* surrounded by a halo of smoke and flame. Well, the SBS had at least left their calling card, he thought. But next time . . . The party piled into the back of the truck, tripping over jerrycans, some full of water, others full of fuel, and a Bren gun which had been set up on an anti-aircraft tripod.

'We're going to have to fight our way out,' said Tommy calmly as he put the engine into gear. 'Know how to use a Solothurn?' he asked Pountney, who, with Ayton, had climbed into the front. Tommy pointed at a large, circular hole in the roof above Pountney's head. The butt of a long-barrelled rifle was sticking down through it.

'Fucking right I do,' said Pountney.

All SBS men went through a course which taught them how to fire and maintain the enemy's weapons. The Solothurn was the Italian Army's Swiss-made anti-tank rifle. It fired a 20mm, armour-piercing bullet which was quite effective at close range against armoured cars and the like. It was certainly more lethal than the British equivalent, the Boys rifle, which fired a half-inch bullet that couldn't penetrate tissue paper.

Pountney pulled himself to his feet as the truck lurched forward.

'Hold tight!' Tommy yelled and let in the clutch with a jerk. The Solothurn was secured to the truck by a simple bipod. Pountney swung the butt upwards with one hand, then squeezed himself through the hole until he could fit the butt securely into his shoulder. The rifle kicked like a mule, he knew, and he needed a broken collar-bone at this particular moment like a hole in the head.

He made sure that the magazine, which clipped on to the left-hand side of the breech, was secured, then cocked the weapon, felt the first round slide easily into the breech and squinted down the sights. Provided one of Rommel's Mark III Panzers didn't interrupt their progress, he felt confident that the Solothurn could deal with whatever vehicle appeared in their path.

'Hold on!' Tommy yelled as he accelerated and swung the truck around the first corner, its tyres screeching. Ahead of them a group of Germans with lanterns were running across the road. Ayton, his tommy-gun thrust out of the passenger window, caught a glimpse of one enemy soldier by the roadside working frantically to load a magazine on to a light machine-gun. The truck was past the machine-gunner before he could fire and it scattered the others like leaves in the wind. Bursts of tommy-gun fire from the back dropped two of them before the truck squealed round another corner and was gone. A cheer went up in the back.

'Good driving,' Ayton yelled at Tommy.

Tommy flashed him a grin. 'I won at Brooklands in

'37,' he yelled back. 'Keep a look out on your side. We're not out of trouble yet.'

Tommy was right.

From his vantage point it was Pountney who saw the tank first, just a split second before Tommy. He swore under his breath. He had thought it was one of the open half-tracks that had started in the vehicle compound. But ahead of them, emerging cautiously from a side-street, was the unmistakable outline of the square-sided CV3.

The tank's two machine-guns were still trained fore and aft, so its crew had not yet seen the truck. Once they did, all they would have to do was stop in the middle of the street and there would be no way past them.

Pountney and Tommy acted simultaneously, for as Pountney shouted to Tommy to stop, the driver was already bringing the truck to a juddering halt by the side of the road.

The tank was moving very slowly; only the front half was visible. Pountney saw the turret beginning to swivel, first left, then right, as the crew peered through the slits.

Pountney trained the Solothurn on the tank. He could try his luck by attempting to put a shell through one of the slits; but for once he ignored his gambler's instincts. If he missed, there wouldn't be a second chance. It was better to wait for the tank to move forward enough and so expose its engine, housed just behind the turret.

He could hear the squeal and clank of its tracks as the CV3 crawled forward. The turret began to swing purposefully towards the truck and Pountney knew then that the tank crew had seen the vehicle.

'For Christ's sake, fire!' Tommy roared up at him.

'He knows what he's fucking doing,' Ayton yelled at Tommy.

127

Inch by inch the tank moved forward and inch by inch the muzzles of its machine-guns trained round towards the truck. Calmly and deliberately, Pountney pumped three 20mm shells into it in quick succession, just below the armoured skirt which protected the engine.

The tank stopped and smoke started cascading out of the engine, but the turret, with its two machine-guns, continued to swivel. Pountney aimed carefully, and squeezed the Solothurn's trigger. There was a loud crack and a whine, and a spark of metal hitting metal, as the bullet ricocheted off the side of the turret. He fired once more, and again there was a crack and a whine and a spark.

Ayton watched in helpless fascination. Tommy revved the truck and put it into reverse, but Pountney shouted to him to keep it still. He saw now that the slit in the front of the turret was larger than the ones at the sides. Yet he had to fire before the machine-guns did. The black oblong of the slit seemed absurdly small, but the range was very short, no more than a hundred yards. He squeezed the trigger again and felt the butt thud into his shoulder.

This time there was no ricochet or spark, and the turret jerked and stopped. Pountney knew the mayhem an armour-piercing bullet caused inside such a small space. He worked the Solothurn's breech mechanism and fired again, and the tank slewed sideways as if the driver had fallen on the controls.

'Let's go!' cried Tommy, slamming his foot on the accelerator. The truck bounced forward and skidded round the front of the tank. Ayton gave it a burst of fire as a farewell. 'Save your ammo,' Tommy yelled.

Suddenly they were clear of the town. The unmetalled road became a rutted, sandy track over which the truck bounced and heaved. To their left the sky was already salmon pink against the rain clouds.

Soon after sunrise Tommy took the truck off the track into a wadi, where they camouflaged it with desert netting. They brewed tea and ate cold rations, then took it in turns to stand guard while the rest slept under the truck or beneath nearby scrub.

During the morning the clouds cleared away and the sun blazed down, bringing with it a crawling, maddening mass of flies and other insects. There was no escaping them. They crawled everywhere: on the men's faces, up their nostrils, across their eyelids.

By midday the heat was intense, making it difficult to touch anything, move or even breathe. In mid-afternoon they heard the sound of an aero engine and out of the shimmering haze a biplane with Italian markings appeared, skimming low across the desert. It droned around in circles for a few minutes before disappearing westwards.

'The hunt's on,' said Pountney, watching it go with a hand shading his eyes.

Tommy snorted. 'Needle in a haystack. Know how big the Libyan desert is?'

Pountney shook his head.

'As large as India,' Tommy said, then rolled over and went back to sleep.

The biplane was the only sign that the SBS were being pursued. When darkness came they continued their journey southwards towards the oasis. With the coming of night the temperature plummeted and the desert cold seeped into them. At first they drove without lights at a snail's pace, but after some hours Tommy turned on the headlights and increased his speed. When dawn came he did not stop.

They reached the oasis that evening just as the blistering red sun was dipping below the desert rim. There they found a circle of tatty palm trees, a brackish pool of water, a small Arab encampment full of tethered camels and half a dozen heavily armed open trucks around which were clustered a group of men in assorted khaki clothing. Several were bareheaded and had driving goggles pushed up on to their foreheads; others wore Arab head-dress; many were bearded.

As the truck drew up, one of them came over to it and proffered his hand to Tommy. 'Crichton-Stuart. G Patrol, Long Range Desert Group. Glad to see you. You're in good time.'

Ayton looked at the officer with curiosity. He had heard of G Patrol, made up of members of the Scots and Coldstream Guards. Earlier in 1941 it had launched a famous raid with Free French troops on the Italian stronghold of Murzuk in southern Libya. He knew they were in good hands. He wandered over to look at the trucks and introduced himself to the other LRDG men.

'Seen these before?' one of them asked Ayton, tapping the long bonnet covered in camouflage paint. Ayton shook his head. It bristled with weapons.

'Thirty-hundredweight Chevrolet truck, specially converted for our nefarious purposes,' the man said, 'Left-hand drive, of course. Not that that makes any difference in the desert. Extra-wide tyres, extra-large fuel tanks, extra everything.'

The truck's windscreen lay flat on the bonnet. There was no roof over the driver's cabin, so that the Lewis gun, easily identified by the cowling over the barrel and its ammunition pan, could be fired as an anti-aircraft gun by the front passenger. Sticking up behind the driver was the aerial for the wireless mounted in the back of the truck. Also in the back was a half-inch Vickers machine-gun on a vertical swivel. Along the sides of the truck were jerrycans, boxes, batteries and an array of other equipment. Not an inch of space was wasted. Even the front mudguards had a folded tent on one side and a roll of camouflage netting on the other. Ayton pointed to two steel troughs strapped to one side and asked what they were for.

'Unsticking is what we call it,' came the prompt reply. 'When we get stuck in the sand – which is often – we put those steel channels under the wheels. Colonel Bagnold took similar ones with him when he crossed the desert during the 1920s. These Chevrolets carry fuel for eleven hundred miles and enough food and water for their crew for three weeks. Not bad, eh?'

Ayton nodded. 'But how the hell do you find your way about?' he asked.

'We use a sun compass. It's not affected by magnetism, like an ordinary compass is, and gives the true bearing of the truck's course. With that and the odometer we can end up within two miles of our objective after a hundred-mile run. But we also use sextants to take star sights – and a noon-sun sight if we can.'

That night they ate roasted goat meat and drank harsh arrack, which they traded with the Arabs camping nearby. Then at dawn G Patrol and its seven passengers headed eastwards towards Egypt.

9

General Marker's replacement was a different kettle of fish, Pountney could see that immediately he was ushered into his office.

Several weeks had passed since the raid on the *Rommel-Haus*, mostly spent on a very pleasant leave in Beirut. Now it was back to business.

Poutney gave his smartest salute. He had his hand shaken and was asked to sit down. The hubbub of Cairo's street life floated through the open window as the two men sat for a moment in friendly silence, weighing each other up.

Pountney's personal file was tucked safely away in the General's top drawer, but the man knew it by heart and had been much intrigued by the thumbnail sketch that each file always included. Pountney, he had read, had been a professional hunter and gold prospector in East Africa between the wars and had paddled down the Nile in a canoe with a sack of potatoes and an elephant spear, his sole possessions at the time, before becoming a sergeant in the Palestine police. When the war had started he had been commissioned in the King's Royal Rifle Corps before secondment to the Commandos. Then the sketch had given a brief description of how Pountney had demonstrated the potential of canoes as a weapon of war. The assessment ended with the verdict: 'is not easily assimilable into any normal infantry role.'

The General had chuckled at that. They could say that again.

In a way it was a pity the war was rapidly changing from being a romantic battle for survival into a cold-blooded, scientific, calculated drive for victory. But that's how it was.

Time for business.

He leant forward and offered Pountney a cigarette from a silver box bearing the engraved crest of the General's old regiment. Pountney refused the cigarette. He did not recognize the crest, a rose within two laurels surmounted by a crown. The General, who had been watching him closely, said: 'Intelligence Corps. Newfangled outfit. I dare say you've never heard of it.'

Pountney hadn't, but he didn't like to say so. He was slightly unnerved by the General's perspicacity.

'Its motto is "Knowledge Gives Strength to the Arm."'

Pountney noticed for the first time that the General was formidably young, not much older than himself, and the red tabs and the crossed swords and the pips on the epaulettes of his bush shirt, which showed he was a major-general, were brand-new.

The General looked at Pountney shrewdly. 'Shows the nature of the war is changing, Captain.'

Pountney nodded politely. As far as he was concerned the war hadn't changed at all. However you looked at it, it was still kill or be killed. No good taking it personally, as Davidson had, but that didn't make it any less clear-cut. Obviously the General didn't agree with him, for he now said: 'Not as straightforward as it was at the start. Nothing's quite black or white any longer. Do you agree?'

'I suppose so.' Pountney was being cautious. 'I hadn't really thought about it.'

'Take what happened in Syria. The Vichy French fighting the Free French as well as ourselves. Complicated situation. Downright tricky, really.'

The General's words hung in the heavy Cairo air, inviting a response.

'As far as I'm concerned, sir, those who aren't for us are against us,' Pountney replied. It seemed simple enough, not complicated at all. But he knew now that the General had heard about the little tiff he'd had with a French Navy lieutenant in a Beirut nightclub the previous week. Well, the man had got what he'd deserved and a few days in hospital might cool him off. Pountney held no particular brief for the Royal Navy, but he'd been their guest aboard their submarines on a number of occasions and had come to appreciate their total reliability and steadfastness, and he wasn't going to have any Froggie saying otherwise.

'Fair comment,' said the General, 'but officers must set an example, Captain. I'm sure you would agree.'

It was the gentlest of rebukes, not even a rap over the knuckles. Best let it pass, not argue the toss.

'I understand, sir.'

'Good. Just a little misunderstanding, I think we can call it.'

Perhaps war itself was just a little misunderstanding, Pountney thought bitterly. He noticed that the General had only one medal ribbon, and that was a decoration for distinguished service, not bravery. No Great War campaign medals for the new generation. The General would have still been in short trousers when it began. Here was the new British Army.

Again, the General seemed to read Pountney's thoughts, for he said: 'Congratulations on your MC, Pountney. A very well-deserved one, from what I hear. How many aircraft did you destroy at Maritsa?'

'Fifteen, sir, I believe.'

'Fifteen, eh?'

The General was doing some quick calculations in his head. 'At the beginning of the year the Italian order of battle included three hundred front-line bombers in the Med. So far they have sunk nine of our merchant ships for the loss of twenty-one bombers, or seven per cent of their total bomber force. From our point of view that means they lose three bombers for every ship they sink. You destroyed five times that amount, or five per cent of their total bomber force, and we didn't lose one ship. That's good going by any standards.'

'I hadn't thought of it like that, sir,' said Pountney, bewildered.

The General opened the silver cigarette box, offered it once again to Pountney, who shook his head, and tapped his cigarette on the top of his desk. 'Why should you? That's my end of the business.' He paused. 'Sorry you had no luck in the Rommel operation. It was a good idea. We might try that again sometime.'

'Count me in, sir, if you want to have another go at him.' 'Not at Rommel perhaps,' said the General, smiling. 'There are one or two softer targets we might try.'

He flicked open the top of a silver cigarette lighter and spun the flint, then looked over the flame at Pountney as he lit the cigarette. He seemed to have made up his mind about something, for he said: 'Let me come to the real point of our meeting, Captain Pountney. The War Office are playing merry hell about the establishment and administration of your unit. It's highly irregular for an Army outfit to be attached to the Navy in the way yours is. Put simply, the war can't be run like that. If it was, everyone would have their own private armies and navies. Everyone would be fighting their own private war, rather like you and that French gentleman were.'

'But sir . . .'

The General raised his hand. 'Don't get me wrong. Vice Admiral submarines, in Alexandria, is absolutely tickled pink having you around and you're raising the prestige and the morale of his submarines no end. But that's not the point.'

'Isn't it, sir?' Pountney retorted. 'I would have thought it was very much the point. Especially if we can destroy five per cent of the Italian bomber force without any losses to ourselves.' He thought of Daly and the loss of the team in the *Salmon*, and added: 'Not any material losses, anyway. There's bound to be a loss of personnel occasionally.'

Leaning back in his chair, the General studied Pountney through a pall of cigarette smoke. 'I was told you would fight your corner, Pountney, and I like that. I also happen to think you're right; and so, obviously, did General Marker. It took my staff weeks to find the necessary files. Unfortunately, that doesn't alter the situation.'

The General paused as the cry of an Arab street vendor wafted through the window. The wail was loud and persistent. Pountney wondered what he was selling. His camel? His house? His daughter? The General stubbed out his cigarette and said: 'Here is what I propose. You know Major Stirling?'

Pountney scratched his head. 'David Stirling? Scots

Guards? He was in Eight Commando when I last heard of him. He's part of Middle East Commando now, isn't he? Something called L Detachment?'

'That's the chap. Well, he's rather like you, Pountney: a persuader, someone who's got an idea and is determined to see it fulfilled. God knows how, but after the fall of Crete he managed to convince the Commander-in-Chief to let him form L Detachment – parachutists trained to attack German airfields in Libya. The Prime Minister probably had a hand in its formation. Anyway, Stirling's men recently carried out their first operation at Gazala. They weren't parachuted in but were taken behind the lines by the Long Range Desert Group. It was not dissimilar to your operation against Maritsa, though between ourselves it was not as successful. I think your men would fit in very well with this outfit. Officially, it's still part of Laycock's force, as you are. But Laycock's about to return home to command a new formation. So it makes sense to put your men with Stirling's lot. His unit is now unofficially known as the Special Air Service Regiment.'

'Never heard of it, sir,' said Pountney. He didn't like the trend of the conversation.

The General nodded. He understood how Pountney felt. But business was business.

'Quite. I think the best solution would be to put your chaps nominally under Stirling.'

He saw Pountney's reaction and added: 'There's no question of complete absorption, of course. Everyone's very keen that the name Special Boat Section be retained, and doubtless it will still operate independently with the Navy. But the matter would have been *regularized*, Pountney. I'm sure you understand how important that is from Whitehall's point of view.'

'Yes, sir,' Pountney said stiffly.

It was all a foregone conclusion, he knew that now. While he had been out risking his neck in the desert, in Cairo they had been busy stabbing him in the back.

'I presume I still retain command, sir?'

The General rubbed his chin thoughtfully. 'I'm not sure that would be desirable. I think the C-in-C's keen to spread the talent around a bit – not concentrate it all in one unit.'

Pountney's gloom deepened, though he appreciated the way the General sweetened what was a bitter pill. The bastards were not only intent on fucking up his ideas; they were busy fucking him up, too.

'Besides,' the General went on airily, 'Combined Operations at home are very keen on your concept. Lord Louis Mountbatten, who has recently succeeded Admiral Keyes at Combined Ops, wants you to expand the SBS.'

Pountney tried to keep the eagerness out of his voice. 'He does, sir?'

'He does indeed, Pountney. He wants you back in the UK as quickly as possible so that you can recruit and train men for a second section which will then almost certainly operate here in the Mediterranean. This is where all the action's going to be for the foreseeable future. It's pure speculation, of course, but I wouldn't be surprised if, with the Americans now in the war, there wasn't a large-scale operation in the Med next year. I don't doubt that the SBS will play its part in that. And, oh yes, I forgot. You're promoted to major as of today. Congratulations. Now who's going to fill your shoes here?'

'Ayton,' Pountney replied promptly. 'Lieutenant Philip Ayton. He's a Marine, but we mustn't hold that against him.'

10

'Captain Ayton, sir.' Maitland's rasping Glaswegian accent jerked Ayton awake. 'The Captain says quarter of an hour, sir.'

Ayton swung his legs off the narrow cot in the torpedo compartment and folded it back against the bulkhead.

The *Sentinel* was submerged at eighty feet and Ayton could feel no motion under his feet. As always when they had been submerged for any length of time, the atmosphere in the submarine was stuffy and hot. He dressed, pulled on his woollen hat and rope-soled shoes, checked that the soft leather holster containing his Welrod snuggled comfortably under his left armpit, then walked the few feet along the narrow gangway to the wardroom, where a plate of fried eggs and sausages, supplemented by a pile of toast, was placed before him.

He ate absent-mindedly, thinking of what he might have forgotten, or what possible incident might arise which would need quick action. Raiding from submarines had now become so second nature to him that he had to force himself consciously to try to anticipate trouble. For there was no doubt in his mind that anticipation – thinking through every scenario – saved lives.

Maitland put his head around the mess curtain. 'The Captain says, when you're ready, sir.'

Ayton nodded and wiped his mouth. 'Thanks, Jim. Have you eaten?'

'My usual porridge, sir. The cook's a dab hand at it now that I've shown him how.'

Ayton followed Maitland into the control room. It was daylight on the surface, so the lights had not been dimmed, and he could see that the whole control room crew was 'closed up' and ready for action. Only Timber Woods, who had continued to be a regular conveyor of No. 1 Special Boat Section during the year the unit had been in action in the eastern Mediterranean, seemed inactive as he waited for the navigator to tell him they had reached the right spot. He stood with his feet apart, his hands stuck in the pockets of his reefer jacket with his thumbs outside.

'I make it we're about a mile offshore, sir,' said the navigator from the chart table.

'Thank you, Pilot. Take her up to thirty feet, Number One.'

'Aye, aye, sir.'

The planesmen swung their wheels and the needles flickered back around their dials. When they reached thirty feet Woods ordered the main periscope to be raised. He waited for the water to drain away, made a quick, all-round scan of the surface, then handed over the periscope to Ayton, who eagerly grasped the handles and peered into the eyepieces.

Out of habit he first took a quick sweep round the horizon in low power, noticing that the lens was thinly coated with oil, which created a rainbow haze across it. Probably there had been a sinking close by. The Mediterranean was choppy and waves slopped against the lens as Ayton slowly swivelled the periscope through a full circle. But the horizon, burnished by the evening sun, was unbroken by mast or hull, and the sweep of sea was empty. He changed to high power and concentrated on the stretch of shore that lay directly ahead of the submarine.

He had never seen Crete before. It looked very much like any other part of the Mediterranean coastline. At first the shimmering sun on the water made it difficult for him to see properly, but as his eyes adjusted he began to follow the contours. The submarine was moving forward slowly, which encouraged the waves to slap against the lens, sometimes obscuring his view completely. But as the *Sentinel* neared the shore, he was able to identify the landing beach which he had studied on the chart: a promontory to the left with a low, crumbling cliff, then a semicircle of sandy beach to the right which ended in a rocky point.

Sensing Woods at his elbow, he snapped the handles closed and stood back.

The Captain looked at him questioningly. 'Well?'

'It looks fine,' Ayton said. 'But let me just check the chart again.'

'Be as quick as you can, there's a good chap. At this depth we're a sitting duck to any aircraft which happens to spot us.'

Ayton didn't need to be told that and he knew Timber knew that. He wondered, as he pored over the chart, if the man had been sent on one patrol too many, for he was as jumpy as a bloody kangaroo. But Ayton was determined not to be rushed; in the year the SBS had been operating with the First Submarine Flotilla out of Alexandria, too many mistakes had been made. Understandable mistakes, caused by pressure of time, or the proximity of the enemy, but ones that could have been avoided.

He had made some himself.

If he made one now the submarine would be sitting waiting for contact from the shore which would never come, because they would be waiting in the wrong place. And as everyone aboard was, for the first time, under the orders of some highly secret outfit in Cairo, he was doubly determined that there should be no avoidable errors.

He began checking the chart methodically against his memory of what he had just seen through the periscope. He saw for the first time that to the right of the sandy beach the chart marked a small chapel and cursed himself for not noticing it before. It could easily be an enemy observation post.

'I need one more quick look,' he said to Woods, who nodded reluctantly.

The rays of the sun, now almost touching the horizon, glinted on the rocks, sending sparks of light through the periscope. Ayton swore under his breath.

'I need to identify a building for verification,' he told Woods, 'but sunlight is refracting through this and I can't see a bloody thing.'

'What do you want me to do? Go in further, or wait until morning?'

'Go in,' said Ayton unhesitatingly. An alternative rendezvous had been made for the following night, but Ayton knew that this only increased the odds that something might go wrong.

'Course, Pilot?'

'Two-eight-five, sir. That should alter the angle sufficiently.'

They stood in silence until the navigator looked at his

watch after some minutes and said quietly: 'That should do it, sir.'

Ayton immediately saw the chapel, or rather its ruined remains, lit by the glow of the evening sun. Only part of one wall still stood, not enough protection for it to be used as an OP.

'Down periscope.'

'Satisfied?'

Ayton nodded.

'Take over, Number One. We'll lie one mile offshore until it's time to go in.'

'Shall I wake our two sleeping beauties, sir?' Maitland asked as the submarine slid back into the depths.

'I think we should,' Ayton agreed. 'They'll not be getting much sleep once they're ashore, but they should have some grub inside them before we land.'

Their passengers were members of the secret organization called the Special Operations Executive, which had 'hired' Ayton to get their men ashore, and the two SBS men had then been ordered to tag along as extra fire-power.

The tempo and type of operations had changed since Pountney had returned home to recruit and train a second SBS section. Beach reconnaissance and coastal sabotage had become too risky for the submarines involved, so such operations been replaced by small-scale assault raiding on enemy-occupied islands, and there were now more clandestine missions such as dropping agents ashore – and picking them up again if they were lucky. So the mission to occupied Crete to deliver, and then work with, two members of Cairo's Special Operations Executive had come as no great surprise.

The two passengers, escorted by Maitland, were ushered into the tiny wardroom. They were both tall men, rugged and deeply tanned by the desert sun. With a stab of surprise Ayton saw that they were dressed in German desert army uniforms complete with the spread wings of the Nazi eagle over their right breast pockets and Afrika Korps cuff titles on their right sleeves. One wore the chevrons of a *Stabsgefreiter*, or senior staff corporal, on his upper arms; the other the braided silver shoulder straps and collar insignia of an infantry major. Both men had tucked under their epaulettes the floppy forage cap with its pronounced peak that all German soldiers wore in the desert.

The infantry major saw the look on Ayton's face and, with a grin, snapped to attention and raised his right arm in a Nazi salute.

'Heil Hitler!'

'Jesus, Tom,' said Ayton, 'I've delivered some odd customers in my time, but nothing like you two.'

'Wait till you see our reception party,' Tom Brotherton's sidekick, Bill Mainwaring, replied cheerfully. 'Half the *andartes* on Crete will be there if I know my friend Manali. Now they *are* odd customers.'

'Very odd,' Brotherton agreed.

'*Andartes?*' Ayton had not heard the word before.

'Guerrillas, my friend, Greek guerrillas. I swear the Cretan variety are brigands to a man. They take positive pleasure in cutting a man's throat, particularly if he is a Kraut.'

'Ear to ear,' Mainwaring added. 'They get plenty of practice – that's how they kill their sheep.'

'What's this all about, exactly?' said Ayton.

The two men looked at him in astonishment. 'You mean Cairo didn't tell you?'

'Only that we were to deliver you on to a certain

beach and then work with you until the sub picked us up.'

Brotherton and Mainwaring exchanged glances, then Brotherton shrugged and said: 'It's a kidnapping caper.'

'*Kidnapping*?' Said Ayton. Now he had heard it all.

'Why not? We're going to kidnap the commander of the Crete garrison.'

'What the hell for?'

Mainwaring grinned a grin that reminded Ayton of a shark opening its mouth for a particularly delicate morsel. 'Your guess is as good as ours, old boy.'

'Does it matter?' said Brotherton.

'What do we do with him once we've kidnapped him?'

'Take him back to Alexandria, of course.'

'Dead or alive.'

'Preferably alive.'

Again the shark's grin. 'In our game the preferable option isn't always open to us.'

'Timber knows he might have to take back a dead German general?'

'Naturally.'

'Haven't actually told him he might be dead. Must look on the bright side.'

'Now, how about checking us over?' said Brotherton, making a poor effort at a mannequin's twirl. 'We were told you're an expert on German uniforms.'

Ayton inspected them closely, knowing their lives might depend on the authenticity of their appearance. They looked faultless to him, and they went away to change back into civilian clothes. When they reappeared they were wearing nondescript sweaters and trousers tucked into knee-high boots. Brotherton was also sporting a trilby.

They were joined in the wardroom by Woods and after they had eaten breakfast they whiled away the time playing poker for matchsticks. Brotherton, Ayton noticed, played with an icy, calculated calm, whereas Mainwaring bluffed outrageously. It seemed to fit their characters.

When it was time to make the rendezvous Woods went to the control room and gave his orders for the submarine to re-enter the bay. The lights were dimmed. As soon as they had surfaced, Ayton was called on to the bridge. It was a cloudless, moonless night. A slight haze covered the myriad of stars. Ayton waited for his eyes to become fully accustomed to the dark before raising his binoculars in the direction in which Woods was pointing.

'See it?'

At first he didn't, but then the prick of light flicked on and off in a regular rhythm.

'It's an "R"', Ayton said.

Woods grunted. 'That's a grass-line job, then. I wonder how many we'll get this time.'

'Not many,' Ayton replied. 'They must nearly all be in the bag by this time.'

It had become standard practice for submarines on patrol off Crete to exfiltrate any Allied troops who had managed to stay at liberty after the fall of the island to the German airborne invasion the previous summer. This was done by sending ashore a 'grass line', a coir rope. Made from coconut fibre, this was light enough to float and guide swimmers to the submarine.

'Trim up,' Woods ordered into the voice pipe. 'Gun crews, close up.'

The submarine's forecasing slowly emerged above the surface and water streamed in cascades off the huge swellings of the main ballast tanks. The gun crews appeared from below and two ratings with a Bren gun came with them. The gun was positioned on the landward side of the bridge. Two more seamen emerged from below and descended on to the forecasing to open the torpedo hatch so that the two folbots could be fed through it.

When they saw their craft were ready, Ayton and Maitland went on to the forecasing to make a last check and to supervise their lowering into the water. After the folbots had been secured alongside the submarine, Woods ordered the two passengers on deck. Moments later Mainwaring and Brotherton appeared, carrying their German uniforms in small waterproof rucksacks.

The long 'grass line,' as thick as a man's arm, was fed up the torpedo hatch and one of the ratings coiled it down neatly on the deck. When it was all on deck the rating expertly attached a much thinner heaving line to one end and ran the heaving line through his hands to make sure there were no knots or snags in it. Then he coiled that down, too, beside the coir rope. When he came to the Turk's Head knot at the end of it he handed the cricket-ball sized lump to Ayton, who was standing by his folbot, and Ayton tucked it under his belt.

The SBS men helped their passengers into the rear cockpits of their folbots, then stepped in themselves. Ayton unhitched the Turk's Head and wound the heaving line around the small towing post that protruded above the rubberized canvas deck in front of him. So long as the rating fed out the heaving line smoothly it would not impede the folbot's progress.

The canoeists cleared the bulbous sides of the submarine with a quick sweep of their paddles, and made directly for the signal still winking at them from the shore. The smell of thyme, faint at first, but then strong and distinct, was wafted towards them by the gentle offshore breeze. The sea was flat, the waves lapping gently on to the beach, and moments later they grounded on to the sand.

The SBS men swung themselves out of their folbots and steadied them while their two passengers scrambled ashore. Out of the dark, figures began to emerge. Instinctively, Ayton pulled out his Welrod and levelled it at the nearest, but the man began waving his arms and protesting in Greek. Brotherton put his hand on Ayton's arm. 'It's only Manali.'

Ayton let the muzzle drop and Manali, a rock of a man with an outsize moustache, flung his arms around Brotherton, lifted him off the sand in a bear hug, then, with loud greetings in Greek, kissed him on both cheeks. Brotherton untangled himself and slapped the big man on the back. 'The best and bravest *andarte* on Crete,' he said to Ayton. The Cretan grasped the SBS man's hand with both his. 'You welcome,' he said in broken English. Then he stepped forward and threw his arms around Ayton. The moustache rasped uncomfortably across his face, but it was the man's smell, quite indescribable, which made him flinch.

Other *andartes* were now gathered around the four men, all talking at what seemed the top of their voices.

'Hadn't we better get off the beach?' Ayton said to Brotherton.

'No worry,' boomed Manali. 'No German post for ten mile.'

'They must send out patrols.' Ayton objected.

'Bah!' Manali dismissed the idea.

'Not at night,' Brotherton explained. 'They would get their throats slit before they had gone a mile.'

One of the *andartes* had unhitched the heaving line

from Ayton's canoe and was being helped by two others to haul in the grass line. When it appeared, snaking across the smooth surface of the bay, one of the guerrillas turned inland and waved while the other two continued to haul in the rope until it was taut.

From the darkness three figures appeared, then two more. They were all dressed in British Army battledress in various degrees of disintegration, and they all carried weapons.

Before wading into the water the soldiers unlaced their boots and left them on the sand, where they were quickly pounced upon by the *andartes*.

'All British troops being taken off by grass line leave their boots behind,' Brotherton explained. 'There is such an acute shortage of them on the island.'

One by one the soldiers grabbed the floating line and began hauling themselves out to the submarine while the *andartes* holding the rope dug their heels into the sand as if they were in a tug-of-war team. When all the escapees had reached the submarine, the *andartes* let go of the line, which snaked slowly away from them across the water.

A lone figure now approached them from the back of the beach. Brotherton introduced him to Ayton as Major Paddy Marne.

Paddy was short and wiry, and dressed in the same curious mixture of clothing as the *andartes*: a cloth wound round his head rather like a flattened turban, a black waistcoat and the traditional Greek baggy black trousers – nicknamed 'crap catchers' by the British – tucked into high boots. A pistol and a pearl-handled knife were tucked beneath a wide cummerbund and some kind of automatic weapon was slung over his shoulder.

The *andartes* carried the two folbots off the beach and

hid them in a crevice between two large rocks. Then the whole group, Manali leading, set off in single file straight towards the ridge of mountains which cut the skyline in half ahead of them. Soon after they left the beach the ground began to rise sharply, and they began to follow a narrow goat track which wound its way up into the mountains. They walked for two hours, rested for twenty minutes, then walked for another hour. It was bitterly cold.

Just as the first light of dawn began showing in the east the track flattened out and ran into a broad gully surrounded by a horseshoe of rocky outcrops on three sides and trees and bushes on the fourth. No one challenged them as they entered the camp, but in the slowly growing light Ayton could see several bodies wrapped in blankets sleeping under the trees to which were tethered a number of mules.

A fire was lit, and Ayton and Maitland were handed blankets. Paddy passed them a water bottle full of raki with the comment that the local poison was an excellent inducement to sleep. Thirst made them drink deeply and the raki, fermented from the skins and stones of raisins, scorched their throats. But it warmed them, too, and they settled down to get what rest they could.

Ayton was awakened, not by the shaft of sunlight which lay across his face but by the bleating of a goat nearby, quickly followed by a strange, unnerving sound not unlike water draining with a gurgle from a bath. He opened his eyes and, rolled over, to see Manali wiping his knife on the goat's carcass as its lifeblood pumped out of its throat and seeped into the dry earth.

Manali grinned at him. 'Breakfast,' he said.

He slashed open the dead animal's underbelly and

worked away with his knife. He cut out bits of entrail, kidney, liver and genitals and threw them into the embers of the fire. Then, with the tip of his knife, he gouged out the goat's eyeballs and tossed them in, too.

Ayton looked away. He stood up and stretched, then lit a cigarette. Maitland was already up and was watching Manali's preparations with interest. He handed the raki to Ayton, who took a deep draught. Manali bent over the fire and, with the end of a stick, began picking out pieces of the goat, now covered in white ash, and handing them round.

Paddy came up to them and said: '*Meze* . . . appetizers. They taste better than they look.'

'They'd better,' said Ayton, taking a piece gingerly between his fingers and dropping it in his mouth. It was warm, but it tasted of ash and very little else.

'We'd better kit you out,' said Paddy. 'You'll need proper clothes.' The two SBS men followed him to a cave half hidden by gorse bushes. Inside, the floor was covered with dried grass and leaves which crackled under their feet. Paddy shone his torch on a pile of boots, then on a line of weapons propped up against the wall. Most of them were the standard British infantryman's rifle, the .303 Lee Enfield, but there were several automatic weapons and even a two-inch mortar, though Paddy said they had no mortar bombs for it. Maitland picked up what looked like a cross between a carbine and a tommy-gun. It had twin magazines underneath it – something Ayton had never seen before.

'A 9mm Marlin,' said Paddy. 'It's a Yank automatic weapon. Fast rate of fire, but I'm told it's inclined to jam.'

There was a heap of clothing from which they were

able to find replacements for their uniforms, as Paddy insisted they wore civilian clothes. 'News spreads like wildfire on this island,' he said, 'and not all Cretans are loyal. If the rumour gets about that soldiers are working with the *andartes* the Germans might pay too much attention to us.'

Ayton chose 'crap catchers', puttees and a shirt which felt like cardboard, while Maitland opted for some ancient corduroy breeches and a ragged black jacket. When they had dressed, Paddy led them to a nearby spring, where they washed. As they dried themselves the smell of cooked meat drifted in their direction, and when they returned to the fire Manali was carving hunks of meat off the goat, which had been roasted over a makeshift spit, and handing round the slices on the tip of his knife. Washed down with raki, it was one of the best breakfasts Ayton could remember.

When they had all eaten their fill, and drained the water bottle of raki, Paddy explained his plan to the three other officers. He spread out a map on the ground. The others bent over it and watched him trace a path with a stick to a village called Kastamonitsa.

'This is where we stay tonight,' he said.

The stick moved on northwards towards the coastal town of Heraklion, which Paddy tapped significantly with the tip of his stick. 'German headquarters. That's where the General drives to every day from his villa and back in the evening.'

'And where's his villa? Brotherton asked.

'Here.' Paddy tapped the map some fifteen miles inland. 'Villa Paratsa, it's called. It's in the foothills, which makes it cooler and more pleasant in the summer than Heraklion.'

'Do we take him in the villa?' Mainwaring asked.

Paddy shook his head. 'Not a chance. It's surrounded by an electrified fence and there are dog patrols night and day. The *andartes* have been stirring things up all over the island and the Krauts aren't going to take any chances with their precious general.'

Ayton looked again at the map. There was only one road northwards towards Heraklion, snaking down what, judging from the map's contours, was a fairly steep mountainside.

'An ambush somewhere here, then. On his way into Heraklion.'

'That's the idea. But it would have to be on his way out, to give us time to get away. If he didn't turn up at his headquarters in the morning they'd want to know why, but he often works late or goes out to dinner in town. So his staff in the villa wouldn't worry if he was late back.'

Ayton nodded. That made sense. 'Presumably you'd lay the ambush at a bend in the mountains, where his car would be going slowly?'

Paddy shook his head. 'The road is too narrow to turn the car round. We're going to have to make it farther from the villa, at this junction here.' He tapped the map at a point about halfway between the villa and Heraklion. 'This road heading west is our escape route and the car must slow right down to turn on to the road leading to the villa.'

'But it's open countryside,' Brotherton objected.

'True. But there are ditches on either side of the road, so it will be easy to hide.'

'Any checkpoints?'

Paddy grimaced. 'Plenty on the escape road. I think I know how to deal with them, though.'

'When do we do it?' Ayton asked quietly.

'Tomorrow night.'

11

They lay on a flat piece of rock and took it in turns to scan the villa with Paddy's binoculars. There wasn't much to see, except for the formidable perimeter fence and the sloping red roof of the villa and one of its whitewashed walls. The rest of the building was screened by eucalyptus trees. But from where they were hiding they had a good view of the road which skirted the villa and wound its way northwards until it disappeared into a wood of conifers.

They had marched all the previous day and stayed the night at Kastamonitsa. There had been scouts ahead of them and the guerrillas had moved across the mountains in daylight without seeming to worry about German patrols. Throughout the day the scouts came and went to report what was ahead, what this shepherd had seen, or what rumour that villager had heard. A German patrol had passed through Kastamonitsa the previous night, but long before any Germans appeared, Paddy told the SBS men, doors would have been locked, lights doused, dogs tied up, children cleared from the street. On this occasion the soldiers had not lingered, though they sometimes stayed to search the houses if they suspected *andartes* were in the area.

It was a waiting game, Paddy explained, each side

watching to see if the other made a false move. If the Germans strayed from the main routes on to the mountain tracks their movements were always closely monitored. The *andartes* watched and waited, and sometimes pounced. Few escaped from a Cretan ambush, for the *andartes* were mountain people who knew every inch of the countryside and the ferocity with which they fought the hated occupiers meant that no prisoners were ever taken. The Germans reacted to any clash by taking hostages or burning villages, but this only intensified the islanders' hatred and determination. If anything, the ambushes increased in number after such atrocities. A sentry would be shot or a motorcyclist decapitated by wire strung across his route. Occasionally, the German commander of Fortress Crete, as it was called, would lose his patience and mount large-scale operations to flush out the *andartes* from their mountain hide-outs. But they always failed, for the guerrillas would slip through the cordons and regroup in another area among the rugged peaks.

It was a grim and relentless game of hide-and-seek.

Ayton tapped Paddy's arm. 'Here it comes.'

The villa's gates were swung open by two guards and moments later the long black bonnet of a powerful-looking car nosed its way out. On one wing flew the pennant of a general of the Infantry – the British equivalent of a lieutenant general – and on the other the pennant of the General's command, the 22nd Sevastopol (Bremen) Division, which garrisoned the island.

Paddy adjusted his binoculars carefully and tracked the vehicle. It drove along the outer drive of the villa, then turned left on to the narrow, unmetalled road.

'It's a Mercedes-Benz,' he said; and then: 'There are

two people in the back as well as the passenger in the front.'

Once it was on the road, the car accelerated. Paddy kept his binoculars trained on it until it disappeared into the woods, leaving a cloud of dust in the shimmering air.

'That doesn't tell us much,' said Brotherton.

'It tells us,' Paddy replied, 'that the car doesn't have an escort and that the General likes to drive at a leisurely pace. Even on that straight stretch the driver wouldn't have been going more than twenty-five or thirty miles an hour. We've also got to reckon with there being passengers in the back.'

'Time spent in reconnaissance is never wasted,' Ayton said, repeating the age-old military adage.

They skirted the perimeter of the villa and by midday had rejoined Manali and his *andartes* in their hiding-place in the mountains above the villa. A grizzled old man from a nearby village brought them bread, *misithra* – local cheese not unlike yoghurt in consistency and taste – and several bottles of retsina.

While they ate and drank, Paddy sketched out on the dusty ground exactly where he wanted each man to be positioned and what his task was. When he had finished they synchronized their watches and the *andartes* began to leave the hide-out in small groups at intervals.

It was dusk by the time the five Britons had positioned themselves in the ditch a few hundred yards north of the road junction. The ambush party carried coshes and Ayton had his Welrod tucked under his armpit, though Paddy had told him to use it only in a dire emergency.

As night closed in the temperature dropped. Several vehicles passed them, their headlights carving through the blackness, and then a motorcycle combination roared by.

Paddy glanced at his luminous watch and cursed under his breath.

'Just when we want him to be prompt, he decides to work late,' he muttered to Ayton, but even as he spoke, Maitland, who was watching for the signal, dropped down into the ditch and said: 'They're coming, sir.'

Then he moved to the other side of the road. Brotherton and Mainwaring clambered out of the ditch, brushed down their German uniforms and stood waiting.

The sweeping cones of the headlights flickered in the distance and then they could hear the sound of the Mercedes' powerful engine.

The car came round the last bend. The headlights played on the side of the road and flared in the eyes of the waiting ambush party. It seemed to Ayton that the car was travelling up to the junction much too fast, and he wondered if the chauffeur had been alerted. But then it slowed with a screech of the brakes and at that moment Brotherton and Mainwaring stepped into the headlights waving a torch.

The car stopped and Ayton could hear quite plainly Brotherton's question as he bent down by the chauffeur's open window, and the chauffeur answering that, yes, it was the General's car, but what was going on?

He'll soon know what, Ayton thought.

'Here we go,' said Paddy quietly, then was out of the ditch in one quick movement. Ayton saw the glint of Paddy's pearl-handled knife, tugged out his Welrod and followed close behind. They both wrenched open the nearside doors of the car at more or less the same moment. Paddy had the General by the scruff of the neck and in one swift movement dragged him out and on to the roadside.

Ayton peered into the back of the car, his Welrod at the ready. The door on the offside had been locked by the rear passenger and he could see Maitland wrestling to open it. Ayton caught a quick glimpse of the outline of a peaked cap before the man flung himself at him. Feeling a hand grasp his collar, he stepped back and pulled the trigger of the Welrod. It jolted in his hand and made its cork popping sound. The man, half in, half out of the car, slumped head downwards and a Luger clattered on to the road.

Close to Ayton, Paddy had wrestled the General to the ground and was bending over him, his knife at his throat. In the darkness Ayton could see the whites of the German's eyes bulge in terror.

'*Halt's Maul!*' Paddy warned him quietly. 'Shut up!'

On the other side of the car Brotherton had grabbed the chauffeur's arm as he reached for a Schmeisser tucked beside him. With his other hand he hit him over the head with the cosh. The man slumped forward, blood pouring down his face.

Unable to open the offside rear door, Maitland ran round the back of the Mercedes to join Ayton, his cosh in his hand.

'I think he's dead,' Ayton said, indicating the slumped body to Maitland with his Welrod, 'but you'd better have a look.'

He returned the pistol to its holster and said to Paddy: 'Want any help?'

He saw Paddy's grin flash in the dark as he answered: 'I think he's got the message.'

Ayton extracted a ready-made gag and taped it over the General's mouth. The man's eyes bulged hideously.

'Not too tight,' Paddy warned.

Mainwaring manhandled the unconscious chauffeur out of the car and dragged him on to the side of the road. Manali and several *andartes* now appeared, and the chauffeur was handed over to them.

With the help of a shaded torch Maitland inspected the officer who had been sitting in the back of the car. A thin rivulet of blood was coursing down his cheek, but his eyelids fluttered when the torch played on his face.

'The bullet creased his skull, sir,' said Maitland. 'He'll be right as rain.'

Ayton peered down at the man and saw the line of blood along his temple and the right side of his head. It was as well for the German that the Welrod was a .22-calibre weapon. Anything heavier and he'd have been a goner. As it was, he was beginning to regain consciousness, so he was quickly bound and gagged and passed to the *andartes*.

Paddy handed Ayton the General's cap and Ayton climbed in beside Mainwaring, who took the wheel.

'Good luck,' said Maitland through the open window.

'And you, Jim. And Jim . . .'

'Sir?'

'Keep an eye on those Krauts, will you? Major Marne wants them alive. I don't trust those cutthroats.'

'I'll do my best, sir.'

Mainwaring ground the Mercedes into gear. The car lurched forward and he swung it right and headed westwards. Ayton looked at the petrol gauge and was relieved to see that the tank was almost full.

They drove in silence for a few minutes and then the tension broke and they were all talking at once. Paddy took the gag off their prisoner and told him in halting German that he was a British officer and that if he behaved himself the gag would stay off. The General nodded that he understood, and asked if anyone spoke French. No one did.

'He obviously doesn't think my German's good enough,' said Paddy.

'It isn't,' Brotherton laughed. 'It's bloody awful.'

'He seemed to understand me well enough when I had my knife at his jugular.'

Ten minutes later a red light glimmered ahead. It was being swung to and fro in the middle of the road. Ayton adjusted the General's hat carefully and sat up straight in his seat. The German was ordered to lie on the floor, which he did with some grumbling.

There were two men. One had his rifle slung over his shoulder and was waving the red light steadily in front of him, the other, farther away, was standing on the grass verge next to a wooden guardhouse.

'Slow right down, Bill,' Paddy ordered. 'But don't stop.'

The sentry, thinking the car would stop, stepped to one side, as Paddy had anticipated he would. Mainwaring slowed to a crawl to give him plenty of time to see the pennants fluttering on the wings. The Mercedes drew level with the sentry holding the lamp and, as he stooped towards them, Mainwaring said loudly in German that it was the General's car and put his foot gently on the accelerator.

The sentry straightened up and snapped to attention.

They tensed as the car swept past the sentry and then accelerated towards the guardhouse, where the other sentry was standing, his Schmeisser cradled in his arms. He seemed to look at them for a long time before springing to attention. Moments later they were beyond the checkpoint and round a bend in the road.

'If they're suspicious of anything they might phone ahead,' Brotherton said, but at the next checkpoint the guard waved them through with a flourish.

The road now began to twist and turn as it climbed into the mountains, but the car took the steep gradients effortlessly. After an hour they swept round a bend and saw a third checkpoint ahead. It surprised them as much as their appearance must have surprised the sentry, for, though they slowed right down, he did not step aside.

'Shit!' Paddy murmured and Ayton heard the click as he cocked his pistol.

Mainwaring did the same and laid his pistol on his lap, while Ayton drew his Welrod.

The red light ahead kept swinging in front of them until the bonnet of the Mercedes seemed almost in the sentry's stomach. Those in the car could see now that several Germans were also standing behind the sentry, who was still swinging the light. Mainwaring poked his head out of the window and shouted that it was the General's car, but the sentry seemed bemused. He stopped swinging his lamp, and stood his ground.

'Jesus, do something, Tom,' Paddy hissed.

Without hesitating, Brotherton opened his door, stepped out and shouted something in German. It sounded very authoritative. The sentry looked startled, but he saluted and moved aside, and the men behind him scattered. Brotherton got back into the car and the Germans stood stiffly to attention as it slid slowly between them.

Ayton looked away, towards Mainwaring, to hide his face, but one of the soldiers yelled something.

'Step on it, Bill!' Paddy urged and the engine changed pitch as Mainwaring stamped on the accelerator.

Ayton tensed, expecting a volley of rifle fire. But nothing

happened and within seconds they were climbing steeply, so that Mainwaring was forced to change gear twice in quick succession.

Ayton turned to Paddy. 'Did you hear what that soldier shouted?'

Paddy shook his head. 'I'm guessing, but I think he saw you weren't the General. They must have been alerted by now that he's missing.'

'Is there another checkpoint?'

'One more.'

'Can we take a different road?'

It was Mainwaring who said: 'No. This is the only one which leads south.'

No one had seriously considered that they might have to fight their way through a checkpoint.

'If they know we have him,' Paddy reasoned. 'They're not going to fill the car with machine-gun bullets. They'll just try and stop us. Perhaps with a barricade, or shooting at the tyres.'

Ayton looked out of his window and down over the precipice along which the road was snaking up into the mountains. Ahead of them the full moon had risen above the peaks, casting pale shadows across the road. Even in this eerie half-light Ayton could see that it was a long way down.

'If they want him alive,' he said, 'they won't shoot at our tyres.'

They drove in silence for a few minutes, then Brotherton said: 'Not far now.'

The nose of the Mercedes swung round a particularly sharp bend, after which the road flattened out and ran between two rocky hummocks.

'Any moment now,' Brotherton said.

163

Mainwaring changed up and gunned the engine, making the big car leap forward. They swept round the right hand of the two hummocks and suddenly there ahead was the swinging red light. They wound down all the windows and held their pistols ready, the cold night air rushing into their faces.

The Mercedes' engine growled. They never saw what happened to the guard with the red light. He either went under the wheels or managed to throw himself aside at the last moment. Beyond him, as they had expected, was a wooden barrier and another soldier, signalling frantically with a torch.

'Down!' Mainwaring shouted, and they all ducked as the bonnet smashed into the barrier. The car jumped and swung as it hit something in the road. Splinters of wood flew everywhere. One piece glanced against the windscreen without breaking it; another rattled along the length of the car. The arm of the barrier spun away from them, the headlights catching it as it cartwheeled through the air. Something else scrunched under them, forcing Mainwaring to spin the wheel violently. The car skidded, its back tyres screaming. It bucked and twisted, then straightened out. Calmly, Mainwaring changed gear.

'Bloody good driving, Bill,' Paddy said appreciatively. 'Everyone all right?'

Now they were speeding down the mountainside, along a road which snaked and zigzagged. By the light of the moon it looked alarmingly narrow, but Mainwaring did not slow down.

'All hell will be let loose now,' Brotherton commented, as if he was rather enjoying the prospect.

'Not tonight,' Paddy said. 'What can they do tonight? How much farther, Bill?'

'Not much more than an hour, I reckon.'

They allowed the General up from the floor of the car. He looked shaken and none too happy, but became more cheerful after Paddy handed him a water bottle full of raki.

The bottle was passed round and Paddy began a complicated conversation with the prisoner in fractured German. Every so often Brotherton interjected to help Paddy out with a difficult phrase, but otherwise seemed uninterested in what they were saying.

Gradually the road became less steep and the hairpin bends more easily negotiable. In the far distance Ayton caught a glimpse of the sea shimmering in the moonlight, and soon they were out of the mountains and on the narrow coastal plain.

As the road broadened slightly and straightened, Mainwaring trod down hard. The scenery, dense undergrowth, the occasional tree, whipped by, and then ahead of them Ayton saw a crossroads in the headlights' glare. Mainwaring brought the Mercedes to a halt with a dramatic squeal of the brakes and switched off the lights.

'This is it,' he said. 'Bob and I go right. You go left.'

They climbed out and stretched. Brotherton and Mainwaring stripped off their German uniforms, bundled them up and threw them into the undergrowth before dressing in the Cretan clothes they had put in the boot of the Mercedes at the time of the ambush. After shaking hands with everyone – including the General – they climbed back in the car and drove off.

'What will they do with the Merc?' Ayton asked.

'Leave it on a beach farther west. With any luck the Krauts will assume we've rendezvoused with a sub and won't bother looking for us. Not much hope of that, but it's worth a try.'

'Are they staying on the island?' Ayton asked Paddy.

'They'll replace Dennis and Tim, who are due some leave. Assuming Dennis and Tim have managed to break out of the German cordon, they'll meet us at the rendezvous.'

It was, Ayton thought, going to be a crowded trip back in the submarine. He handed the General his cap, and the German thanked him in English and fitted it carefully on to his head. He had obviously felt undressed without it.

For a while they walked along the road, but when it swung inland again they left it for a goat path which ran parallel with the coast. The ground was not steep, but it was uneven and rocky, and the General, who was middle-aged and none too fit, frequently stumbled and kept asking if they could rest. Paddy gave him ten minutes every hour, which, with the occasional swig of raki, was just enough to keep the prisoner on his feet, though he kept grumbling to himself under his breath.

Dawn broke fresh and sparkling in front of them and, just as the sun cleared the horizon, they came to a shepherd's hut with three mules tied to a nearby tree. Flies were already pestering the animals, which were swishing their tails and stamping in irritation.

As the little group approached the hut, a sack covering its entrance was pulled to one side and out stepped a middle-aged man. Under his *capota*, the sheepskin cloak all shepherds wore, his clothes were ragged and his beard unkempt. He cried out a greeting to Paddy. The two clasped each other's hands and then gave the traditional Cretan greeting of a kiss on each cheek before slapping each other lightly on the face.

'My friend Nikko,' said Paddy to Ayton.

Nikko seized the SBS officer's hand and said something in Greek.

'He says welcome,' explained Paddy.

Nikko indicated that they should sit down, and brought from his hut a bottle of wine and a wooden bowl steaming with potatoes, onions and boiled eggs, all mashed together. He studiously ignored the General, who had sat down apart from them on a slab of rock, and Paddy had to tell the Cretan to give him some food, too. They ate ravenously. When they'd finished, Nikko untethered the mules and led them over to the three men. Ayton's experience of riding had been confined to a donkey on Margate beach when he was a child, but this proved sufficient, for his mule was placid and unhurried, and though there were no saddles each animal had a rope halter.

They said goodbye to Nikko, who embraced them both. Paddy dug out three gold sovereigns from the belt he carried around his waist and pressed them on the Cretan, who made a great show of being reluctant to accept them. He handed Paddy a *sakuli*, a cloth holdall, containing food and wine, which Paddy slung on his back.

Paddy led the way and Ayton took up the rear. The German looked uncomfortable and had trouble keeping his seat, but by midday when they stopped to rest, Paddy said they had made good time and would be at the rendezvous by the following afternoon.

Under a rocky outcrop they found some shade, and rested until the sun had lost the worst of its heat. When they started out again the ground became steeper, for the mountains on this part of the island almost reached the shoreline. The sun cast long shadows ahead of them, before dipping behind the mountains, but even in the dark the goat path was easy to follow.

They kept going until the moon had risen, then camped for the night under a cluster of trees. Paddy unslung the *sakuli* and passed round the food and wine. They ate without speaking, though the German continued to mutter to himself. As they rolled themselves in their blankets Ayton wondered aloud if the General was going off his head, but Paddy said he was just having a hard time of it.

They were up at dawn, and after finishing the last of the food and wine, remounted their mules. An hour later Ayton, hearing the faint sound of an aero engine behind him, shouted a warning to Paddy. They dismounted and led the mules into some thick undergrowth.

'There it is!' Ayton pointed upwards.

The aircraft was tiny. Skimming down the coast towards them, it was wobbling slightly. Once it deviated from its path and circled inland.

'A Fieseler-Storch,' Paddy announced when it was still some way off. 'High-winged monoplane, single engine – no doubt about it. The Krauts use them for gunnery spotting and general reconnaissance.'

It cruised slowly towards them, then swung away towards the coast, but it had come close enough for Ayton to be able to see the passenger scouring the ground with binoculars. The plane flew so slowly it seemed to hang in the air like a hovering sparrowhawk.

'The hunt's on,' said Paddy as he watched it fly slowly along the coast. 'They obviously weren't taken in by our little ruse. The whole island will be swarming with Krauts today.'

They waited until the plane was reduced to a speck before remounting, and kept a wary eye on the sky ahead in case it doubled back. The General, who had seemed enormously heartened by its appearance, relapsed into a muttering gloom again. They kept going through the heat of the day, climbing steadily all the time.

Once they came across a flock of sheep and a young shepherd who told them that two lorries full of Germans had arrived at the nearest village early that morning. They had searched every house before moving on northwards and had left behind hurriedly printed pamphlets which said that the General had been abducted 'by bandits' and that if he was not handed back within three days they would carry out reprisals until he was released.

The Cretans were used to the Germans' threats. When it looked as if they would be carried out, all the villagers took to the mountains, but it worried Paddy that they were inevitably going to suffer. He asked the young shepherd whether Manali and his party were on their way, but the boy didn't know.

They arrived at the rendezvous just after the sun had set and were greeted enthusiastically by the *andartes*, who had heard about the success of the operation. Dennis and Tim had already arrived, having managed to slip through the cordon around their headquarters when Germans had been withdrawn from it to hunt for the General's kidnappers. In the confusion which had followed the kidnapping they had easily eluded enemy patrols and found their way to the rendezvous.

At dawn the next morning Manali arrived with Maitland and soon afterwards the *andartes* in Manali's band straggled in. The group, Maitland told Ayton, had had to break up into twos and threes in order to slip undetected through the cordon the Germans had thrown around the approaches to the southern coastline. Neither the General's chauffeur nor the staff officer who had been in the back of the Mercedes was with the *andartes*, and when Manali was asked where they were he simply shrugged.

Ayton and Paddy took Maitland to one side. 'What happened?' Paddy asked.

Maitland looked uncomfortable. 'They just vanished. Manali said that the chauffeur died in the night and that the officer fell and broke his neck.'

'And you believed him?'

'I did not, sir,' the sergeant answered indignantly. 'But what could I do? That lot would slit their grandmothers' throats if it suited them. I thought the Gorbals were tough, sir, but these *andartes* beat anything I've seen.'

'We'd better take it in turns to guard the General,' said Paddy, 'or he'll be the next one.'

The next day a goatherd from a nearby village brought them news that the Germans had set up a command post there and that the rumour was that they were going to send out patrols along all the southern beaches. If they weren't careful, the messenger warned, the party would be cut off from the coast.

'When is the sub due?' Paddy asked Ayton.

'Tomorrow night.'

'Too long a time to stay here. We must move down to the bay tonight and take the chance that we can find somewhere to hide tomorrow.'

At nightfall, after bidding a long and warm farewell to Manali and his *andartes*, they started off down the goat path up which they had scrambled the previous week.

12

Ayton found the rock-strewn path even more difficult to go down than it had been to ascend. His boots slid on the screed and more than once he thought he would pitch forward but just managed to retain a foothold.

Paddy, who was in the lead, set up a brisk pace. He was followed by Dennis and Tim, who had the General between them on a mule, while Maitland and Ayton took turns to take up the rear. They reached the beach well before dawn and skirted round it to find a convenient place to spend the day. Once it was dark, they planned to go down to the shore to unearth the hidden folbots and await the submarine.

In the undergrowth behind the beach they found the remains of a fisherman's stone hut which would give them some protection from the sun. It stood in the middle of a patch of bare ground, so that it was both hidden by the surrounding undergrowth and fairly easy to defend. By daybreak they had eaten, tied up the mule at the back of the hut and divided the day between them into two-hour watches.

The sun rose hot and burning, and the flies gathered in clusters on them as they rested. The General mumbled in his sleep; the mule stamped its feet. Around the middle of the afternoon Ayton, who was on watch, heard the

Fieseler-Storch again, but it was well inland of their hiding-place and he did not see it.

After the sun had set they ate again and then, before the moon rose, made their way cautiously to the end of the beach, where the folbots were hidden. As they lifted them out from between the rocks, the General muttered something to Paddy, who said to Ayton: 'He hopes he doesn't have to go in one of those things. He can't swim.'

'Then he's going to have to keep bloody still and behave himself,' said Ayton. 'I'll take him out to the sub when it arrives. Jim can take Dennis.'

They lay in the sand at the back of the beach. Ayton studied his luminous watch impatiently and promptly at eleven o'clock began flashing the agreed letter out to sea at regular intervals. The minutes passed, but there was no response. After half an hour Paddy whispered: 'What could have happened?'

Ayton lifted the torch and flashed it again. Anything could have happened. Paddy knew that as well as he did. The sub could have been sunk, or delayed, or could simply have been ordered elsewhere for another operation. It was only the first of three rendezvous. The second was scheduled for the following night and the third for seven nights later, but Ayton doubted if they could remain undetected for another twenty-four hours, much less another week.

He swept the bay with his binoculars. The waning moon came out from behind a bank of cloud, making the water shimmer in his lenses. For a moment he thought he saw the hull of the submarine, but the shadow on the sea dissolved.

Then Paddy, with his binoculars still raised to his

eyes, grabbed Ayton's arm. 'There,' he said. 'Ten o'clock.'

Ayton trained his binoculars to the left, but he knew Paddy must be mistaken, for nothing broke the calm surface of the sea.

'Where?'

'There! Right in front of you!'

The urgency in Paddy's voice made Ayton lower his binoculars from near the horizon into the shallows. Christ! The sub looked as if it was about to beach itself, it was so close in. Only the upper part of the conning tower had broken the water. At first he thought it was stationary, but then he saw it was moving parallel with the beach from left to right, and moving so slowly that the tower caused hardly a ripple on the surface.

As he watched, two figures appeared on the bridge. In his excitement Ayton fumbled with his torch and dropped it in the sand. He picked it up, shook the sand off it, made sure the blue filter was still in place, then sent the recognition signal. Those on the submarine must have seen his signal immediately, for it swung slowly towards them and stopped.

Timber Woods, Ayton noted with approval, still used the bows-on approach, preferring to give those ashore the maximum protection of his guns.

'Let's go,' Ayton whispered to Maitland, who had the General next to him. They picked up the folbots and ran to the water's edge. Paddy and Tim stood guard as Ayton and Maitland carried one of the folbots into the water and held it steady while the General clambered nervously into the front cockpit. Ayton swung himself into the rear cockpit while Maitland held the folbot's stern. Maitland gave the folbot a push and Ayton struck deep into the water with his double paddles.

The folbot's bow climbed and hung on a wave. The wave broke, cascading them with foam. The General cursed loudly in German. Ayton kept the bow at right angles to the incoming waves and the next one swept harmlessly under them. Then they were out beyond the breakers into calm water.

The submarine was still hull down, but most of the conning tower was now clear of the water and Ayton could see the barrel and part of the mounting of the three-inch gun in front of the bridge. As the folbot neared it, the submarine blew the last of its internal ballast and surfaced completely, emerging like a great black whale.

As Ayton came alongside, two seamen in their white sweaters leant over and grabbed the bow and stern of the folbot while a third reached for the General and hauled him on to the forecasing.

'A prisoner,' said Ayton. 'But he's a general, so treat him gently.'

The seaman's teeth gleamed in the semi-darkness. 'If you say so, sir.'

Then Maitland came alongside and Dennis was hauled unceremoniously on to the forecasing. Ayton called out to Woods, who was leaning over the bridge. 'No more prisoners, Timber, but there are still two to be picked up.'

Woods lifted his hand in acknowledgement. 'Make it snappy, there's a good fellow,' he said.

The seamen released both folbots and the two SBS men turned them for the shore. A feeling of elation began to flow through Ayton as he paddled, and the exhaustion of the previous days lifted from him. They were home and dry now.

'We've done it,' he said to Paddy when he reached the beach. 'We've actually fucking done it.'

As he spoke there was a shout from the far end of the beach, followed by a burst of automatic fire. Bullets scattered sand and whined above their heads.

'Krauts!' shouted Paddy. 'Let's get the hell out of here.'

The next enemy burst of fire was more accurate, the bullets ripping across the water and making them duck instinctively. Ayton saw several figures running along the back of the beach and Maitland turned and fired a burst at them with his tommy-gun. More bullets kicked up the sand. Suddenly Maitland gave a grunt and slumped down.

'Shit!' said Ayton. He felt transfixed.

'Get going!' yelled Paddy at him as he dodged into the rocks. 'I'll cover you.'

Ayton ignored him and scrambled over to Maitland while Tim dragged one of the folbots into the water. Even before he touched him, Ayton knew Maitland was dead. He felt for his pulse; there was nothing. He rolled him over. Sand covered his eyelashes. Instinctively, Ayton brushed his fingers over the eyelids, closing the Scot's sightless, staring eyes. It was the least he could do.

Under Paddy's covering fire, Ayton ran into the water and thrust hard on the stern of the folbot, then shouted at Tim to get in and use his paddles. Behind him as he clambered into the rear cockpit he heard Paddy firing in short, steady bursts. Ayton hoped he had plenty of ammunition. He would need it.

He thrust his paddle into the water and the folbot gathered way. There was an outside chance that the Germans had not yet seen the submarine, but as the folbot reached it a Very light arched into the sky, illuminating the beach.

'There's still one of us ashore,' Ayton shouted to Woods as Tim was hauled on to the forecasing. 'In the rocks on the right. They may not have seen you yet.'

'They will,' Woods replied grimly. 'I'll make sure of that. Close up, gun crews,' he said into the voice pipe before shouting down to Ayton: 'I'll give you covering fire while you fetch your friend. But for Christ's sake don't hang about.' He turned back to the voice pipe. 'I want the Bren up here, too. Pronto!'

Another Very light burst over the beach and in the brightness Ayton could see more figures moving along the back edge. He would have to be quick, for the Germans were obviously moving to outflank Paddy, who was hiding in the rocks. As he moved the folbot away from the submarine he saw the barrel of the three-inch gun begin to traverse towards the shore, and heard the gun layer shout instructions. Seconds later the weapon fired behind him with an ear-splitting crack. The shell screamed over his head and exploded with a blinding flash behind the beach. The figures there scattered, and Ayton heard himself cheering.

If the first shell was slightly high, the second was rather too low, for it exploded on the beach close to the edge of the water, throwing up a great gout of sand and shale; but the third dropped right on the back fringes of the beach. Then the Bren gun opened up. One in five bullets was tracer and Ayton could see the flickering line of lead seeking out the range of the German patrol. Then he had to concentrate on beaching the craft.

The sea was rougher now and one of the breaking waves nearly spun the folbot out of his control. But a moment later he was through the breakers and almost aground. As he leapt out, Paddy, crouched down low, came running out of the rocks. One determined German started to fire at him and bullets ricocheted off the rocks and whined into the night. But he did not fire for long, for the Bren gunner on the bridge of the submarine soon zeroed in on him.

The two men scrambled into the folbot as a third Very light blossomed into the sky, but there was no more firing.

'Thanks,' Paddy breathed.

Extra seamen waited for them on the submarine's forecasing as they came alongside, and the folbot was fed hastily down the torpedo hatch. Woods was the only one on the bridge when they climbed up to it. He motioned them down the conning tower's ladder and pressed the button to start the klaxon, whose raucous blare was supplemented by Woods shouting: 'Dive, dive, dive!' down the conning tower.

The two men half climbed, half slid down the ladder and heard above them the clang of the bridge hatch being closed by Woods. They moved quickly across the control room, which was in darkness except for the lights on the depth gauges and the eerie red glow of the emergency lights.

'Both engines full astern,' the First Lieutenant ordered. 'Eighty feet.'

The engine-room telegraphs rang full astern and the planesmen spun their wheels.

'Jesus,' said Paddy calmly when they reached the wardroom. 'That was close.'

He took his tommy-gun off his shoulder, unclipped the magazine and worked the breech mechanism to make certain the weapon was unloaded. The General sat at the wardroom table, his eyes closed, his mouth moving, as he repeated some incantation to himself.

'How is he?' Ayton asked Dennis.

'Scared as hell.'

'He isn't the only one.'

When the submarine reached eighty feet Woods turned it round and headed out to sea. They ran for an hour, then surfaced to charge the battery and to signal Alexandria that the party, including its guest, had been picked up safely and with only one casualty. However, instead of being ordered back to base immediately, the submarine was instructed to move to a position off the southern tip of Greece.

The First Lieutenant broke the news to the party, who had taken over the tiny wardroom to grab some sleep. 'Sorry, chaps, but it must mean there's an Eyetie convoy coming through.'

At dawn, its battery fully charged, the submarine dived. The loud throb of the diesel engines was replaced by the quiet whirr of the electric ones, and all motion of the vessel moving through the water ceased. It was, thought Ayton, who was immediately awakened by the change, rather like leaving the hustle and bustle of city life for some remote country location.

He dozed off again, only to be woken some hours later by a shake on his shoulder. It was the First Lieutenant. 'We've reached our new billet. The Captain says you might like to come into the control room. We could be in for some fun.'

Ayton rubbed his eyes, eased his way out of his narrow bunk and headed for the control room. The submarine was already at periscope depth, for Woods, his back bent, his legs slightly apart in the crouching position, had his eyes glued to the main periscope. As Ayton entered, the Captain snapped shut its handles and ordered the periscope to be lowered.

Turning to Ayton, he said: 'There's a two-ship convoy approaching, escorted by what looks like a destroyer. You SBS characters have always used us as mere transports. Now you can see what our real task is.'

While its members were unstinting in their hospitality and support, Ayton knew that the submarine service sometimes regarded SBS operations as an additional hazard it could well do without. It had always been firmly understood from the start that the safety of a submarine and its forty-man crew was never to be put in jeopardy for a handful of SBS men. But there was nothing in the rules, as far as Ayton could recall, to say that members of the SBS, even if they had a German General as a captive, should not be put at risk if there were two valuable Axis merchant ships to be sunk.

For several minutes the submarine ran on towards the approaching convoy. The crew, ready to carry out their various tasks, sat in silence. The electric engines whirred and hummed. They had been submerged for only a few hours, but to Ayton the atmosphere was already stuffy. Woods glanced at his watch.

'Any HE, Number One?'

The First Lieutenant moved over to the asdic operator, who was bent over his dial with his headphones over his ears, and tapped his shoulder. The operator removed his headphones and said something, then replaced them.

'Only faint HE dead ahead, sir,' the First Lieutenant reported. 'That'll be the convoy.'

'Up main periscope!'

Woods swung the periscope through a complete circle before concentrating on a section straight ahead. After a few moments he stood up and gestured to Ayton that he could look. Ayton bent to the eyepieces.

At first he could see nothing but the turmoil of broken water, but then, as the wave drained away, three indistinct black blobs came into view. He switched to high power and suddenly the trio of vessels leapt out at him. The two merchant ships, in line ahead, were moving diagonally towards the submarine at an angle that gave Ayton a good side-on view of them.

The leading one looked modern, its low, slightly raked funnel indicating that it was almost certainly diesel-powered; the other, box-shaped and ugly in contrast to its companion's sleek lines, was an ancient coal-burner, its straight, high funnel belching black smoke.

Their escort, off the port quarter of the coal-burner, was moving from starboard to port, probably circling its two charges to maintain with its asdic a constant watch for underwater intruders. Its long, low outline, twin raked funnels, and gun turrets on its fore and after decks, identified it as a destroyer, or possibly a large corvette.

As Ayton watched, it swung under the stern of the coal-burner and, with a white bone of foam at its bows, came hurtling towards them. Ayton stepped back hurriedly and Woods took his place. But instead of ordering the submarine to crash-dive, as Ayton had expected him to, Timber just chuckled and gave the control room a running commentary as he watched the Italian warship manoeuvring.

'Pretty duff tactics,' he said eventually. 'With luck, he's not going to cause us many problems. Group up. Both engines full ahead. I'm going to take out the diesel one first. Close up for the attack!'

The First Lieutenant moved to the 'fruit machine', a device which calculated at what angle ahead of the target to aim the torpedoes. The device was connected electrically to the gyro compass, which gave it the heading of the submarine, and the First Lieutenant fed into it the target's speed, course and range as estimated by the Captain and his attack team.

The asdic operator lifted off his headphones. 'Sorry, sir, can't pick up her revolutions clearly enough.' Sometimes an asdic operator could count the revolutions of a target's engines and from this its speed could be calculated.

'I'd say it's about nine knots,' said Woods after a moment, his eyes riveted to the periscope lens. He hesitated, then said: 'Her course is one-two-zero degrees. Range two thousand yards and closing.'

The navigator began to plot the attack on his chart.

The target's speed and course had to be calculated by eye, but, provided the Captain could estimate the height of the target's mastheads, the range could be obtained by a device on the periscope which made two images of the target, one above the other. After balancing the water-line of one image on the mastheads of the other, the target's range could be calculated with help from a scale on the lens.

'Plot suggests target speed of nine knots, sir,' said the navigator. 'Course one-three-zero. Range one thousand five hundred yards.'

It all seemed very unhurried to Ayton and he was not surprised when the gunnery control officer murmured in his ear that it often took an hour or more for a submarine to be manoeuvred into the right position to fire its torpedoes.

Yet calculations from Woods flew thick and fast, and the SBS man could feel the tension in the control room increase as the minutes passed.

'Course and speed constant. Range one thousand yards and closing. The target's bearing is green ten. I want a course for a sixty track.'

'Steer zero-eight-zero degrees, sir,' the navigator said after a few minutes. 'That will give you an angle of sixty degrees.'

'Starboard thirty, then.'

'Thirty of starboard wheel on, sir,' the helmsman reported, swinging his wheel, then: 'Steering zero-eight-zero degrees, sir.'

'Course and speed constant. Range six hundred yards and constant.'

Now the submarine was the right distance from the target, and in the right position, as the diesel merchant ship was now steaming across the submarine's bows.

'What's the DA?' Woods asked the First Lieutenant, straightening up from the periscope.

'DA ten red, sir,' the First Lieutenant replied, reading off the 'director angle' from the fruit machine.

'Put me on ten red.'

Once the Captain knew what angle to aim ahead of the target, he could put the submarine on the director angle, or correct course, to fire the torpedoes.

There was a pause as the helmsman altered course to starboard. Then Woods set the periscope at the 'aim off' angle by using the bronze bearing ring around the periscope where it passed through the pressure hull.

'Stand by, one and two tubes.'

The hand of the engine-room artificer in charge of the torpedoes gripped the firing handle of the first tube on his panel. Woods waited until the merchant ship was in the middle of the vertical graticule on the periscope's lens.

'Fire one! Fire two!'

Ayton felt an abrupt increase of pressure on his eardrums as the torpedoes, propelled initially by compressed air and then by their own electric power, left their tubes. The submarine gave a slight lurch backwards as if it had run into a large, soft pillow.

'Torpedoes running, sir,' the asdic operator called out.

'Good. Down periscope. Starboard forty. Take her down to eighty feet.'

The seconds ticked by. Everyone in the control room was motionless, almost as if they were holding their breath. Woods glanced at his watch. To Ayton time was suspended. The suspense lasted so long he was sure the torpedoes must have missed, when two sharp explosions, one coming rapidly after the other, hammered against the submarine's pressure hull.

Immediately the atmosphere in the control room changed from anticipation to relief. If the relief was muted it was because all knew the attack would draw retaliation.

After a couple of minutes Woods ordered the submarine to be taken to thirty feet and the attack periscope to be raised.

'We got her all right,' he said matter-of-factly. 'And now for the coal-burner.'

'Diesel HE dead astern, sir,' the asdic operator announced.

'Is it on a steady bearing?'

'Coming straight at us, sir.'

'It's the destroyer,' the gunnery control officer said quietly to Ayton.

'Down periscope! Hard-a-starboard. Take her to one hundred feet. Group down. Shut off for depth-charging.'

One by one the watertight doors were clamped shut.

'Stop the fans. Steer one-five-zero.'

A blanket of thick, heavy, hot silence descended. Any careless, noisy movement, such as dropping a spanner, could be picked up on the destroyer's asdic as it began scouring the area for the submarine. Ayton felt the sweat beginning to form on his forehead.

'HE bearing green four-five, sir,' the asdic operator said quietly.

'Hard-a-port. Steer three-five-zero.'

'HE astern and increasing, sir.'

'He's on to us,' said the gunnery control officer.

'Stop one engine.'

The submarine hung suspended. Its single propeller turned just enough to move it forward without emitting enough sound to be detected by the enemy's asdic. Now all they could do was wait. And hope.

'HE constant, sir. Bearing green one-seven-five.'

'She's starting a hunting pattern, sir,' the navigator said to Woods, looking up from his plot.

'I know what she's doing, Pilot,' Woods said irritably.

'HE constant, sir. Bearing green one hundred.'

The wireless operator at the rear of the control room smothered a cough.

'HE fading slightly, sir. Bearing green eight-zero.'

'He's drawing ahead of us,' Woods said quietly. 'Hard-a-starboard. Take her down to a hundred and twenty feet.'

'Clever move,' the gunnery control officer whispered

to Ayton. 'The Wops usually search in an anticlockwise pattern.'

'Steer zero-nine-zero.'

'Zero-nine-zero it is, sir,' said the helmsman.

'HE still fading, sir. Bearing red one hundred.'

The tension in the control room seemed to ease.

The one electric motor hummed and whirred as the minutes ticked by.

'HE still fading, sir. Bearing red one hundred.'

No one moved, then Ayton saw the asdic operator's back stiffen slightly.

'HE constant, sir. Bearing red zero-nine-zero.'

'Shit,' said the navigator. 'She's turning clockwise.'

'Hard-a-port,' ordered Woods calmly. 'Group up. Both engines full ahead.'

The telegraph engines clanged.

'She can't hear us increase speed at that distance,' the navigator said. 'We'll cut back across her path before she gets too near us.'

'Steer two-seven-zero.'

'Two-seven-zero it is, sir.'

'HE fading slightly, sir. Bearing green one hundred.'

'We're now moving roughly parallel with one another, but in opposite directions,' the gunnery control officer explained to Ayton.

'HE continuing to fade, sir. Bearing green one-one-zero.'

Ayton, who was beginning to grasp the intricacies of underwater hide-and-seek, said: 'That must be good.' But the gunnery control officer shook his head and told him: 'She's just completing part of the search box. She won't give up yet.'

Sure enough, the asdic operator said: 'HE increasing,

sir. Bearing green one-two-zero.' Then: 'HE increasing, sir. Bearing green one-two-five.'

'She's turning out of her pattern,' said the navigator. 'She must have heard us.'

'Hard-a-port,' said Woods. 'Steer one-eight-zero. Group down. One engine only.'

'HE constant, sir. Bearing red one-six-zero.'

The air, heavy and stale, seemed to be getting more difficult to breathe. Ayton could see the strain on the faces of the First Lieutenant and the navigator, but Woods remained outwardly unconcerned.

'HE constant, sir. Dead astern,' said the asdic operator. Then: 'HE fading slightly, sir. Bearing green one-seven-zero.'

'She's maintaining her course,' said the navigator in wonderment. 'She's lost us.'

Woods glanced across at him. 'You always were an optimist, Pilot. I like that.'

The First Lieutenant grinned at the navigator. 'Like to put a ten-shilling note on that, David?'

'HE increasing slightly, sir,' said the operator. 'Still bearing green one-seven-zero.'

'No,' replied the navigator.

'What's happened?' Ayton asked the gunnery control officer.

'She's turning towards us.'

'HE definitely increasing, sir. Bearing green one-seven-five.'

'Now we're for it,' said the gunnery control officer.

'Hard-a-port. Absolute silence in the ship. Steer zero-nine-zero.'

'Zero-nine-zero it is, sir.'

'HE still increasing, sir. Bearing red zero-eight-zero.'

Ayton recalled Pountney's orders on how to behave when under a depth-charge attack. 'When you are privileged to be on one of HM submarines during an enemy depth-charge attack,' the orders had stated, 'be calm, hide yourself away in a corner of the control room, or anywhere else, out of everybody's way. Be seated, say nothing, hold an open book and look at it. It does not matter if it is upside down – they will not notice it.'

Ayton liked that 'privileged', and tried to remember where exactly he had put the book he had been reading. It was in the wardroom somewhere, but he couldn't remember where.

The first pattern of depth-charges exploded with four cracks in quick succession. The submarine bounced and shuddered as if some giant unseen hand was shaking it to and fro. A slab of cork insulation fell from a bulkhead on to the floor of the control room. For an instant the lights flickered.

'Not very close,' said Woods. The navigator raised his eyebrows in mock surprise.

The explosions died away and were followed by a series of rumbling echoes like some distant but violent thunderstorm.

'He can't hear us when he's dropping his depth-charges,' the gunnery control officer said to Ayton. 'With any luck he's started his attack too early.'

They waited for the next pattern to fall. Faintly at first, then more distinctly, Ayton heard the destroyer's propellers as it approached.

Schoo . . . schoo . . . schoo . . .

He held his breath.

Schoo . . . schoo . . . schoo . . .

The sound swelled and faded as the destroyer passed over and then ahead of them.

Crack! Crack! Crack! Crack!

It was like being inside an empty oil drum with someone hitting the sides with an iron bar. The noise was deafening. Ayton found himself being hurled across the control room, then the lights went out and the submarine staggered as if it had been hit by a giant fist.

Ayton grabbed the after periscope standard and hung on to it for a few seconds before levering himself up.

The submarine seemed to be tilting. Compressed air hissed out of a broken pipe.

At the other end of the control room he heard Woods say sharply: 'Get those emergency lights on. Now.'

'HE fading, sir,' intoned the asdic operator.

There were more sharp explosions as the destroyer laid down a third pattern of depth-charges, and their rumbling aftermath filled the submarine and drummed on its hull. But the explosions were much farther away and hardly shook the submarine at all.

'Is she turning?' Ayton heard Woods say to the asdic operator.

'HE continuing to recede, sir,' the operator replied after a moment. 'Bearing green zero-nine-zero.'

The emergency lights flickered on, casting a dim glow through the control room.

'Everyone all right?'

No one said they weren't.

'Check the engine-room, Number One.'

'Aye, aye, sir.'

'Pilot, see that everything's all right for'ard.'

The navigator nodded and knocked aside the levers that held closed a watertight door. This divided the control room from the forward part of the submarine containing the seamen's and petty officers' messes as well as the torpedo stowage department and the torpedo tubes. The tubes were not enclosed by the submarine's pressure hull, which made them the most vulnerable part of the vessel when it was submerged.

'HE continuing to recede, sir. Bearing green zero-eight-zero.'

There was a slight haze in the control room and an acrid smell. The submarine still seemed askew, too, the floor tilting slightly; but then Woods gave orders for her internal trim to be altered and she slowly righted herself.

'No HE, sir.'

The First Lieutenant and the navigator returned to say that there was no major damage, though one of the engine-room artificers had been knocked unconscious when he had been thrown across the engine-room by the force of the explosion. However, there was plenty of minor damage, mostly to the electrical wiring and the compressed-air pipes. Temporary repairs were carried out to the latter, but the damage to the wiring made it difficult to continue the attack, and rather to the relief of everyone in the control room Woods decided not to pursue the coal-burner.

They waited an hour and then the Captain ordered the submarine up to periscope depth. Everyone waited while he scanned the whole horizon before settling on an area off the port bow. He racked up the periscope to high power, then ordered it to be lowered.

'We got her all right,' he said. At this everyone cheered. 'She's about to go down. The destroyer is standing by her. The coal-burner's legged it. Let's go home.'

13

Major Pountney covertly watched his general's face as Pountney's chosen elite for No. 2 Special Boat Section demonstrated their latest skills on the chilly October waters of the Firth of Clyde off Ardrossan-Saltcoats. The section had officially come into being the previous March and was now fully operational.

'You seem to have done a good job of collecting as fine a bunch of hooligans as I've ever laid my eyes on,' Laycock said as they were driven back to the officers' mess after the demonstration. Pountney knew the commander of the Special Service Brigade well by now. 'Hooligans' was a term he used sparingly, for it was one of praise.

'Thank you, sir.'

'How do you do it?'

The guard at the gate presented arms smartly and the other raised the barrier and saluted. Laycock acknowledged them by saluting briefly.

'Select the right men and let them get on with it,' Pountney replied promptly. 'Choose your other ranks with more care than you would a wife and keep them in the picture as to what is going on as much as you can. I won't tolerate creepers. I don't allow petty charges to be brought against any man. If he's no good, I return him to his regiment pronto. Above all, I make sure I'm accessible to my officers and men at all times. I'm Daddy. If anyone has to be bawled out, I let my second in command do it. It seems to work.'

'I'm told,' said Laycock, the amusement he felt showing in his voice, 'that you have a notice on your desk saying . . . well, what does it say exactly?'

' "Are you tough?" ' Pountney quoted promptly. ' "If so get out. I need buggers with intelligence." '

Laycock laughed. 'I like that. Very good, very good indeed, Roger.' He paused and went on more seriously: 'I'm glad you've found them, as we're going to be needing them before this war is won.'

Laycock's staff car drew up by the steps of the officers' mess, one of the smaller stately homes which had been requisitioned for the duration. All the officers who were sitting in the ante-room rose to their feet as Laycock entered, but he immediately waved them back into their armchairs and approached the bar.

'Two large pink gins,' he said to the barman, then turned to Pountney. 'It seems to me, Roger, that the new section works very well together. Most of them came from No. 6 Commando. Am I right?'

Pountney nodded, added a modicum of water to the pink tincture in his glass, raised it to Laycock in thanks, and swallowed most of it in one gulp. The warmth of the near-neat gin fuelled the glow inside him which had been caused by Laycock's words of praise. Now, at last, he was pretty sure the General was going to tell him what was in store for the new SBS unit.

But if this was so, Laycock was in no hurry to raise the matter. Instead he asked with genuine curiosity: 'You say you choose your men with care?'

Pountney drained his glass and the General signalled

to the barman to refill their glasses. 'I do, sir. If I can, I choose ex-bandsmen.'

Laycock's eyebrows shot up. 'Good God. Why?'

'It's their training, sir,' Pountney explained. 'They have to march and counter-march while playing an instrument and reading their music. They also have to watch their feet to make sure they don't run into the musician ahead of them. Doing so many different things at once makes them excellent marksmen, as that's what you have to do when you're firing any weapon, as you know. Align the foresight, the backsight, and the target. It makes them nimble, too.'

Laycock laughed. 'Any other favourites?'

'I look out for anyone with Boy Scout training, as they've been taught self-reliance. They're also taught to look carefully and to move quietly.'

'And?'

'If I can, I recruit the studious, artistic type,' said Pountney promptly. 'He is infinitely better than the swaggering, tough individual who can usually only display his toughness in pubs. You've got to be super-sensitive and alert if you're going to land successfully on enemy-occupied coastlines.'

'From what I've seen this morning, Roger, you've chosen well.'

Laycock paused as if making up his mind to say something. Pountney knew better than to prompt him. He waited in silence. Outside, on the parade-ground, he could hear the drill sergeant shouting at the Special Service Brigade's latest batch of recruits. Laycock emptied his glass, indicated that Pountney should do the same, and said: 'Let's take a stroll outside, shall we?'

A cold, autumnal, north-westerly wind blew in off the

Firth. Pountney turned up the collar of his greatcoat as they walked briskly around the edge of the parade-ground.

'I'm under pressure to regularize the Special Boat Sections,' Laycock said abruptly. 'They're neither fish nor fowl as far as the Admiralty and the War Office are concerned. The Admiralty seems to be winning the argument for your lot to be absorbed into the Royal Marines. What's your view on that?'

'May I be frank, sir?'

'Of course.'

'Bugger that, sir.'

Laycock laughed. 'I thought you might not agree.'

He turned to look at Pountney and his face became grave. 'But we have a war to fight, Roger, you know that. Personal preferences have to be put aside. Becoming part of the Marines would mean the survival of the SBS. If such an integration is opposed, then you could be disbanded before your section has even seen action.'

Pountney hesitated. 'What about No. 1 SBS?'

Laycock shrugged. 'One of life's little ironies, I'm afraid. Ayton's a Marine but it looks as if Stirling and his SAS outfit are about to put in a take-over bid.'

Fuck the lot of them, Pountney thought. But he said: 'Put like that, sir, I have no alternative.'

Laycock smiled. 'Good man. I shall report back that you concur. No point in getting up their nostrils. However, between ourselves I have every intention of hanging on to your section for the immediate future, as I want to use them for cross-Channel raiding.'

'Sounds interesting, sir,' Pountney said eagerly.

'But I am sending *you* back to the Med, Roger.'

'Into the arms of my old mate Stirling, sir?'

Laycock shook his head. 'No. I've been asked to provide

three reliable SBS officers for an important clandestine mission. I want you to be one of them. Do you have a good man to take command of the section here?'

'Yes. Captain Montanaro. My number two.'

'Chap who sunk that freighter in Boulogne harbour in April?'

'That's him, sir.'

'Good. I'll have a chat with him in due course, but it's your role I want to tell you about. So far as I can.'

They left the edge of the parade-ground and took the path to the seashore. The north wind sharpened.

'It won't have escaped your notice that a large number of American troops have arrived here and in Northern Ireland during the last few months.'

Pountney nodded. It hadn't. You'd have to be deaf, dumb and blind not to know the Yanks had arrived. Having the Yanks here made one wish one was deaf, dumb and blind. The local female talent was the best source of information about them.

'They're commanded by a chap called Eisenhower. Heard of him?'

Pountney shook his head.

'He's tough and he's bright. And he's got a grin that even Brooke, who's no admirer of the Americans, admits is worth a couple of divisions.'

Pountney knew Laycock was referring to Field Marshal Brooke: the Chief of the Imperial General Staff – the head of the British Army – the chairman of the British Chiefs of Staff, and Churchill's right-hand man. Laycock was certainly moving in exalted circles, Pountney thought, but he knew Laycock wasn't a name-dropper; he didn't need to be. He knew that the General, without breaking any of the ground rules about secrecy, was trying to give him some background to whatever it was he was going to tell him.

Laycock paused on the path and looked straight at Pountney. 'I had to get you the highest security clearance to tell you this, but I insisted you knew, as naturally I must give you the opportunity to volunteer for the job that needs doing. There's going to be an invasion by Allied troops somewhere in the Mediterranean shortly.'

'Somewhere?'

Pountney couldn't help echoing the word. The Mediterranean was a large place.

'Somewhere,' Laycock repeated firmly. 'I can't give you more details than that. But the job is a top-secret operation which entails ferrying ashore a group of high-ranking American officers by folbot. They will, hopefully, negotiate terms with the French military authorities so that the invasion will be unopposed.'

That narrowed the options and Pountney's mind raced through the likely places. There was the southern half of France, which was under Marshal Pétain's Vichy regime, which collaborated with the Germans; but there were also the French colonies of Morocco, Algeria and Tunisia in North Africa.

Pountney was well aware that what Laycock had told him was pure dynamite.

'Who do I do this with, sir?' he asked cautiously as they resumed walking towards the shore.

'That's up to you. They'll have to come from No. 1 Section. You can choose them, but they must be officers and they must be utterly discreet. Any ideas?'

'Ayton, for one,' Pountney said immediately.

'But he's a Royal Marine, Roger,' Laycock said jokingly. 'I know what you think about Marines.'

'There are always exceptions, sir.'

'I'll see what I can do. He helped pull off an invaluable task for us in the summer by indulging in a little kidnapping. Who else?'

Pountney thought for a moment, then said: 'Bob Harmon would be ideal. He's a strong paddler and he's as cool as they come. He's a Marine, too, but he knows how to keep his mouth shut.'

'Good. So you'll do it?'

Pountney misunderstood. 'You mean, arrange their transfer, sir?'

Laycock gave Pountney an amused look. 'No, Roger. I'll arrange that. You won't be speaking to anyone until you arrive at Gibraltar tomorrow night.'

Pountney whistled. 'Like that, is it?'

'I meant, you'll volunteer?'

'Of course, sir.' Pountney felt momentarily aggrieved that the General felt it necessary to ask. But Laycock was punctilious in following the rules. He had already asked too many men to go on operations from which they had never returned.

'Your batman has had orders to pack all your belongings. They'll be at RAF Leuchars by the time you arrive there. A Liberator is on stand-by to fly you straight out. Ah, here we are.'

The path petered out by the coastal road. A little way down the road Pountney saw a jeep and a dun-coloured staff car drawn up behind it. The jeep was full of Military Police, their red caps and blanco standing out against the olive green of their vehicle.

A lieutenant in battledress with a revolver strapped to his belt was leaning against the staff car. When he

198

saw Laycock he jumped to attention and saluted. They crossed the road.

'Here's your charge, Merrick,' Laycock said. 'Major Pountney understands he is not to talk to anyone.'

'Very good, sir.'

Laycock turned to Pountney and extended his hand. 'Sorry, for the rush, Roger, and for all the cloak-and-dagger stuff.' He waved his hand apologetically towards the two vehicles and their armed occupants. 'Is there any uncleared business you want me to deal with?'

Pountney grinned. 'No, sir. My tailor is just going to have to wait a bit longer for his bill to be paid, that's all.'

He shook Laycock's hand, then saluted him. Laycock returned his salute, and said: 'Good luck, Roger.'

The driver of the staff car held open the rear door. Pountney ducked his large frame into the back seat and the lieutenant slid in beside him. The car, preceded by the jeep, moved away smoothly and Pountney settled back and wondered what the hell it was all about.

'How long is it going to take us to get to Leuchars?' he asked his escort after they had driven in silence for ten minutes.

'I'm sorry, sir,' the lieutenant replied, 'but I am under the strictest orders not to allow you to talk to anyone. That includes me, sir.'

The autumn day faded. Darkness wrapped the countryside and the staff car's shaded headlights just about picked out the rear of the jeep. Pountney's training, to relax when you can – a lot of war is about hanging around waiting for something to happen – allowed him to stop his mind speculating on what he had let himself in for. He closed his eyes and slept until he was woken by a shake on his shoulder. He glanced at his watch. It was after ten o'clock.

'We're here, sir,' said the lieutenant.

The airfield's guard commander, a sergeant in the RAF Regiment, bent down and briefly shone a torch in Pountney's face, then switched it to a piece of paper in his hand. He handed back the paper to the lieutenant through the car window and saluted.

'I'll give you an escort, sir. Corporal Stammers,' he shouted. A corporal appeared out of the darkness and climbed into the staff car beside the driver.

'Officers' mess, Sarge?' the corporal queried.

'No. Hut B for these gentlemen.'

They drove round the airfield perimeter, past a line of hangars with the large, black outline of bombers parked outside them, and eventually reached a far corner where two Nissen huts stood side by side in the darkness.

Pountney climbed out and stretched as the RAF corporal fetched the officer in charge, who turned out to be an elderly captain in the Pay Corps. The lieutenant had a short conversation with him, saluted Pountney and drove off.

The reception room of Hut B, the larger of two, was empty. Blackout blinds covered all the windows, but otherwise it was surprisingly bright and cheerful. There was even a small bar and a gramophone playing jazz records the Americans had brought with them.

The Pay Corps captain introduced himself, offered Pountney a drink and said: 'No flight tonight, I'm afraid. Bad storms coming in from the Atlantic. They'll clear by dawn, so it will be an early start. I expect you'd like something to eat before turning in.'

Pountney found all his kit in his room. He sorted out

what he thought he might want to take with him and packed the rest in boxes that had been provided.

It was still pitch-black when he was wakened, given eggs and bacon, and driven to the Liberator B-24 bomber, easily identifiable by its twin tailfins, which was standing at the end of the runway with its four engines warming up. Pountney found he was the only passenger, though there was a lot of cargo.

The Liberator's engines bellowed into a deafening roar and the whole fuselage shook as it began trundling down the runway. It gathered speed and lifted off, climbed right into the first glimmers of dawn, gained height over the North Sea, then turned to head south-west.

It was a long, tedious journey, broken only by coffee from a vacuum flask which one of the crew brought to him, and by the invitation of the pilot to visit the cockpit. But there wasn't much to see except the tops of the storm clouds and Pountney soon returned to his seat. Later the clouds began to break up and eventually he saw, bathed in late-afternoon sunlight, the Rock of Gibraltar, the only foothold the Allies had retained in Europe.

Pountney had never landed on Gibraltar's airstrip, but it had a fearsome reputation, as there was little room for error. However, the Liberator pilot touched down right at the start of the strip and had plenty of time to stop before he ran out of runway. He turned and taxied to the concrete apron which lay right under the shadow of the Rock.

Pountney climbed out of the bomber just as a staff car drew up alongside it. A naval commander in white drill shirt and shorts jumped out and shook his hand. 'Roger Pountney, I presume. I'm David Garnett.'

Pountney gestured to the mass of aircraft that were assembled in every corner of the airstrip. There were row upon row of them.

'What goes on?'

'Something big,' said Garnett. 'Very big. You'll hear soon enough.'

They drove through the town with its yellow stone buildings and crowded pavements, and down to the harbour. This was packed, too, with warships of all sizes. Freighters, moored alongside one another, crammed the wharves. Barrage balloons floated in the blue sky above this extraordinary armada. Beyond the confines of the vast harbour with its stone piers lay the curve of neutral Spain's Ceuta Bay.

'Where to, sir?' the driver glanced over his shoulder.

'The *Maidstone*,' said Garnett. He turned to Pountney. 'Depot ship for the Eighth Submarine Flotilla,' he explained.

HMS *Maidstone* was an old freighter which had seen better days. Even the Navy, with its reputation for keeping everything spick and span, seemed to have given up on her. She was moored to a quay and on her outboard side lay three submarines which Pountney immediately recognized as identical to the ones he had operated with the previous year.

'Some out on patrol?' he asked, knowing a full flotilla consisted of twelve submarines.

Garnett shook his head, but did not elaborate. They walked up the gangway, acknowledged the salute of the Marine sentry and went below to the wardroom, which had been turned into a temporary conference room. A trestle-table covered in a baize cloth stretched the length of the room. Otherwise it was empty except for three lieutenants standing by the bar, whom Garnett introduced as being the captains of the three submarines which lay alongside.

Garnett bought drinks all round, then said: 'Roger was asking where the other subs are.'

The oldest-looking of the three lieutenants, Jack Jewall, smiled wryly through his luxuriant black beard. 'Have you not heard our little rhyme for the S Class?'

Pountney shook his head.

'Twelve little S-boats searching earth and heaven,' quoted the youngest lieutenant, who looked hardly more than a schoolboy. '*Starfish* goes a bit too far – then there were eleven.'

'Eleven watchful S-boats doing fine and then,' Jewall intoned, '*Seahorse* fails to answer – so there are ten.'

'Ten stocky S-boats in a ragged line,' Garnett chimed in. '*Starlet* drops out of sight – leaving us nine.'

'Nine plucky S-boats all pursuing fate,' said the third lieutenant, who looked as if he never spoke much. '*Shark* is overtaken – now we are eight.'

There was a pause and Pountney said: 'Is that it?'

'No,' said the Commander. 'Unfortunately not.'

'Eight sturdy S-boats – men from Hants and Devon, *Salmon* now is overdue – and so the number's seven.'

'Seven gallant S-boats trying all their tricks,' said the schoolboy lieutenant. '*Spearfish* tries a newer one – down we come to six.'

'Six tireless S-boats fighting to survive.' They were taking it in turn now, building up the litany of destruction into a kind of chant. 'No reply from *Swordfish* – so we tally five.'

'Five scrubby S-boats patrolling close inshore. *Snapper* takes a short cut – now we are four.'

Everyone paused for breath at this point, but then a voice behind them said: 'Four fearless S-boats too far out to sea. *Sunfish* bombed and scrap-heaped – we are only three.'

Pountney turned round. A tall, cadaverous, balding officer with a lot of gold on his epaulettes stood in the wardroom doorway. Everyone sprang to their feet.

'I've heard a lot about you chaps,' said the Captain after he had been introduced to Pountney by Garnett as Barney Hawkes, the Captain SM Eighth Flotilla. 'What do you think of our little ditty?'

'An exaggeration, I hope,' Pountney said.

'Sadly not,' said Hawkes gravely. 'The Med's not the ideal place in which to operate a sub. The water's too clear, it's too shallow, and the enemy's airfields are too close for comfort. I know you've lost men in some of those submarines.'

Pountney nodded. Besides the two lost in the *Salmon*, he knew that Bailey and Davidson had not returned from a routine submarine patrol earlier in the year. And only the previous week he had been told that the experienced and reliable Tim Robertson and his paddler were missing after taking part in an operation off Sardinia in which their submarine had been reported sunk by Italian destroyers.

Hawkes tossed back his drink and said: 'Well, we'd better get down to it before the Yanks arrive.'

Two of the lieutenants took that as a signal to leave. Jewall stayed behind and seated himself next to Hawkes, who slapped a thick file on to the baize-covered table and indicated that Pountney should take one of the chairs opposite him.

Hawkes asked Pountney how much he knew, and when

Pountney told him, he said: 'I can't add much at this point except to say that the landings will be in French North Africa and that it is an American operation, though British troops and ships are involved.'

'Why American?' Pountney asked.

'Oran,' Hawkes replied. 'That's why. We want to avoid fighting if possible. If the French Navy knew it was a British operation it would fight to the last man and the last ship. Need I say more?'

Pountney recalled his fracas with the French naval officer in Beirut, and shook his head.

'"He that is not with me is against me,"' he quoted inscrutably.

Hawkes raised bushy eyebrows. 'Very profound, Major. I hope you're not given to spouting too many Biblical quotations.'

'Eye for eye, tooth for tooth,' Pountney added. 'Hand for hand, foot for foot, burning for burning, wound for wound, stripe for stripe.'

The two naval officers looked at Pountney doubtfully.

'Just giving you the SBS philosophy, that's all.'

Hawkes coughed into his hand; Jewall tried to hide his smile.

'Quite,' said Hawkes. There was a pause, then Hawkes said: 'Jack here will be taking you across in the *Seraph*. He had three folbots of the latest design delivered to him this morning.'

'How will we know where to land?' Pountney asked.

'Tony Eden did a submarine recce two nights ago and made sketches of the area. It's a lonely beach at a place called Messelmoun, about twelve miles west of Cherchell and seventy-five miles west of Algiers. You know Tony, of course.'

Pountney nodded. He had not seen Eden since he had reconnoitred that possible landing beach on Rhodes with him the previous year. It seemed a long time ago now. Since then Eden had made great strides in forming the Combined Operations Pilotage Parties – known to everyone by their initials COPP – whose purpose was to survey landing beaches and guide the invasion forces on to them. This had been one of the original purposes of the SBS, but Pountney had been glad to relinquish it for more active pursuits such as blowing up railway lines and attacking enemy airfields and shipping.

As Hawkes finished speaking there was a knock on the wardroom door and Eden entered carrying a large folder. There were greetings all round, then Eden spread out a long strip of paper on the table, a pencil sketch of the shore where Pountney was to land.

'The powers that be wouldn't let me go ashore,' said Eden. 'This is the best I could do.'

The sketch was remarkably detailed and neat, considering it had had to be assembled from looking at the coastline through a periscope. It showed a lonely stretch of beach with a solitary two-storey villa in the middle, half hidden from the sea by tall pine trees. The house was labelled simply 'white with red roof'.

'No beach gradients?' Pountney asked, though it wasn't really a question. He knew Eden could not have obtained beach gradients without leaving the submarine.

'I have aerials,' said Hawkes, producing a wad of photographs from his file and spreading them out on the table. 'They'll have to do. The pattern of the waves shows that there are no sand bars in front of the house.'

'I hope you're right,' said Pountney, studying the prints

closely. 'I don't want to land our precious cargo on a spit of sand a mile from shore.'

He could see that in front of the house the succession of waves produced a uniform, evenly spaced pattern. But to the right they became uneven before re-forming and breaking on the shore.

'There's a bar here,' Pountney pointed out. 'And another one on the left edge of this photograph. Not much margin for error.'

'If we can get in near enough,' said Jewall, 'I can guarantee to drop you off in exactly the right spot.'

'Can the *Seraph* get in close?' Hawkes shot at Eden.

Eden nodded. 'We got to within half a mile of the shore and there was plenty of water under us.'

'You'll need to get in much nearer than half a mile,' said Pountney. 'Remember, we'll have passengers, not expert paddlers, with us.'

'Let's have a look at those aerials,' said Jewall.

He thumbed through the photographs, studying them carefully, before handing them back. 'They need expert analysis, but I'd say the distance between the waves shows that the seabed is sufficiently steep-to. If I had a long gangplank you could walk ashore.'

'Good,' said Hawkes. 'That's something settled.'

There was another knock on the door and a seaman entered with a signal which he handed to the Captain.

'Something else that's settled,' Hawkes said to Pountney as he read it. 'Your two colleagues will be here in an hour. A Catalina's flying them in from Malta.'

'Officer of the watch told me to inform you two staff cars approaching, sir,' the seaman said, adding with some awe: 'One of them's the Admiral's car, sir. The other's the Governor's.'

Hawkes stood up. 'You must excuse me. I should be on the quarterdeck to greet them.'

'Who's the Admiral?' Pountney asked Jewall when Hawkes had left them.

'Vice Admiral Sir Frederick Edward Collins,' Jewall replied. 'Flag Admiral, North Atlantic station.'

'And the Governor?'

'General Sir Noel Mason-MacFarlane,' said Garnett. 'Headed the British Military Mission to Moscow until recently.'

Pountney whistled. Even he was impressed. 'Big guns indeed. And where are the Yanks we're meant to be delivering?'

'They'll be with them.'

The door opened and the three men waiting at the conference table stood to attention. Suddenly the wardroom was full of American accents, lots of gold braid and unfamiliar uniforms.

The Governor, easily distinguishable because he was in civilian clothes, said: 'At ease, gentlemen. There will be no formalities. I want everyone to speak their mind.'

His aide-de-camp ushered the Americans to their seats. There were three of them, two Army officers and a Navy captain. The tallest Army officer – he stood literally head and shoulders above everyone else in the room – particularly caught Pountney's attention. He was, Pountney could see from the two stars on his shirt lapel, a major-general. His long, oval face, youthful, vigorous and almost unlined, was dominated by a prominent hooked nose that had given him, Pountney soon learnt, the nickname 'The Eagle' from the British Prime Minister. His demeanour was patrician, almost regal.

The Governor, an amiable-looking man with a clipped

moustache who was dressed in a tropical suit, sat at one end of the table. Hawkes sat at the other with Jewall and Pountney on either side of him. The Admiral took the chair on the Governor's right. His flag lieutenant pulled out a notebook, ready to take notes.

'We haven't had time to brief our side,' the Governor said to the American general. 'Perhaps you could do so?'

'Sure,' said the General. 'Gentleman, my name's Clark. Mark Clark. I am General Eisenhower's deputy for the upcoming operation, which has been given the code-name Torch. I have the authority to reveal to you that at this moment two large convoys of Allied troops are readying to sail, one from the United States, the other from Great Britain. Nearly seventy-five thousand troops in all. They will land simultaneously on the shores of Morocco and Algeria.'

A ripple of astonishment went round the table and Clark acknowledged it with a slight smile.

'As you know, both countries are French colonies. They are defended by one hundred thousand fully armed and equipped French troops. If the operation is to be a success, it is essential that the landings are unopposed. I have been assigned to conduct the negotiations which will bring that about.'

Clark paused and the Governor smoothly intervened. 'I think we should explain that the French are governed by agreements with the Germans that they will defend any French territory attacked by the Allies. If the French stand by these agreements there will be bloody fighting ashore, though there's no doubt that, with our air superiority, we would prevail.'

Pountney was gripped by the enormity of what was being unfolded.

'On the other hand,' said Clark, 'if the French fail to comply by fighting, Hitler will certainly occupy Vichy France. The whole country will then be under the Nazi jackboot.'

Heads I win, tails you lose, thought Pountney. Poor bloody Frogs, they were going to get it in the neck either way.

'How do we know they're willing to negotiate?' Admiral Collins asked.

'As you know, we still have diplomatic relations with the French,' Clark replied. 'The French Resistance in North Africa have been in touch with our people there. There is no doubt that elements of the French Army are prepared to back the Allies.'

'At whatever cost?'

'At whatever cost,' Clark said quietly.

The silence that descended was profound. There was no one present who did not realize the gravity of what was being proposed. After a moment the Governor broke it by asking: 'And who is the leader of these elements?'

'General Mast, who commands the Algiers garrison,' Clark replied. 'He has pledged that his troops will not fight, provided a certain French general assumes control of all French forces in North Africa and announces they have joined the Allies.'

The Governor nodded. 'I see. Is that General de Gaulle? As leader of the Free French, I assume he is mixed up in this somewhere?'

Clark shook his head. 'Emphatically not. Most of the French Army regard him as a traitor who has flouted the authority of Marshal Pétain, the legitimate leader of

France. De Gaulle knows nothing; nor will he until the landings have taken place.'

'Who else is there?'

'There is such a man,' said Clark. 'We have code-named him Kingpin. That's all I can tell you at this moment.'

The Admiral grunted. 'I hope he lives up to his code-name.'

'So do we, Admiral,' said Clark. 'So do we.'

Another silence followed, which was again broken by the Governor. 'That is the background. Now for the detail. First of all we need to know if we can we deliver the General and his colleagues to the rendezvous. Captain Hawkes?'

The Captain outlined the result of Eden's reconnaissance and the availability of the submarine and of the SBS with folbots to take the party ashore.

'So it's a practicable proposition?' the Governor asked.

Before Hawkes could reply, the Admiral intervened. 'Are you seriously suggesting that one of my submarines should surface close to the enemy coastline during a three-quarter-moon period to deliver these officers ashore? It's madness.'

A silence again descended on the conference. If an admiral said 'no' to an operation, that operation did not take place. It was as simple as that.

'You must understand, Admiral,' Clark said quietly, 'that a lot of lives hang on the success of my mission.'

'And I have the responsibility of protecting my men and my ships,' the Admiral stated flatly. 'Not to mention trying to protect the lives of valuable personnel belonging to the United States Army.'

The Governor looked at the faces on one side of the table and then at the other. Deadlock. He turned to the US naval officer sitting on Clark's right.

'Captain Wright?'

'The Admiral's right,' the Captain said immediately. 'Such an operation poses unjustifiable risks.'

'So, if there was an American submarine available to mount such an operation, you would refuse permission?'

Wright shifted uncomfortably in his seat. 'I didn't say that, exactly.'

The Governor had made his point, and he said quietly: 'This operation has the highest political backing, gentlemen. The very highest. That is why I am chairing this meeting. It is not a military decision but a political one. I must know if it can be carried out by the Royal Navy. If the Royal Navy can't do it, I must find another way.'

The Americans murmured their agreement. The Admiral sat back in his chair, his bluff face suffused with repressed anger. But when he spoke his words were soft and slow. 'I hear what you're saying. Then you must address your questions not to me but to the officers who will be risking their lives.'

All eyes turned to Hawkes, who said: 'I should like to introduce you to Lieutenant Jewall. He is captain of the *Seraph*, which has been allotted to this operation.'

'Lieutenant Jewall,' said Clark, fixing the young officer with an intent stare. 'Can it be done?'

Jewall glanced at the Admiral. The Admiral's face was wooden.

'Certainly, sir,' Jewall said eagerly. 'I can get you there. And with any luck get you back.'

Clark's face relaxed. 'Thanks, son. That's all I need to know.'

The Governor turned to the Admiral. 'We have your permission?'

The Admiral, his expression still set, said gravely: 'You have.'

The Governor smiled. 'I'll inform London immediately that it can be done and that the submarine will be sailing tonight.'

He rose from his seat.

Pountney rose, too. 'Excuse me, sir.'

All faces turned towards the large, taut figure of the SBS officer.

'Yes, ah . . . Major . . .?'

'Pountney, sir,' Hawkes said briskly to the Governor. 'He and two of his officers will be delivering the General and his colleagues to the rendezvous in their canoes.'

'Yes, Major Pountney?'

'Our passengers will need to practise, sir.'

'Practise?'

'Getting in and out of the folbots. It needs practising. It can be tricky.'

Clark leant forward. 'We are going to be in your hands, Major. You tell us what to do and we'll do it. Practise all night if we have to.'

'That won't be necessary, sir. Just an hour or so of your time will do.'

'You have it, Major.'

The meeting broke up and Jewall took Pountney abroad the *Seraph*, where he found Ayton and Harmon unpacking their kit in the torpedo stowage department. The spare torpedoes had been offloaded and the space converted to bunks and a stowage area for the three folbots.

'What's it all about, Jumbo?' Ayton asked.

'You'll know soon enough,' Pountney replied. 'It should be an interesting little jaunt.'

'I know your interesting little jaunts,' Bob Harmon laughed. 'The last one involved a tour of the desert.'

At sundown General Clark, Captain Wright and one of the American Army officers arrived and settled into the tiny wardroom, and after dusk the submarine sailed. It ran on the surface across calm water illuminated by a three-quarter moon that almost turned night into day.

Below, Jewall and the three SBS men crammed around the wardroom table with the Americans to study the large-scale map of the Algerian coast which the General had spread out. He pointed to a cross on the map. 'This is our destination. You can see it's an isolated part of the coast. You've had it surveyed?' he said to Jewall, who nodded and handed over Eden's sketch.

Clark studied it intently. 'Yeah, that's the one – white walls and a red-tiled roof. Apparently it sits on top of a large sand-dune about halfway between the beach and this coastal road here. A path leads up to it from the beach through a small olive grove which sounds a good place to hide the canoes.'

Jewall looked at the sketch, then at the map. 'With respect, that sounds like all Algerian coastal scenery, sir. The whole coastline is covered with holiday villas like that. Are there any additional landmarks?'

Clark pointed with his forefinger. 'They told me this hill here to the left of the house is shaped like a sugar loaf. Very distinctive. As you can see, a small wadi empties into the sea from that area. There should be no trouble identifying it.'

Neither Jewall nor Pountney commented. They had heard that casual remark from senior officers before.

Clark sensed their doubts and added: 'The people in the house will have a powerful light shining seawards from the first floor if it's all right for us to land, and there will be a reception committee on the beach to meet us.'

The eyes of the two British officers met briefly and each knew the other had the same nagging doubt. Americans, they had heard, tended to be naive, though Clark certainly didn't look or behave that way.

'May we know who owns the house, sir?' Pountney asked gingerly.

'It's the weekend retreat of one of General Mast's friends, who is a member of the French Resistance,' said the other Army officer. He wore gold-rimmed spectacles and the eagle insignia of a full colonel, and spoke with an inflection that overlaid his American twang. At the conference the General had introduced him as Walt Meredith, his interpreter and an expert on the French Army and French foreign policy, adding: 'He's completely trustworthy.'

Pountney had heard that one before too, and asked: 'Is there going to be any way we can identify the reception committee before we land, sir?'

Clark shook his head and looked hard at all three SBS officers: 'You guys are worried we might be walking into a trap, aren't you?'

'There's always that possibility,' said Pountney, glad that it had come out into the open.

'Well, it's something we're going to have to risk,' said Clark briskly. 'We'll have to play it by ear. I'm going in whatever the consequences. We're playing for big chips, gentlemen, very big chips.'

It was now the turn of the SBS men to exchange glances. They knew how vulnerable a folbot was approaching the shore; it was obvious that the General did not.

The impromptu conference broke up and Jewall returned to the bridge. The SBS officers dragged one of the folbots along the narrow passageway and into the wardroom and laid it on the floor, so that the three Americans could practise entering its rear cockpit from the table.

Ayton showed them how. 'You sit on the edge of the deck like this and then you lower your leg, placing your foot just there. Then straighten up very carefully, balancing on one leg. Good . . . Now place the other leg here and grip with both hands on the side. Lower yourself gently . . . That's it.'

Once the Americans had got the hang of it, Pountney requested permission to go on the bridge to speak to Jewall. The bearded lieutenant did not lower his binoculars when Pountney appeared, but kept studying the horizon. He disliked being on the surface when visibility was so good, but the battery had to be charged – there was no escaping that.

'Yes, Jumbo. What can I do for you?'

'We've had a trial run in the wardroom, but I want to put them through real boat drill now. Could you stop this battleship for a moment?'

Jewall lowered his binoculars as he turned in amazement. 'You're asking me to stop my ship? Here? Now?'

''Fraid so, old boy. Won't take long.'

'You know bloody well that would contravene all the accepted rules governing submarines at sea in wartime.'

'Of course,' said Pountney cheerfully. 'But I assume you want to deliver and pick up our passengers without losing any of them.'

Jewall groaned. It went against his well-developed instinct for survival, but he saw the sense in what Pountney was saying. He gave the necessary orders and a folbot was quickly delivered on to the submarine's forecasing as the submarine came to a halt. It wallowed awkwardly in the swell, which had been hardly noticeable when the submarine had been under way.

Under such conditions the Americans found it difficult to apply the lessons they had learnt in the wardroom, but eventually they all managed the difficult manoeuvre of dropping into the folbot's rear cockpit as the tiny canvas craft bobbed in the water, and of then climbing out again. Satisfied, teachers and pupils went below, the folbot was returned to the torpedo compartment and the submarine resumed its course and speed.

At dawn Jewall ordered the submarine to run at eighty feet and shortly afterwards he ordered it up to periscope depth. He carefully examined the coastline ahead, then asked for Mark Clark to come to the control room. In moments the General was beside him, and Jewall handed over the periscope.

'That must be the villa,' said Clark after a moment. 'It has a red roof. And, yes, there's the olive grove and the sugar loaf on the left. That must be it.'

Clark stood back from the telescope and thrust out his hand to Jewall. 'Thanks, son. By getting us here you've almost certainly saved hundreds if not thousands of lives. Now, I guess, it's down to me.'

The young lieutenant took the American's hand and saw the emotion in the elder man's eyes. 'The Royal Navy, sir,' he said gravely, 'never lets anyone down.' Then he gestured at the three SBS officers standing behind him.

'And the Royal Navy includes these cutthroats here, as they are Royal Marines.'

'Don't count me in with that mob yet,' Pountney grumbled good-naturedly. 'It'll take more than a few sweet words to convert me into a bloody bootneck.'

14

The *Seraph* spent the day two miles off the Algerian coast, one hundred feet below the calm surface of the Mediterranean. At dusk Jewall started to close with the coast and surfaced half a mile from the landing area. The moon was not yet up; the stars glittered brightly in the night sky. Immediately Jewall focused the periscope on the villa he saw a white light shining from its first floor: the signal that it was all clear for Clark to go ashore.

The folbots were brought up through the torpedo hatch and launched on to a swell which was more pronounced than it had been the previous night, so that the three canvas craft bobbed and weaved in the water. The three SBS officers agreed that one of the folbots would land first and its occupants would signal the other two to come ashore if the reception committee was a friendly one.

Pountney and Jewall took some time to devise a simple, unambiguous code when using their walkie-talkies to contact one another. Eventually Jewall produced a pin-up photograph of a scantily dressed, dark-haired starlet Pountney immediately recognized as Jane Russell.

'I'll prefix any message by describing her top half,' Jewall suggested, 'and you can answer by telling me about her lower half. A different description each time in case anyone overhears what we say the first time round.'

'Suits me,' Pountney replied. 'But keep it brief.'

They both laughed.

All three men were armed with coshes and with Welrods. Bob Harmon was assigned the task of reconnoitring the beach first to ensure that their reception was a friendly one. He took Colonel Meredith with him, as the American had done some canoeing and knew how to handle a paddle. Ayton and Pountney watched them go, their blades throwing up glowing streaks of phosphorescence as they headed for the shore. Ayton, with the naval captain, Jerry Wright, went next. Finally Clark and Pountney pushed off from the submarine, which began to back off into deeper water so that it could crash-dive if it had to.

The last two folbots held back from the beach, their occupants straining to see what was happening ashore. Shadowy figures approached the water's edge and they could see Harmon and Wright pulling the folbot up the sand. The moments passed and no signal came. Pountney could hear Clark sitting behind him muttering under his breath and was amused to know that even generals got edgy when things didn't go right. The minutes ticked by.

Pountney peered ahead of him at the moving figures on the beach. It seemed inconceivable that Bob had allowed himself to be captured without firing a shot. Then at last Harmon's torch flicked on and off, signalling the dot . . . dot . . . dash . . . dot of 'F', to indicate that the reception had been friendly. At once Pountney drove his paddle blade deep into the water.

They soon reached the surf, which the folbot took in its stride, and seconds later they were borne by it on to the sand. They scrambled out as willing hands clutched the folbot.

'What the fuck happened?' Pountney asked irritably when Harmon came up to him.

'Dropped the bloody torch in the water,' Harmon said apologetically. 'Someone had to go up to the house to get another.'

The moment passed. Later Pountney reprimanded himself for allowing the tension to get to him, but then reasoned that it wasn't every day that he had the responsibility of landing an Allied general on a potentially hostile beach.

Clark reacted by slapping everyone on the back and shaking hands with the reception committee: three rather mysterious individuals in berets who spoke to Meredith in rapid French.

Pountney dug out his walkie-talkie from a pocket in the folbot, slid up the aerial and turned it on.

'Hello, *Seraph*, how do you hear me? She's got thighs as soft as butter.'

'I hear you loud and clear,' Jewall replied. 'She has the most gorgeous tits. Over.'

'All safe and sound,' said Pountney. 'We're going up to the villa now. Over.'

'We'll get the hell out of it,' said Jewall, and even over the walkie-talkie Pountney could hear the relief in his voice. 'See you as arranged. Over and out.'

Two of the Frenchmen led the way up to the villa while the third obliterated any traces of the landing. They dumped the folbots in the olive grove, covered them with a camouflage net and scattered leaves and loose grass over them.

The signal light had been turned off and the villa was so heavily blacked out that even when they were right up to its walls not a chink of light showed. But inside, its large rooms with marble floors were brightly lit. The landing party was shown into the main sitting room, where they were greeted by a group of French officers and an American in a civilian suit who was introduced as Dave Murphy.

The conference began immediately and the three SBS men were taken to another sitting room, where they gratefully accepted coffee and brandy before settling down to sleep on the sofas with which the room was liberally equipped. It was morning when one of the reception committee shook Pountney's shoulder roughly and told him in broken English that the conference was over, that General Mast and his advisers had departed, but that they were now expecting new visitors. '*Les flics*,' the man said. 'Police. You must 'ide.'

Pountney grabbed his tommy-gun, woke the other two and followed the man down into the cellar, where the SBS men found their three charges and the American civilian. Clark and the other two seemed worried by this turn of events, but Dave Murphy looked quite unconcerned. A single bare bulb lit the large room, which was lined with row upon row of wine racks. Most of them were empty, the SBS men immediately noted, but not all.

'They sent the servants away several nights ago,' said Meredith in a low voice. 'One of them had been fired. This guy, to get his own back, reported to the police that there might be smuggling going on.'

'If they find us we're in deep shit,' murmured Clark.

After a short while they heard the measured footsteps of the police above them as they searched the villa's ground floor. Everything went quiet for a while, then near the entrance to the cellar they heard raised voices, a scuffle and a single shot.

Clark pulled his Colt automatic pistol from a canvas holster he was wearing on his belt, but Pountney put a restraining hand on his arm. 'Allow us, sir,' he whispered.

Nodding, Clark slid the weapon back into its holster.

Pountney gestured to Ayton and Harmon to stand to one side of the door while he stood at the other, then indicated to the Americans that they should move farther away, which they did immediately.

'How many?' Pountney mouthed at Meredith, who stuck up four fingers.

There was more scuffling above them, then footsteps on the cellar steps.

For the three SBS men it was routine work. Pountney and Ayton drew their coshes from inside their shirts while Harmon, acting as the backstop, carefully and quietly drew back the hammer of his .22 Welrod and balanced the integral silencer on his raised forearm.

The door handle turned and rattled, and the gendarme on the other side shouted an order. They heard the jangle of keys and the lock being turned, then the door was flung open.

A torch beam stabbed the dark corners of the cellar and Pountney noted that they were dealing with a cautious customer. But not seeing anything unusual, the policeman stepped into the cellar.

Harmon covered him carefully with his Welrod while Ayton hit him behind the right ear with one well-directed stroke of his cosh. The man's peaked cap flew off and his cape furled round him as he pitched forward. Pountney caught him neatly and pulled him, as quietly as he could, over to where the Americans were standing. Pountney gestured that they should bind and gag the unconscious gendarme.

Then he put up four fingers and drew one down. Three to go.

He went back to the door, tossed the gendarme's cap in the direction of the Americans and resumed his position beside the open door. When the first gendarme did not return Pountney knew that two of them would come next time, or perhaps all three, because that was the way the police the world over worked, whether it was the local constabulary back home or the German Gestapo.

Nothing happened for some minutes, then someone above began shouting what must have been the gendarme's name. Silence again, then heavy footsteps on the cellar stairs. Was it two or all three? It was impossible to tell.

A shadow fell on the shaft of light coming through the door.

'Gaston?' The door creaked wider open. 'Gaston?'

Pountney smoothed his hand over his cosh and raised it above his head. Ayton did the same.

The second gendarme was taller than the first and had drawn his revolver from the highly polished leather holster at his waist.

The SBS men let him come farther into the cellar than they had the first one, but when the second gendarme didn't follow directly behind him, Pountney hit the first one hard with his cosh.

At the same instant Bob Harmon stepped into the gap and shot the second policeman who was still hovering on the cellar steps. In the confined space the sound of the silenced Welrod, like a bottle being uncorked, seemed louder than normal.

As the second gendarme pitched forward there was a

frantic scrambling of boots on the stone stairs. Harmon moved quickly through the cellar door, stepping sideways to avoid him as he fell. 'Plop' went the Welrod again.

'Shit!' Harmon snarled. 'Missed the bastard.'

He ran up the steps and flung himself at the door the third gendarme had just slammed in his face. He wrenched it open and went down on one knee, holding the pistol steady in both hands.

Plop.

The third policeman staggered slightly, but kept running. Moments later he was out of the house and staggering down the path towards the coastal road, his cloak billowing out behind him.

'Shoot him!' Harmon yelled at one of the beret-wearing Frenchmen who was guarding the back entrance with a Sten gun. The Frenchman raised the Sten and fired at the policeman's legs, and the man rolled over like a shot rabbit.

Harmon raced down the path past the writhing figure of the wounded gendarme. Parked to one side of the coastal road was the policemen's car, an old blue Buick. Harmon, who thought another one of them might have remained with the car, was relieved to see it was empty. The keys were still in the ignition and Harmon started it up and drove it down the path, then off the path and into some undergrowth where it would be hidden from both the road and the air.

When he returned to the villa he found Pountney and Ayton bent over another beret-wearing Frenchman, who was sprawled in the sitting room. He had been shot at close range by one of the gendarmes and died as Pountney tried to stem the flow of blood from the bullet hole in his neck.

The two gendarmes who had been shot were having their wounds bound by Ayton. Both of them, he said, would survive. The Americans had come out of the cellar and were conferring.

'We think Dave should beat it,' Clark said to Pountney, 'and we should get the hell out of here, too. Can you signal the *Seraph*?'

Pountney stood up and shook his head. 'She'll be seven miles out and a hundred feet down, sir. She won't surface until dusk.'

Clark turned to Murphy. 'You know the set-up here, Dave. How long do you reckon it will be before they start searching for these guys?'

Murphy shrugged. He seemed quite unconcerned by what had happened. 'Two hours, maybe three. We're a long way from anywhere and they won't come looking yet.'

He said his farewells and walked off along the path on his own. His car, he said, was concealed half a mile down the road.

'A great guy,' said Clark, watching him go. 'If we succeed in this crazy mission it'll be because of him. So how long have we got to wait, Roger?'

They were all on first-name terms by now, though no one called the General 'Mark'.

'Until an hour after dusk,' Pountney said. 'I'd suggest we pass the time by sampling the wine from the cellar.'

They carried up a variety of vintages and enjoyed them with their lunch. Afterwards they slept off the effect of the wine and in the evening strolled to the beach to watch the sun go down and to crack open the remaining bottles from the cellar. When the last glow had left the sky, Pountney began calling up the submarine on his walkie talkie.

'Hello, *Seraph*, how do you hear me? She has dimples on her knees. She has dimples on her knees.'

'And you guys call us Yanks sex-mad,' said Clark, pouring himself another glass.

After ten minutes or so the walkie-talkie crackled and Jewall said: 'She's got black hair and bedroom eyes. I hear you loud and clear, Roger. What's happening?'

'Mission completed,' Pountney replied. 'We're ready to be picked up. But be quick about it. The police could be on to us.'

'Switch on the light and we'll home in on it. We'll have you out in a jiffy.'

Pountney turned to Meredith. 'The sub needs to home in on the light. Can you tell our French friends to turn it on?'

'Sure,' said Meredith, scrambling to his feet.

The SBS men carried the folbots down to the water's edge. The surf was higher than the previous night and each wave produced a subdued roar as it broke on the sand. It pounded on the beach, throwing spray in all directions.

Meredith returned. 'They've cleared off. The villa's locked.'

Pountney cursed. 'What about *les flics*?'

'They must have taken them with them.'

More likely they'd cut their throats and buried them, Pountney thought.

'We'll have to use the RG equipment,' he said and started calling Jewall on the walkie-talkie.

'She's got a beautiful bottom.'

'Her cheeks are red and rosy,' Jewall replied. Pountney explained they could not switch on the signal light.

'All I can do is steer on a reciprocal bearing and hope we find you.'

'How close can you come in?'

'Five hundred yards, no more.'

'We've got bad surf here and the police are on our tail.'

'I'll do what I can.'

Pountney switched off the walkie-talkie and quickly considered his options. 'Phil, go and watch the coastal road. Bob, I want you ready to take the General out once we've found the *Seraph*.'

Pountney took the RG screen out of his bergen and went to the water's edge. To his right Harmon dragged the folbot forward while Clark stood ready with the waterproof bag which held all the documentation from the conference. Pountney held up the screen and moved it slowly in an arc. The minutes passed. Then, right at the end of one sweep, the beam of the signal lamp was intercepted by the screen. Pountney switched on his walkie-talkie.

'You're much too far to the right,' Pountney said urgently after he had swapped more praise of the female anatomy with Jewall. 'There must be a bad lateral current.'

'I'll move to starboard,' said Jewall. 'Once the moon is up I'll be able to see more.'

'By the time the moon is up the police will be here,' Pountney replied. It was, he thought grimly, a case of the blind leading the blind.

When the *Seraph* turned, Pountney lost contact with the RG lamp on her bridge. He glanced at his watch. On the surface the submarine could move at a healthy fourteen knots under her twin diesels, but at night and under such conditions he knew Jewall would not risk more than half that speed. Assuming she was at least half a mile off her correct position it would take about ten minutes for her to reach it and then she would have to be exceptionally careful as she began to manoeuvre closer inshore.

It seemed much longer than ten minutes when Pountney at last re-established contact with the submarine's infrared beam. She was a little too far to the left now, and he called Jewall to tell him. Slowly the beam moved from left to right, then stopped.

Now the *Seraph* was in position opposite the villa, and Pountney called Jewall to tell him. Jewall said he would edge in as close as he could. Pountney searched the horizon with his binoculars.

'See her?' Harmon was at his shoulder.

'No, but she's there all right.'

Both turned when they heard the crunch of footsteps in the sand.

'Car lights,' said Ayton breathlessly. 'A long way off, but they're coming in this direction.'

'Shit,' breathed Pountney.

'I'd better get going with the General,' said Harmon.

'You, too, Phil,' Pountney ordered. 'Take Jerry with you. Stick together.'

Because Meredith spoke French, Pountney reckoned he would need him if they fell into the hands of the police. He handed Harmon the RG screen, and he and Meredith helped launch the folbots. Up to their knees in foam, they struggled to hold the fragile craft as their occupants clambered in. By keeping the folbots' bows head on to the breaking waves, they prevented them from capsizing. Then they moved into deeper water before giving one huge shove to propel the craft through the last breaking wave.

First one folbot, then the other, shot forward, with the SBS officers flailing their double paddles frantically.

Somehow, no one quite knew how, they did not capsize and were soon swallowed up in the dark.

'Two folbots on their way,' Pountney told Jewall. 'They'll home in on you by RG.'

'How will you find us?' Jewall asked anxiously.

'By smell, I expect,' Pountney said with a facetiousness he did not feel. He turned and saw car lights playing on the side of the villa wall.

'Time we went,' he told Meredith. 'Know how to wield a paddle?'

'Sure. Done a bit of kayaking in my time.'

'Just keep time with me if you can.'

They dragged the folbot to the edge of the water, waited until one wave had receded, then Meredith clambered into the front cockpit. Pountney, holding the stern, pushed hard as the next wave swept forward and they were afloat. Meredith steadied the folbot with his paddle as best he could as Pountney slipped in behind him. But they were fractionally slow and the craft began moving backwards and another wave broke with a viciousness that sent them careering sideways out of control. Once broadside on to the force of the waves, the folbot capsized.

They tried again and the same thing happened. This time the craft rolled right over after they had scrambled out of it.

'Now what?' Meredith asked after they had tipped out the water from the folbot.

Pountney glanced up the beach and saw several men moving round the villa, their torches playing on the ground, then on its walls and windows.

'Third time lucky,' he said.

This time he guided Meredith right through the breakers. One wave broke over his head, leaving him gasping for breath. But he hung on and was towed out by Meredith until the folbot was beyond the surf.

Once in calmer water, Pountney hauled himself, one leg on either side of the craft, on to its stern, moving carefully so as not to upset its precarious balance. Then, after edging forwards until he was close enough to the rear cockpit, he put his hands behind him and, by gripping the sides of the folbot to keep his balance, swung his legs up out of the water. When they met above the cockpit he swung them down into it, at the same time edging the rest of his body forward. For a moment he was crouching half in and half out of the cockpit before he managed to slide his legs forward and straighten them as he sat down.

'OK?' shouted Meredith over his shoulder.

'OK,' Pountney shouted back. 'Hand me the walkie-talkie. It's in that waterproof pocket on your right.'

The American handed it over his shoulder, but the pocket had not been closed properly and the walkie-talkie refused to work. Behind them powerful lights began to play on the sea, and Pountney, looking back, saw that the police had brought a car, its headlights blazing, right on to the beach.

'They'll see our footmarks,' Meredith said over his shoulder as they rested.

'They'll think it's smugglers,' Pountney replied, trying to reassure himself as much as Meredith. They watched until the car and the men withdrew and Pountney then signalled 'F' continuously out to sea with his torch. The *Seraph* wouldn't answer, he knew, as it was much too dangerous to signal towards the shore where anyone could see it, but Jewall might spot it and be encouraged to draw nearer.

They bent to their paddles once more. Behind them

the shore dwindled into darkness, but the moon was shining strongly now and Pountney was confident that they would spot the submarine soon. Sure enough, after another ten minutes' paddling, he saw her bulk almost straight ahead.

He flashed his torch again and this time someone struck a match and held it briefly against the bridge structure.

Fifteen minutes later they were safely aboard the submarine.

In the tiny wardroom a bottle of brandy was produced and everyone was talking at once. Clark rapped the table and said: 'I propose that all of us who went ashore tonight, plus Lieutenant Jewall and all his officers, be made founding members of a new club.'

There was a murmur of approval.

'What shall we call it, General?' Meredith asked.

'How about the Panoe Club.'

The Americans roared with laughter.

'Panoe Club?' said Pountney.

'That's right. None of you Limeys ever heard the joke about three Canadian businessmen who went off on a hunting trip?'

None of them had.

'A fourth was going to join them later,' Wright explained.

'When they arrived at the hunting ground they discovered they needed three punts and a canoe,' said Meredith. 'So they sent a telegram to their fourth friend telling him to ship them up to them.'

He turned to Clark so that the senior officer could tell the punch-line.

'The next day the fourth friend sent a telegram back,' the General said, his face as straight as a poker. 'It read: "Girls are on their way; am now searching for a panoe."'

15

'It's on then?'

Clark smiled. 'Sure is.'

The Governor leant back in his chair and breathed a loud sigh of relief. 'Congratulations, General. A real coup.'

'I couldn't have done it without those Seraphims,' Clark said. 'Those guys did a first-rate job.'

'So Mast has agreed his troops won't oppose the landings?'

'Yes. Provided Kingpin assumes command of all French forces in North Africa and announces that they have joined the Allies.'

'And the French Navy?'

Clark hesitated. 'Mast is certain the Navy will toe the line if Kingpin plays his part.'

The Governor looked at Clark shrewdly. 'Are you as certain, General?'

Again Clark hesitated. 'Frankly, no. Especially if they suspect any British involvement. After Oran you guys are about as popular with the French Navy as Admiral Horatio Nelson must have been.'

The Governor rubbed his chin. 'So what's the answer?'

'There is an alternative,' Clark said with slow emphasis. 'Murphy told me the Navy's Commander-in-Chief,

Admiral Darlan, is in Algiers right now. He's visiting his son, who's sick.'

The Governor looked aghast. 'But that's impossible. Darlan is one of Pétain's right-hand men. He has treated with Hitler. Oh, no, no, General. That would not do under any circumstances.'

Clark bent forward and said urgently: 'Only Darlan has the power to command the Army and the Navy. Mast wouldn't like it, as he's for Kingpin; but he'd have to obey Darlan. I urge you to consider it.'

'Impossible,' said the Governor firmly. 'My government would never allow it.'

Clark shrugged. 'If you Limeys won't have Darlan – just supposing he would change sides – then we must go for Kingpin.'

'And Mast thought Kingpin could sway the Navy as well as the Army?'

'Sure. But he would, wouldn't he?'

The Governor rose. 'Kingpin it is, then. I shall issue the orders immediately.'

Clark remained seated. 'It's not quite as simple as that, sir.'

The Governor sank back in his chair.

'If we go for Kingpin, Murphy believes it will be necessary to neutralize the French Navy's ships in Algeria.'

'How?'

'The planners say the best way is to send a small force a few hours before the invasion takes place to persuade the Navy not to act.'

'That means into Oran?'

'Exactly. But this time the ships will be flying the Stars and Stripes, not the white ensign.'

'And supposing they choose not to cooperate?'

Clark smiled. At that moment the eagle looked more like a hawk. 'Then they will have to be stopped from leaving harbour.'

'What now? I wonder,' Pountney said as he and Jewall walked up the gangplank of the depot ship. It was forty-eight hours since they had returned to their Gibraltar base and Pountney was already getting itchy feet; and he knew that Ayton and Harmon felt the same way too.

'Barney only said to report on board with you immediately,' Jewall answered. 'Another flap, I suppose.'

Hawkes was waiting for them in the wardroom. Before him on the baize-covered table was a pile of files a foot thick through which he was ploughing one by one. 'Don't ever become an administrator,' he said by way of greeting.

'The day they make me become one,' Pountney said, 'is the day I retire to my old pursuit of hunting big game in Africa. War or no war.'

Hawkes motioned them to seats opposite him and gave them both a hard look before saying: 'I've got another job for you two. Another hush-hush one. Think you're ready?'

'I'm sure we are, sir,' Jewall answered. 'My Seraphims have got quite a taste for cloak-and-dagger operations now.'

'Seraphims?' Hawkes queried.

'General Clark's term, sir, for all of us who were on board the *Seraph*.'

'Seraphims, eh,' Hawkes chuckled. 'Very good. They've got quite a sense of humour, those Yanks. Sharp as a needle is General Mark Clark. President Roosevelt has just announced he's to have a third star. Makes him the youngest lieutenant general in the US Army.'

'He's got a good thirst, I'll say that for him,' said Pountney, remembering how many empty bottles they'd left behind them. 'What's the job you've got for us?'

'Sail for southern France tonight to pick up a very distinguished – I repeat, very distinguished – high-ranking French officer who is in hiding there and take him to a rendezvous with a Catalina flying boat. The Catalina will fly him here. The convoys for Torch have sailed and we must get him here as quickly as possible.'

'Kingpin?'

Hawkes nodded.

'What's his real name?'

'It's in your orders. For now you'll know him only by his code-name.'

'Sounds simple enough, sir,' Jewall said airily.

'There's just one more thing,' said Hawkes.

There always was, thought Pountney.

'Kingpin has stipulated that he won't have anything to do with the British and we can't afford to offend him. Thousands of lives could depend on his cooperation. So he must be picked up by an American submarine.'

'But the Yanks haven't got a submarine within three thousand miles of Gib, sir,' Jewall objected.

'We know that. The Yanks know that. But Kingpin doesn't know that.'

'So the *Seraph* is going to have to fly the Stars and Stripes?' said Jewall.

'Exactly,' said Hawkes. 'But she's also going to have to have an American captain.'

'My accent would hardly be convincing,' said Jewall.

'Which is why Jerry Wright will be going with you as

captain,' said Hawkes. 'He'll greet Kingpin when he comes aboard and will appear to captain the ship once you're under way. Any sign of a British presence and Kingpin could demand to be taken ashore. Like all Frenchmen, he's a very proud man.'

'So the crew's going to have to brush up on their American accents,' said Jewall.

'That won't be necessary. We've been told Kingpin doesn't speak English. Just make the sub look like a Yank one, that's all.'

'Pin-ups,' both officers said together.

Hawkes grinned. 'You have my permission to put pin-ups wherever you like.'

'If he doesn't speak English, how the hell are we going to communicate with him, sir?' Jewall asked.

'Colonel Meredith is also going with you,' said Hawkes. He slid Jewall's sealed orders across the table to him. 'It's all in there. Thank you, Jack, you can go. Jumbo, wait one, will you?'

What now? Pountney wondered.

'I want you and your two offsiders to return in the Catalina with Kingpin,' Hawkes said after the door had closed behind Jewall. 'One reason is he has to be guarded night and day.'

'And the other reason?' Pountney queried.

'General Clark has personally requested that the SBS should help mount an operation that is an important part in the invasion. Overall it's an American show, of course, but frankly the Yanks don't have the know-how for the particular job they want done. It's one for volunteers, of course. But I take it none of you would have any objection?'

Pountney grinned. 'None at all.'

'Good. You'll be fully briefed when you return with Kingpin. Jack has in his orders what you are to do. Good luck.'

Jewall was waiting for Pountney on deck. 'What the hell was that all about?'

'Barney didn't really say,' Pountney replied. 'But it sounds like it'll be fun.'

They strolled back to the *Seraph* together and Pountney and the other two SBS officers spent the rest of the day checking their folbots and equipment, and preparing for the four-day voyage. The Americans came aboard at dusk and the submarine sailed shortly afterwards. Pountney thought the coxswain had rather overdone his orders to fix pin-ups to any available space in the wardroom, but it certainly made the tiny cubicle more cheerful.

Once at sea Jewall broke open his orders, then called the others into the wardroom. 'Cap d'Antibes is our destination,' he said. 'Kingpin is a man called Giraud. General Henri-Honoré Giraud.'

Hawkes had included a photograph of their prospective passenger. It showed a tall, lean, straight-backed officer with hollow cheeks, keen eyes and a large moustache. He carried a walking stick and was looking straight into the lens. His expression, which must have made the photographer nervous, was just slightly out of focus.

'A real martinet by the looks of him,' said Pountney, examining the portrait closely.

'At least he'll be easy to recognize with a moustache that size,' Ayton commented.

'The name's familiar,' Jewall said. 'But I can't think how.'

'French First World War hero,' said Captain Wright,

who was the oldest among them. 'The Germans took him prisoner, but he escaped on a horse. He put up a fight in June 1940, too, before the Jerries captured him again.'

'How come he's in France if he was made a prisoner of war. I thought they were all shipped to Germany.'

'Search me,' said Wright. 'I guess he escaped just as he did in 1916. He's quite a guy, though he must be in his fifties now.'

'Says here he limps from a war wound,' said Jewall. It adds: 'Treat with extreme caution.' Sounds as if he is some sort of explosive.'

In the following days and nights the *Seraph* ran on the surface in the dark at maximum speed, diving only during daylight to avoid the attention of enemy aircraft. On the evening of the fourth night they reached a point two miles off Cap d'Antibes on the French Riviera. Jewall brought the submarine up to periscope depth and ran in towards the bay where they were to pick up General Giraud.

Through the periscope it looked a fine night, no moon and a calm sea; perfect weather for the operation. Jewall handed over the periscope to Pountney so that he could examine the exact spot where he and the others were to land.

'What's their call-sign?' he asked Jewall, who was standing beside him.

'The letter "S",' Jewall replied.

'Looks to me as if that's being flashed from a house on the left-hand end of the bay.'

He stood back and Jewall took his place.

'Right place, but they're early,' said Jewall doubtfully. 'There's another hour to go before they're meant to call us.'

For a moment there hung between them the spectre of a trap. Any minor deviation from the accepted plan always alerted the taut nerves of those undertaking a clandestine operation.

It was Wright who gave them their answer. 'Remember the French are an hour ahead of us,' he said.

Jewall swore in relief. 'You'd think they'd have told the poor old bastard that. Ready to go?'

Pountney nodded.

'Down periscope. Stand by to surface. Blow main ballast.'

Jewall was first on to the bridge, followed by the two lookouts and then the three SBS men, who immediately went forward with two of the crew to receive their folbots from the torpedo hatch. Pountney and Meredith went in the first folbot; Ayton and Harmon followed in the other two. They would not land until Pountney had signalled it was safe for them to do so.

'Let's have the Bren up here,' Jewall said into the voice pipe. 'Better safe than sorry.'

From the periscope it had seemed a perfect night; on the water the surface was ruffled by a chilling westerly wind which blew straight out of the Pyrenees.

The 'S' winked regularly from the left end of the bay, coming, Pountney could see now, from a large, blacked-out villa situated well behind the curving beach.

The folbot grounded and the two men leapt out and crouched on the sand. Pountney held his tommy-gun at the ready. The sea murmured behind them and in the distance a dog barked persistently; otherwise there was nothing except the signal which kept winking.

'Guess we can call the others in,' whispered Meredith, but Pountney put a warning hand on his arm. In the shadows below the villa something was moving now, he was sure of it. He eased his weapon forward. He felt the American tense under his hand and knew that he, too, had seen the movement. They waited. The dog stopped barking; a clock somewhere in the town struck twice. Then they saw a man emerge from the shadows and walk on to the beach. As he approached they could see he was wearing a trilby hat, a polo-neck sweater and canvas trousers, his hands deep in the pockets.

Pountney felt rather silly crouched on the sand while the man strolled across the beach towards them. He stood up and Meredith did the same. The signals stopped. The man began to talk rapidly in French as he approached them, taking his hands out of his pockets to gesture as he spoke. He didn't seem particularly friendly. Meredith replied, then told Pountney: 'He asks if we're Americans.'

Pountney gestured to the United States Army patch on the shoulder of Meredith's uniform. The man responded with an expressive Gallic shrug.

'Show him something American, Walt,' Pountney suggested.

Meredith dug in his pockets and produced a packet of Lucky Strikes. He held the packet out to the man, who took it, turned it over, then pocketed it. He still looked sour, but now he shook Meredith's hand and spoke in rapid French.

'He'll take us to the General,' Meredith said.

'He's not taking us anywhere,' Pountney snapped. 'The General's coming to us. I trust him as much as I would a rattlesnake.'

If it was a trap, Pountney reasoned to himself, they wouldn't want shooting on the beach, because they would know there was a submarine out there somewhere. Much better to lure Meredith and himself off the beach and dispatch them quietly behind one of the villas which lined the bay.

'He says the General's not quite ready.'

'We'll wait,' said Pountney phlegmatically.

This brought a volley of French which made Meredith raise his hands in a conciliatory gesture. 'He says it's dangerous to stay on the beach. Sometimes police patrols come down here.'

'Great,' said Pountney. 'They choose a beach which has police patrols.'

'I think the guy's genuine,' said Meredith.

'We'll soon know,' Pountney replied sceptically.

They picked up the folbot and followed the Frenchman to the fringes of the beach, where there was a small park guarded by ornamental railings. They left the craft under some bushes near the gate and followed the Frenchman into the park, in the middle of which stood a bandstand, its white paint peeling, its wooden frame in bad repair.

The Frenchman indicated that they should stay by the bandstand, and vanished quickly into the dark. Before long he returned with a tall figure who walked briskly with a walking stick. The tall man was dressed in civilian clothes and wore a raincoat over his shoulders like a cape. Only when he got close did Pountney detect a slight limp. He was accompanied by several civilians, all of them armed with Sten guns.

There were brief, hurried introductions before the group moved to the edge of the beach. Pountney and Meredith carried their folbot back down to the water's edge and then flashed the recognition signal out to sea. Moments later the other two folbots slid smoothly out of the dark. Without waiting, and without even looking to see if the coast was clear, the General strode down the beach to meet them, and his aide hurried after him.

'Walks as if he bloody owns the place,' Pountney muttered to Meredith.

'Probably does.'

Giraud proved to be extraordinarily agile for so tall a man and he had little difficulty in fitting himself into Ayton's folbot. In fact he was rather like a schoolboy on an outing, giving Meredith a running commentary on his youthful canoeing adventures as they steadied the folbot for him. The aide kept quiet but looked permanently terrified, not only for his own safety but also for Giraud, who seemed totally oblivious to danger.

Jerry Wright, wearing the full uniform of a US Navy captain, saluted Giraud when he stepped on to the submarine and a large American flag fluttered in the breeze above the bridge. The General was hurried below and Jewall watched impatiently from the bridge as the folbots were fed through the torpedo hatch as in the distance the lights of a fishing fleet were gradually growing brighter.

Pountney lowered the hatch as the last folbot disappeared below, applied the clips and hurried back to the bridge. Jewall ordered the submarine to turn and head out to sea, and water sloshed across the forecasing as Pountney ran along it towards the conning tower. He reached its footholds and swung himself over the bridge casing.

'About time, too,' said Jewall.

He pressed a large brass button and the sound of the klaxon clamoured in Pountney's ears as he half climbed, half slid down the ladder into the control room. He heard the hatch of the conning tower slam shut above him and Jewall shouting that all clips were on. Moments later the submarine's captain was standing beside him in the control room.

'Take her to eighty feet, Number One,' Jewall told the First Lieutenant. 'I don't want to tangle with any fishing nets.'

Beyond the dividing curtain Pountney heard the General's aide speaking rapidly in French to Meredith and there was a good deal of laughter, generated by relief that the operation had been successfully completed.

Pountney joined them and Jewall followed him and produced a bottle of rum and some glasses. Soon the bottle was half empty. Giraud, flushed and smiling, sat bolt upright at the head of the table. Pountney had never seen anyone with such dignity and presence. The General stood up, shook Pountney's hand with both of his and said something in grave, slowly spoken French.

'He thanks you on behalf of France,' Meredith explained.

Giraud turned to Wright, then Jewall, and shook their hands too, and repeated his short speech. Wright told the General through Meredith that he was going to be flown back to Gibraltar. Giraud asked the date of the invasion and when Wright told him the Frenchman's eyebrows shot up in amazement. The General had hoped, Meredith translated, to persuade the Allied governments to divert their forces to southern France, as the Germans would occupy it if North Africa were invaded.

'Christ,' Pountney said to Jewall. 'I thought de Gaulle was bad enough. This chap obviously thinks he can give Winston and Roosevelt orders.'

Wright then asked Meredith to explain that, as Eisenhower's naval representative, he was empowered to ask the General to approve the contents of a speech that he, Giraud, would be asked to broadcast to North Africa immediately he reached Gibraltar. It called on all French forces there to join the Allied forces when they landed. He placed the sheet of paper in front of Meredith, who translated it and handed it to Giraud. The General drained his glass of rum, took the piece of paper in his hand and spoke so quietly that Meredith had to strain to hear him.

'He says he cannot do it,' said Meredith. 'He is a soldier, not a politician. And now he needs to sleep. Tomorrow he has to take command.'

'Take command?' Wright queried. 'What does he mean? There's nothing for him to take command of at the moment. And there never will be if he doesn't make that broadcast.'

Meredith grimaced. 'He's under the impression that he has been rescued in order to command all Allied forces taking part in the invasion.'

There was a moment's stunned silence, before Wright broke it by asking: 'Who put that in his head, I wonder?'

'Search me,' said Meredith.

After the Americans had argued fruitlessly with the General in an attempt to change his mind about making the broadcast, the party broke up in a sombre mood.

'We seem to have risked our bloody necks for nothing,' Ayton grumbled when Pountney explained the situation to the other two SBS men.

'I hope bloody not,' said Pountney, 'for all our sakes', and he described the conversation he had had with Hawkes.

Once past the fishing fleet, the submarine surfaced and ran for the rest of the night towards its rendezvous with the Catalina flying boat seventy miles off the coastline. Just before dawn Wright broke wireless silence to send a coded signal to Gibraltar saying that the operation had been successful but that Giraud had refused to sign the communiqué.

By the time this had been done, and confirmation that the message had been received had been transmitted to the submarine, the sun was edging above the horizon and it became too dangerous to stay on the surface. The klaxon honked its warning and the *Seraph* dived to eighty feet. An hour later it reached the rendezous and Jewall brought it up to periscope depth.

The submarine's officers took it in shifts to watch for the Catalina through the periscope. At ten o'clock the First Lieutenant said excitedly: 'Aircraft dead ahead, sir', and stood back to allow Jewall to look. The silence in the control room was broken only by the whirr of the electric motors as Jewall concentrated on the dot above the horizon. The dot turned into a blob and the blob into the distinctive shape of the high-winged, twin-engined Catalina, with floats at the end of its wings and the twin blisters of the gun turrets in its fuselage.

'Down periscope! Stand by to surface! Shut main vents.'

The rating on the control panel on the starboard side of the control room moved a series of small levers and there were several muffled thuds as if someone was banging the submarine with their fist.

'All main vents closed, sir.'

'Blow all main ballast!'

The roar of high pressure air expanding into the ballast tanks filled the control room, and the planesmen spun their wheels to put the planes to the correct angle to surface. Jewall unclipped the lower hatch and entered the conning tower, and the First Lieutenant shouted out the changing depth of the submarine to him. 'Twenty-five feet . . . twenty . . . fifteen.'

Jewall swung open the hatch and a blast of fresh air swept through the control room, mixed with a sprinkling of Mediterranean sea water. Wright followed him up, ready to play his role when the General appeared.

'Stop blowing,' shouted the First Lieutenant above the roar of the compressed air.

'Signaller on the bridge!' Jewall called down through the voice pipe. 'Make it snappy. He's almost on us.'

The signaller carrying a small lamp and the wide-barrelled Very pistol scrambled up the ladder, followed by the two lookouts with their powerful binoculars and the crew of the Oerlikon gun. Those below heard the steady throb of the Catalina's engines and the dull thump of the Very pistol being fired.

The throb of aero engines grew louder, but then receded, and the Very pistol was fired again. The Catalina's engines dwindled, then steadily increased.

'Major Pountney on the bridge,' Jewall called down through the voice pipe. 'Unstow folbots. Oerlikon crew, close up.'

When Pountney reached the bridge he saw that the sea was flecked with white. The occasional wave slapped hard against the *Seraph*'s ballast tanks and cascaded spray over the forecasing. Overhead the Catalina was circling in a cloud-flecked sky, a lamp winking from one of its gun blisters.

Wright had joined them on the bridge. 'What do you think, Jumbo?' he asked anxiously.

'Looks bloody choppy,' said Pountney doubtfully.

Jewall watched the Catalina as it made a pass across the water before landing.

'We'll get it to taxi as close as possible,' he said.

'Can you pick up the folbots?'

Jewall shook his head. 'You'll have to sink them if the Catalina can't take them aboard.' He bent over the voice pipe. 'I want the General ready to come on the bridge. But he's not to come until until I say so.'

The flying boat skittered across the water, founts of spray flying from its floats, then the pilot revved the engines and it lumbered into the air again.

'He doesn't like it,' Jewall commented.

'Neither do I,' said Pountney.

The Catalina gained height and circled.

The signal lamp blinked from its blister and the signaller said: 'Oil, sir. He wants oil.'

'Good idea,' said Jewall. 'Chief ERA on the bridge,' he said into the voice pipe. The long, lugubrious face of the chief engineer peered out of the conning tower's hatch almost immediately. 'You wanted me, sir?'

'Chief, we need oil on the water. Plenty of it.'

The ERA disappeared without comment. Submarines always had spare oil. As a last resort it could be pumped out while a submerged submarine was under depth-charge attack. If bits of old clothing and other debris were added to it the attackers could sometimes be duped into thinking the submarine had been sunk.

They watched the oil being pumped out of the leeward side, to be spread across the water by the wind. It had a remarkable effect on the waves, damping them down and suppressing the spray.

'Tell him to land as close to leeward of us as possible,' Jewall instructed the signaller.

The oil slowly turned a large patch of water into a dark-brown, velvety slop. The Catalina did one dummy run, then landed in the middle of it. The pilot revved its engines and taxied slowly towards the submarine.

'The General on the bridge,' Jewall said crisply into the voice pipe. Pountney clambered down from the bridge and on to the forecasing.

Giraud appeared on the bridge wearing his raincoat and carrying his walking stick. He looked less gaunt and seemed to be enjoying himself, though his aide, who followed him on to the bridge carrying a briefcase, looked seasick.

'Aircraft dead astern, sir,' one of the lookouts suddenly shouted. 'Elevation fifteen degrees. About ten thousand yards.'

Jewall and Wright exchanged glances.

'Talk about being caught with our pants down,' said Wright drily.

'You'd better be ready to take him below,' Wright warned the aide, who spoke some English.

Jewall turned to the lookout. 'Can you see what it is?'

'Bit far away, sir, but it looks like a Junkers 88 to me.'

'Warn the Catalina,' Jewall snapped at the signaller. The signaller raised his lamp.

'The General asks if he can stay on the bridge,' the aide said haltingly. Giraud was looking around with immense detached interest, like a tourist admiring the view.

'No, he bloody well can't!' Wright replied testily. 'Get him below immediately.'

'Elevation twenty degrees, sir. Eight thousand yards. Still looks like a Junkers.'

'The Catalina's going to take off, sir,' the signaller reported. 'He says a Hudson escort for him is due around now.'

'It'll be too bloody late for us,' said Jewall above the noise of the flying boat's revving engines. On the forecasing Pountney and two seamen had already launched the first folbot.

'Secure that torpedo hatch,' Jewall shouted down to them. 'Get away from the sub,' he warned Pountney, who was in the folbot. 'I may have to crash-dive.'

He trained his binoculars on the ever-growing dot astern of the submarine. It couldn't be the Catalina's escort, as it was coming from the wrong direction. Whatever it was, it was very slow and probably hadn't spotted them yet.

'Do we dive?' he asked Wright. It was a submariner's nightmare to be caught on the surface by an enemy aircraft.

'No,' said the US Navy captain calmly. 'We fight it out. Otherwise we'll never get him to Gib on time. Do you agree?'

'We might never get him there at all,' said Jewall grimly. 'But I'm game if you are.'

'Elevation thirty degrees, sir. Six thousand yards. Almost certainly a Junkers.'

'Only fire on my orders,' Jewall shouted to the Oerlikon crew on the bandstand aft of the bridge. He was relieved to see that Giraud had disappeared below without further argument. Stubborn old bastard.

The Catalina took off in the direction of the approaching aircraft and lumbered into the air. Jewall had no idea how, if it came to it, the aircraft would fare in a dogfight with a Junkers, as neither was equipped for such an encounter.

'Elevation thirty-five degrees, sir. Five thousand yards. Definitely a Junkers, sir.'

'Shit,' Jewall muttered under his breath. He raised his binoculars again and recognized the pointed wings of the Junkers 88. He saw the bomber suddenly dip and knew that its crew had seen the submarine. He could see the markings now on its black wings and fuselage.

'Stand by to open fire!' he shouted to the Oerlikon crew.

'Elevation forty degrees, sir. Four thousand yards.'

Jewall glanced down to make sure that Pountney was well clear of the submarine.

'Full speed ahead!' he said into the voice pipe. 'Hard-a-starboard.'

'Elevation forty-five degrees, sir. Three thousand yards.'

The Junkers was diving steeply at them.

'Open fire!'

Boff! Boff! Boff!

The quick-firing Oerlikon drummed in their ears as the 20mm shells sped towards the target.

Boff! Boff! Boff!

Empty shell cases rolled off the bandstand and into the sea.

The enemy aircraft continued to dive.

'Get down!' Jewall yelled at the lookouts.

He and Wright crouched under the lip of the bridge. But their eyes did not leave the Junkers and they watched, almost as if hypnotized, as two black objects detached themselves from its belly. At first the bombs wobbled in the air, but then their fins stabilized as they dropped towards the submarine.

'Hard-a-port,' Jewall said into the voice pipe.

But the bomber had misjudged the speed of its small target and both bombs fell well astern, throwing up fountains of water.

The next moment the Junkers was directly over them, filling their ears with the thunder of its engines.

The Oerlikon followed it round.

Boff! Boff! Boff!

The bomber swung upwards and jinked hard to its left, ready to circle round and continue the attack.

Boff! Boff! Boff!

Quite suddenly a small curl of grey smoke appeared under the Junkers which quickly turned to a long, black trail of burning oil as the aircraft lumbered to gain height.

The Oerlikon crew cheered.

Overconfident bastard, thought Jewall. That'll teach him.

The Junkers straightened out, turned north and headed straight for the French coast. Soon it was a dwindling speck, leaving behind it a thin trail of burnt oil which was quickly dispersed by the wind.

No time for congratulations, Jewall thought as he bent once more to the voice pipe. 'Stop both engines. The General can come to the bridge now.'

He waved to the folbot, which was well astern. Giraud reappeared, looking annoyed at missing the action. If he was surprised to see Jewall so evidently in command, he showed no sign of it, but shook hands gravely with the young lieutenant before being escorted carefully by Wright on to the forecasing and loaded into Pountney's canoe when it came alongside.

As he climbed in, the Catalina returned and landed nearby. Meredith and Giraud's aide, the latter clutching the briefcase, were taken across in the other two folbots. It was an anxious quarter of an hour, with the lookouts constantly scanning the horizon, but eventually the Catalina lumbered across the oily water and clawed its way into the air.

Jewall breathed a sigh of relief and pressed the klaxon button.

16

Lieutenant General Dwight D. Eisenhower, Commander-in-Chief of the Allied North African Expeditionary Force, pushed back his chair, stood up and gave one of his famous grins. It split his face from ear to ear. Giraud bowed slightly, gravely shook Eisenhower's proffered hand across the conference table and sat down. His aide, still looking worried and ill at ease, sat next to him. Clark and Meredith came in and sat down on either side of Eisenhower.

Eisenhower's underground headquarters, recently hewn out of the great Rock of Gibraltar, was a hive of frantic activity as the time for the invasion approached. But here in the conference room all was quiet except for the hum of the air-conditioning.

Conducting the negotiations across the conference table was too formal, Eisenhower thought, but that was what the French had wanted. He had wanted an informal talk, but ultimately Giraud had little bargaining power, so perhaps it was understandable that he wished to seem as aloof and as formal as possible. It sure didn't help though, Eisenhower felt, and time was short. It was going to be a difficult meeting.

He resumed his seat and cleared his throat, then made what he considered was an acceptably brief speech about the General's bravery and courage in escaping from Germany and then from southern France, and the privilege of having him in Gibraltar to help the Allied cause.

As Eisenhower spoke, Giraud looked straight at him, his gaze never wavering. Occasionally his hand strayed to the ends of his handlebar moustache, but otherwise he sat perfectly still. He was in uniform now, his chest covered with row upon row of decorations, a visible contrast to the single line of ribbons worn by Eisenhower, who had not so far been in battle.

Eisenhower concluded his speech by saying that having such a glorious nation as France, with her illustrious past, on the side of the Allies would surely tip the balance of the war against the Nazis. A memorable victory would then be theirs for the taking, a victory in which France would have played a crucial role. A politician to his fingertips, Eisenhower spoke with sincerity and conviction, and when he had finished he gestured to the General to speak.

For the first time since the conference had begun Giraud diverted his eyes from Eisenhower's face and read in French from a sheet of paper. He spoke slowly and emphatically and after each sentence he paused while it was translated by Meredith. Occasionally he glanced at Eisenhower as if to measure the effect he was having, but Eisenhower remained inscrutable.

When Giraud had finished, Eisenhower and Clark exchanged glances. It was worse than they had thought. Much worse.

'Regrettably,' said Eisenhower abruptly, 'it is not possible to put the General in overall command of the landings.'

Meredith translated and Giraud acknowledged this with

a slight bow of the head. He turned to Meredith and spoke rapidly.

'He says it was his understanding that he was to take command. He had a personal letter from our President to that effect. Otherwise, he would not have come,' Meredith explained.

Eisenhower groaned inwardly. Giraud might be a brave officer, and a fine one, too, but he seemed extraordinarily naive politically. Eisenhower had seen Roosevelt's letter and it had made no such offer. It had held out promises – but what did promises mean in wartime?

'I profoundly regret if there was some misunderstanding,' Eisenhower said. 'However, I am sure the General will believe me when I say that the circumstances have changed. These now dictate that a distinguished – I repeat, distinguished – Frenchman is present in North Africa around whom all Frenchman there can rally to fight for the Allied cause. You are that man, General. All we need is for you to broadcast a message to your countrymen in North Africa that they are to welcome the Americans as Allies. The lives of thousands of Americans and Frenchmen are in your hands. All the glory is yours.'

Meredith translated. There was a moment's tense silence before Giraud smiled slightly and then spoke.

'The General says he is not a politician,' Meredith said. He can say that again, Eisenhower thought, but not a muscle on his face moved.

'He says that it was the decision of the Allies to invade North Africa, not his. The blood must be on your hands.'

There was a moment's stunned silence. Then Clark leant forward and said to Meredith: 'Render this into

French, Walt, just as closely as you damned well can: "Old gentleman, I hope you know that from now on your ass is out in the snow."'

Meredith glanced across at Eisenhower, who shrugged. 'We've got to get the stubborn old bastard to agree somehow,' he said. 'If flattery is not going to do it, let's try something else.'

It was going to be a long session and he called for more coffee.

17

In a different part of the Rock, a British naval commander from Combined Operations was briefing the three SBS men, the captains of the two ships which were to enter Oran harbour, and a tough-looking American lieutenant colonel, with a Texan drawl, who had been introduced to them as the commander of the small elite force of US Army Rangers who were to accompany the SBS.

The Commander held a snooker cue in one hand and a half-smoked cigarette in the other. With the cue he tapped a map which had been slung over a blackboard on an easel. 'This is Oran, gentlemen, the French Navy's principal North African base in the western Mediterranean.'

'I remember it well,' said the younger of the two ship's captains, an RNVR lieutenant commander called Harvey. 'I was the Jimmy on one of Somerville's destroyers. It left a bad taste in all our mouths.' He spoke bitterly.

'With any luck, Terry,' the Commander replied soothingly, 'this time there won't be a shot fired in anger, as the purpose of this little operation is merely to persuade the French Navy not to react to the landings. But we'll be landing troops to prevent sabotage of port facilities and ships prior to the arrival of American troops of the Central Task Force.'

'Where are they coming from?' the older captain, an

RNR commander called Bill Crean, asked. The RNR, Royal Naval Reserve, was drawn mostly from merchant seamen. Crean had a complexion like leather and looked as if he had sailed all seven oceans of the world, which indeed he had.

'They will be landing on beaches to the west of the Bay of Oran and to the east of the port at approximately 0300 hours. That's an hour after you're due into Oran.'

'You mean,' said Pountney, 'we'll be the first ashore?'

'Exactly. You'll have with you a small force of US Army Rangers commanded by Colonel Budd here. Two companies of them, to be exact. But the ships are ours, as the American Navy has nothing suitable this side of the Atlantic. They will be British-manned and will be commanded by these two stalwarts here.'

'And how do we let the French know what our intentions are?' Crean asked.

'Both your ships will be rigged with loudspeakers. French personnel will be going with you to broadcast the message that you have come as allies of the French.'

There was a sceptical silence, broken eventually by Pountney, who asked: 'So where does the SBS fit in?'

'To see to it that no ship leaves the harbour.'

'And how the hell do we do that?'

'We have a new little gadget for you which should help,' the Commander replied. 'You'll be seeing that next. While you SBS boys are out in your canoes, Colonel Budd's Rangers will occupy the wharves around the harbour and two gun batteries guarding the western and northern approaches to the port.'

'What ships are taking us in?' Budd asked. 'Battleships, I hope.'

A ripple of laughter went round the room, but the

American's underlying meaning did not escape any of those present.

The Commander smiled and drew on his cigarette. 'Ex-US Coast Guard cutters which your Navy loaned to us last year, Colonel. Lake Class. I recommend them. Seaworthy boats.'

'Why Coast Guard cutters?' Ayton asked. 'Seems a funny choice.'

'The French will identify them as American.'

'They're armour-plated, I hope,' said Pountney, half under his breath. What lunatic had thought up this operation? he wondered. The Royal Navy might have sunk half the French fleet in July 1940, but what about the other half?

'Not armour-plated,' the Commander said, 'and they're only 250 feet long, but fast for their size. You won't need armour-plating, as we are confident the French will welcome the Americans as allies.'

'And that includes the French Navy?'

The Commander hesitated, then said cheerfully: 'The French Navy will fall into line, I'm sure. However, just in case they start shooting before they start thinking, I suggest you come in from the east, not from the Bay of Oran. Then you can hug the cliffs along the coastline, which will make you well nigh impossible to spot. You should remain undetected until you appear off the mouth of the port, which won't give the batteries time to get a shot at you. And when the French identify you as American – well, there'll be vino all round.'

He passed around data of the area and sketches of the entrance to Oran harbour, and also handed out the most recent aerial reconnaissance photographs. Some of the verticals showed the layout of the long, narrow harbour.

Its waters were protected from the Bay of Oran by a mole that stretched from the harbour entrance to one of the batteries, Fort Lamoune, which covered the Bay of Oran. Another battery, Ravin Blanc, was sited on the shore to guard the harbour entrance, and under its shadow lay the harbour's main quay.

Most of the French warships, destroyers and corvettes, appeared to be moored at the far end of the harbour under the guns of Fort Lamoune, though there were a number of smaller vessels alongside the main quay. The soundings data showed clearly that the north-south channel into the harbour entrance from the Bay of Oran was wide and deep and well dredged. But there were sand bars to the east of it, with only a narrow channel through them.

The harbour entrance was protected by a boom. The gap in it, to allow the passage of friendly vessels, was protected by several block-ships which could be manoeuvred to close it at short notice. There was also an inner boom constructed with a line of coal barges.

'It doesn't look an easy nut to crack,' Ayton commented and the other two SBS men murmured their agreement.

'You won't have to crack it,' said the Commander cheerfully. 'They'll welcome you with open arms.'

'Are you certain of that?' Harvey asked sceptically.

The smile on the Commander's face faded. He stubbed out his cigarette and said quietly: 'No. But it's the best we can do under the circumstances. You've all been hand-picked. I don't doubt that you will be able to cope with whatever confronts you.'

The briefing broke up and the Commander led the three SBS men along another corridor hewn out of the Rock and into a large, well-lit space that looked like an arsenal for exotic weaponry. At the far end stood a line of prefabricated offices. The Commander knocked on the door of one and was told to enter by a gruff Scottish voice.

'Here you are, Donald,' the Commander said. 'These are the fellows you want.'

A tall, lithe man in the uniform of a lieutenant commander RNVR came round from his desk, which was piled high with paper, and shook their hands enthusiastically. His face was familiar to Ayton, but he could not place it until the officer introduced himself as Donald Campbell. He knew then they were in the presence of the holder of the world land- and water-speed records.

'Donald's our dirty-tricks man,' said the Commander. 'Full of new ideas and new inventions.'

Campbell rubbed his hands together and picked up from his desk a long, cylindrical object. 'My mini torpedo. Twenty-one inches long. Specially designed to cripple vessels in sheltered waters.'

He handed it to Ayton, who weighed it in his hand and then passed it on to the other two.

'It's powered by a car's windscreen-wiper motor,' Campbell said, 'which drives twin opposing screws. Packs a one-and-a-half-pound cavity charge of PE in its nose. What do you think?'

Campbell's shrewd eyes were fastened on Ayton, who opened his mouth, then shut it again. It was Pountney who asked how they were supposed to operate it.

'Easy,' said Campbell cheerfully. 'You just set the screws rotating by pressing this switch here. You then launch it at your target from your folbot.'

'And its maximum range?'

'Fifty yards. It'll make a nice hole in anything smaller

than a cruiser. Damage it enough to keep it in harbour without causing casualties.'

'Except us,' said Ayton under his breath.

Pountney, who liked anything new and knew that ordinary limpets would be much too powerful, agreed that each SBS team should take three of the devices. Campbell seemed delighted and escorted them to the exit, extolling some of the other ideas he was working on.

'I don't like it,' said Pountney after the staff car returning them to the depot ship drew away from the underground headquarters. 'I don't like it at all. In fact it stinks. If there's not going to be any opposition, there are far more of us than necessary; if the Frogs are going to fight, there are nowhere near enough. It just doesn't make sense.'

It had, they agreed, all the signs of a hastily conceived, ill-thought-out operation.

'Nothing unusual in that,' said Harmon grimly.

'Let's just hope that Giraud does his stuff,' Ayton remarked.

They collected their kit from the submarine depot ship and located the two cutters, which were moored alongside each other nearby. They were handsome-looking vessels, renamed HMS *Hartland* and HMS *Walney* after they had become part of the Royal Navy, with a marked sheer and high bows and sterns that reminded Ayton of photographs he'd seen of whaling ships. The superstructure of each was concentrated amidships and mounted on their fore and after decks were single four-inch, quick-firing guns of the latest design.

The three SBS men exchanged salutes with the officer of the watch as they boarded the inboard cutter and crossed to the outboard one, where they were to meet the two captains to discuss the briefing.

'Did you find out anything more?' asked Harvey, after the SBS men had been taken to the wardroom and given what Crean called 'a stiffener'.

'Nothing,' said Pountney, tossing back his drink. 'Hey, what're the ingredients for this? It's a cracker.'

'Smacks to me of an afterthought,' said Crean gloomily. 'Some bright spark woke up last week and thought, hey, supposing those Frogs just do happen to want to oppose the landings. Better send in the Marines or something, then went back to sleep.'

'We've got Rangers, not Marines. What the hell are they? Some sort of Boy Scouts?'

'American equivalent of Commandos, I was told,' said Harvey.

'Rather them than me, whoever they are,' said Harmon. While they waited for Colonel Budd and his men to join them they went over their orders once more and rescrutinized the reconnaissance photographs and sketches. When Budd did arrive he seemed equally sceptical about the operation. 'Just hang in there until we arrive, was all I was told by General Fredendall,' he remarked.

'Fredendall?'

'He's commanding the Central Task Force.'

'Did he tell you what reception to expect?'

'Nope. When I asked him he just said: "Goldarn it, Budd, how the hell do I know?" He seemed to think you Limeys would be able to fill me in.'

The silence which followed this remark was broken by Pountney, who said that as they were all confined to the cutters until they sailed that evening it was not revealing any great secret to say that the Allies had a French general up their sleeve who was going to make sure the landings weren't opposed.

'How?' Budd asked bluntly.

Pountney shrugged. 'Radio broadcast, I suppose.'

'Big deal,' said Budd in disgust.

The British officers looked at the lanky American. They'd heard that Texans didn't pull any punches.

Budd shifted his chewing gum from one cheek to the other and pronounced: 'I reckon they putting us in deep shit, gennelmun. Real deep shit.' He spoke the words slowly, almost with affection. 'Right up to here.' By way of measurement he put the edge of his outstretched hand on his forehead.

'Well, there's nothing we can do about it,' said Crean briskly. 'I'm sure we'll manage. We'll get you into the main quay and then it's up to you.'

'So long as we go in expecting trouble,' said Budd affably, 'I'm happy. I'd put any one of mah men against any dozen garlic-eating sons-of-bitches, if you'll excuse mah language.'

'Our friend Budd doesn't seem to like the French,' Ayton said to Pountney after the meeting had broken up and they had been shown to their sleeping quarters, a tiny double cabin under the quarterdeck. Harmon had already gone aboard the inboard cutter, the *Walney*, where he and his sergeant paddler had been joined by a third SBS folbot team.

'Like? It's not a matter of liking the French,' said Pountney. 'No one likes them. Admire them, yes. Like them, no. Not possible.'

Above them they heard the thud of boots as the contingent of Rangers came aboard and made their way below.

Two hours later, as dusk settled over the Rock, the two cutters sailed for Oran. At dawn those aboard them saw

266

stretched out across the horizon the great armada of ships which shortly after midnight would begin landing troops in the vicinity of Oran and Algiers.

By midnight both cutters had closed with the North African shore and had turned westwards to follow the coastline. It was a dark, stormy night – 'as black as the ace of spades' was how Harvey described it to the two SBS men as they all stood on the bridge of the *Hartland* trying to distinguish some of the landmarks they had seen on the chart. Not a glimmer of light showed along the shore.

'Perhaps they're expecting us,' said Harvey.

'You bet your bottom dollar they're expecting something,' remarked Budd from the far corner of the bridge. 'Them Froggies ain't stupid.'

Behind them they could see the *Walney* pitching badly. Spray flew across her bows as she dipped and lurched. Then all the officers on the bridge had to hang on as the *Hartland* was hit by a large wave. The compass light lit the small bridge with an eerie glow.

'Point Canastel,' Harvey suddenly said, pointing to star-board of the cutter's bow. 'Starboard twenty, Hammond,' he said into the voice pipe.

'Starboard twenty it is, sir,' the helmsman replied from the wheel position directly below the bridge. 'Steer two-eight-zero.'

The ships followed the curve of the land until the tip of the point was reached, then they changed course once more, this time heading south-west, which would bring them directly to the mouth of Oran harbour. Budd left the bridge and minutes later the Rangers began to gather on deck. They huddled where they could to avoid the cold wind and the spray which occasionally swept over the vessel's bows.

'Gun crews, close up, Number One,' Harvey said to his First Lieutenant. 'Make absolutely sure they know not to fire unless given specific orders to do so.'

'Aye, aye, sir.'

The two cutters hugged the coastline, its steep cliffs towering above them. Everyone on the bridge had binoculars trained straight ahead, and they were soon picking up the first pinpricks of light from the port.

Pountney glanced at the radar repeater which twirled steadily in front of the Captain. It showed the ships were some three hundred yards from the shore, the right distance to navigate the narrow channel between the sand bars which would lead them into the main channel just as it curved in towards the harbour's outer boom.

'Port and starboard lights ten degrees on the starboard bow,' said Ayton. Two pinpoints of coloured light glowed through the dark. The starboard light, coloured green, marked the end of the long mole. The red speck of the port light indicated the end of a short mole that jutted out from the land at right angles to the outer mole.

'Obliging of them to have those switched on,' said Harvey. It was in everyone's mind that this was a good omen, but no one said so. Pountney had sketched an aerial view of the harbour from the reconnaissance photographs and had it spread out in front of him on a small chart table at the back of the bridge.

'The outer boom lies about two hundred yards beyond those two lights,' he said. 'The inner boom is no more than fifty yards beyond it.'

'And the Ravin Blanc quay?'

'Less than a quarter of a mile from the inner boom. Right under the battery.'

'The *Hartland* was to land one company of Rangers at the quay, while the *Walney* headed straight for the inner end of the harbour, so that the Rangers aboard could occupy the French naval barracks nearby and the Fort Lamoune battery, which lay beyond them. *En route* it would drop Harmon and a small group of British naval ratings at the Millerand Quay, halfway along the harbour. Many of the merchant ships were moored there, and Harmon's task was to ensure that they were not sabotaged or taken out to sea.

Pountney and Ayton, their folbot filled with Campbell's torpedoes, would be put ashore on another quay farther up the harbour, from where they would be able to attack any warship which attempted to put to sea.

Between the two navigational lights they now saw a white one blinking. The navigator counted the flashes with a stopwatch. 'Group flashing four every fifteen seconds,' he said. 'That's the centre ground buoy in the harbour.'

'That means the entrance to the outer boom hasn't been closed by block-ships,' said Harvey. 'Otherwise we wouldn't see it. Again, very obliging of them.'

'Too obliging,' said Budd, who had come on to the bridge to report that his Rangers were ready to disembark.

'I want the French tricolour flown at the masthead, Number One,' Harvey said, 'and the largest US naval ensign we've got draped alongside the bridge. And tell the broadcasters to stand by.'

He glanced at his watch. 'We're early. Slow ahead,' he said into the voice pipe.

'Watch the current, sir,' the navigator warned as he

looked at the radar repeater. 'Its driving us too far inshore.'

'Thank you, Pilot. Starboard five, Hammond.'

As the harbour entrance drew nearer, its two entrance lights glowed more brightly, and beyond them could be seen, in dim outline, the shapes of buildings. A minaret stuck up in the middle of them like a pencil and to the left, just distinguishable, was the square bastion of the Ravin Blanc battery, which sat on top of a small ridge overlooking the harbour.

'Both ensigns in place, sir,' said the First Lieutenant. 'We've also got a whacking big Stars and Stripes flying astern. The broadcasters are standing by.'

Harvey glanced at his watch again.

'Here goes,' he said quietly, and ordered the cutter's engine half ahead.

Both ships passed through the narrow channel between the sandbanks and entered the main channel. Still nothing stirred ashore. The seconds ticked by. The entrance through the outer boom could now plainly be seen. A shower of rain passed over the ships and a gust of wind eddied off the shore.

Suddenly the silence was broken by the wail of an air-raid siren on shore, then a blinding light cascaded into the bridge, making everyone blink and shade their eyes.

'Searchlight on the outer mole, sir,' shouted the First Lieutenant. As he spoke, a second one sprang to life on the inner mole and flickered along the length of the *Hartland* before moving on to illuminate the large American flag which the *Walney* was flying.

'We'll soon see if the old General has done his stuff,' Pountney said to Ayton. The cutters, now brilliantly illuminated by the two searchlights, continued straight for the entrance through the outer boom.

'Start the broadcasts, Number One.'

The loudspeakers boomed out in French, the words echoing almost mockingly off the cliffs. The *Hartland* was almost abeam of the two harbour lights, with the *Walney* close behind. Both were brilliantly lit up by the searchlights.

Then the French Navy made up its mind. A shell cracked overhead, a second hit the water just ahead of the *Hartland* and a machine-gun on the inner mole began an uneven chatter. One of the windows on the bridge smashed, scattering glass everywhere.

'Full speed ahead!' Harvey shouted into the voice pipe, and the two SBS men felt the cutter shudder under them. The loudspeakers continued their announcements, but were soon drowned by the noise of incoming fire.

'Lay down smoke, Number One. And shoot out those bloody searchlights.'

The increase in the cutters' speed caught those ashore by surprise. For a few vital seconds the searchlights lost their targets and the guns – there must have been half a dozen firing now – began shooting so erratically that one shell extinguished the starboard entrance light on the outer mole.

The quick-firing guns on the fore decks of both cutters opened up on the searchlights and one was quickly extinguished, but the machine-gun on the mole got the range and ran a tattoo of bullets along the *Hartland*'s bridge as the cutter plunged through the outer boom. The smoke containers, fired from mortars, hid the *Hartland* at first, but the wind was in the wrong direction and the smoke soon drifted away. Splinters and bullets flew everywhere, snapping and whining in the confined space of the bridge like angry hornets. The First Lieutenant grunted and slid to the floor.

'Hang on!' yelled Harvey as his ship made straight for the inner boom of coal barges. Ayton crouched down and turned the First Lieutenant on to his back, but then looked away when he saw the neat hole between the man's eyes.

The quick-firing gun on the after deck now found a target and opened up with a sound like wood being chopped methodically at speed. Seconds later the *Hartland* rammed the barges with a tremendous thud which shook the entire ship from stem to stern. The boom buckled and broke under the enormous force of the steel bows of the cutter. The barges scraped and banged along the *Hartland*'s side and moments later the cutter had broken through into the harbour and was heading for the Ravin Blanc quay.

Flashes flickered from the muzzles of the Ravin Blanc battery, but the gunners could not now depress their guns sufficiently and their shells whirred harmlessly over the *Hartland* and exploded on the outer mole.

Ayton, thrown off balance when the cutter hit the inner boom, levered himself on to his feet by gripping the chart table. There was blood all over it and he could feel its sticky warmth on his fingers.

'All right, Phil?' He could see Pountney looking at him anxiously through the pall of acrid smoke that now filled the bridge, and he nodded. If he was hit, he certainly couldn't feel anything.

'Tell the Colonel to stand by to land, Number One,' Harvey shouted without turning round.

'He's dead, sir,' Ayton said.

'Fuck it,' said Harvey irritably. 'You go, then. Tell Budd I won't be stopping. His men will have to jump for it.'

Ayton half slid, half jumped down the ladder from the bridge. He groped his way aft, stepping over Rangers who were spread-eagled on the deck trying to find shelter from the flying fragments of steel and bullets. Already several had been hit. He found Budd crouched behind a lifeboat, calmly rolling a cigarette.

'I sure hope your French general fries in hell,' he said after Ayton had given him Harvey's message. 'If I ever catch him I'll cut his balls off.'

He stuck the cigarette in his mouth, lit it with a Mickey Mouse lighter, slung his tommy-gun over his shoulder and began shouting orders. Moments later the *Hartland* manoeuvred slowly alongside the quay and the Rangers climbed down on to it from scrambling nets which had been lowered by the crew. They scattered quickly and the *Hartland* swung away, its stern jarring heavily on the quay as it turned. Ayton ran back along the deck and hauled himself up the bridge ladder as the *Hartland* rounded the end of the Ravin Blanc quay and headed up the harbour.

The *Walney*, ahead of the *Hartland* now, was caught in the full glare of another searchlight and was under heavy fire from a destroyer which lay alongside the next quay. For a moment it looked as if the cutter was holding its own, but as it drew abreast of the destroyer it slowed and stopped, then, with a colossal explosion, simply disintegrated.

'Jesus Christ,' Ayton said quietly, knowing Harmon and his sergeant, and the other SBS team, were goners. 'Jesus fucking Christ.'

The searchlight switched to the *Hartland*, but the

gunners manning the cutter's fore-deck gun soon found its range and it exploded like an outsize firework.

The destroyer now turned its guns on the *Hartland*. Even without the aid of the searchlight, its gunners were remarkably accurate. The first salvo fell short, sending up great spouts of water which momentarily screened the cutter from the destroyer. Perhaps because of this the second salvo was too high. The shells screamed overhead and fell close astern.

But now that the cutter had been bracketed, Harvey knew the destroyer's gunners had the correct range, and he shouted down to the helmsman to turn to starboard to avoid the third salvo. This exploded on the port quarter, exactly where the cutter had been moments before.

The outer mole loomed close.

'Hard-a-port!'

The cutter kept her course.

'She's not responding, sir! The rudder must be jammed.'

'Stop both engines! Astern both engines!'

At a distance the outer mole had not appeared to be particularly high; close to, it loomed alarmingly on a level with the cutter's superstructure. Everyone on the bridge ducked instinctively as more glass shattered.

With a resounding jolt the *Hartland* hit the outer mole. It seemed that every rivet of its steel hull had been shaken loose.

'Full astern both engines!'

The cutter shuddered and yawed, but refused to move. It had run on to the mole behind a floating dock which protected it from the destroyer's fire, and in the sudden silence which followed Pountney looked at Ayton and said: 'This is where we get off.'

Harvey nodded his assent and as the two SBS men scrambled down on to the deck they heard him shouting orders to get the ship afloat.

Machine-gun bullets twanged above them. The small team of ratings who had been allotted to help them offload the folbot were waiting with it under the bridge. On Pountney's order two clambered down the netting and on to the mole so that the folbot could be handed to them. The SBS men grabbed their weapons and equipment and followed.

Mud and foam churned around the cutter's stern as they launched the folbot and paddled vigorously towards the floating dock. As they reached it the cutter slid back into the harbour and moved out from under the cover of the floating dock. But immediately it did so a searchlight picked it out and the destroyer resumed firing. The destroyer's second salvo blew away the cutter's bridge and the next started a fire raging in its engine-room.

The two SBS men watched helplessly as the *Hartland* slowed, then stopped, wallowing in the water as flames engulfed it. Again and again the destroyer's shells smashed into the cutter's flaming hull as it sank slowly into the harbour.

18

The Commander from Combined Operations and Captain Barney Hawkes scrutinized the two SBS men sympathetically.

'You must have had a rough time of it,' the Commander said.

'Oran military prison was the worst part,' Ayton replied.

They had been locked up for only a few hours before Fredendall's troops arrived and freed them, but it had seemed like a lifetime.

'Many survivors from the Rangers?'

Pountney shook his head. 'Bloody few, to be honest.'

The Commander sighed and tapped the end of his pencil on the desk. 'And Campbell's miniature torpedoes? I don't suppose you had a chance to use them?'

'We launched two before they caught us,' said Pountney. 'One sank immediately. The other went round and round in circles and then hit a quay without exploding.'

'No good then?'

'No bloody good at all.'

The Commander grimaced. 'A proper balls-up from start to finish.'

'That's about it,' Ayton agreed.

A silence settled on the Commander's office for a

moment. Then he lit a cigarette, offered the packet to the two SBS officers and said: 'You'll be pleased to know that the invasion as a whole was a great success. The French offered very little resistance.'

'Giraud did his bit in the end, then?' Pountney directed his question at Hawkes.

'Giraud? Oh, no, he's out of it,' Hawkes replied wearily. 'None of the French in North Africa would have anything to do with him. A has-been, you might say. Missed his moment completely. That is, if he ever had one.'

'Barking up the wrong tree, were we?'

'Seems so. We're negotiating with Darlan at the moment. He's agreed to change sides.'

'I thought Darlan hated our guts,' said Pountney. 'And that we hated his.'

'So we do,' said Hawkes. 'But he's the only man for the job, it seems.'

'And the Germans?'

'Haven't you heard? They've occupied the whole of Vichy France.'

Poor buggers, Pountney thought. He was glad his war was a simple one: kill or be killed, eye for an eye, tooth for a tooth. He wanted to get back to the Section now, as quickly as possible, and said so.

'We'll fly you out tomorrow,' Hawkes promised.

'How soon can you get me to Alexandria?' Ayton asked.

'This will tell you.'

Hawkes pulled out a buff envelope from his pocket and slid it over the desk. Ayton opened it, read the contents, then tossed the sheet of paper across to Pountney.

'"As from 15 November 1942,"' Pountney read out loud, '"No. 1 Special Boat Section will be renamed D

Squadron of the Special Air Service and will therefore in future be directly commanded by Major David Stirling. Captain Philip Ayton MC Royal Marines is granted three weeks' leave in the United Kingdom before reporting to Special Services Brigade at Ardrossan-Saltcoats for further employment." '

Pountney rose from his seat. 'Come on, Phil, it's time we had a drink.'

OTHER TITLES IN SERIES FROM 22 BOOKS

Available now at newsagents and booksellers
or use the order form provided

continued overleaf . . .

MARINE L: SBS

All at £4.99

All 22 Books are available at your bookshop, or can be ordered from:

22 Books
Cash Sales Department
P.O. Box 11
Falmouth
Cornwall
TR10 9EN
Tel: +44 (0) 1326 372400
Fax: +44 (0) 1326 374888
Email: books@barni.avel.co.uk.

POST AND PACKING:
Payments can be made as follows: cheque or postal order, payabl-
to Little, Brown and Company (UK) or by credit cards. Do not
send cash or currency.

While every effort is made to keep prices low it is sometimes
necessary to increase cover prices at short notice. 22 Books
reserves the right to show new retail prices on covers which may
differ from those previously advertised in the books or elsewhere.

NAME ....

ADDRESS ....

....

POST/ZIP CODE ....

☐ Please keep me in touch with future 22 Books publications
☐ I enclose my remittance for £ _____
☐ I wish to pay by Visa/Access/Mastercard/Eurocard

Card number

☐☐☐☐ ☐☐☐☐ ☐☐☐☐ ☐☐☐☐

Card expiry date

☐☐ ☐☐

Please allow 28 days for delivery. Please tick box if you do not
wish to receive any additional information ☐